MARICO MOON

MARICO MOON
by
HERMAN CHARLES BOSMAN

Published by –

The House of Emslie

3 Hatton Place
Edinburgh
Scotland
EH9 1UD

www.emsliesquared.com

ISBN 978-0-9567745-2-1

eBook ISBN 978-0-9567745-9-0

Copyright © in this edition The House of Emslie, 2018
Cover photograph by Samantha Reinders
Cover by MR Design

All rights reserved. No part of this publication may be reproduced, stored, or transmitted in any form, or by any means electronic, mechanical or photocopying, recording or otherwise, without the express written permission of the publisher.

Distributed in South Africa by Flyleaf
Visit: www.flyleaf.co.za   E-mail: orders@flyleaf.co.za
Tel: 071 896 0881   Fax: 086 668 2753

Distributed in the United Kingdom by Central Books
50 Freshwater Road   Chadwell Heath   London   RM8 1RX
Tel: 0208 525 8800   E-mail: contactus@centralbooks.com

This publication is dedicated to Oom Schalk Lourens

who is alive and well

and living in the pages that follow

Introduction

Starting on 24 April 2014, and without fail every Thursday since then, we at Cape Rebel have published – by e-mail – stories designed to entertain and to bring a smile to the faces of our readers, at the same time promoting South African and other literature and folklore that continue to delight and inspire us.

Each of these Cape Rebel stories, distributed *gratis* and as much for our own enjoyment as for that of our 'joiners', provides a short literary diversion for those who spend their days, as we ourselves do, 'late and soon, getting and spending, laying waste our powers' (with apologies to 'the old sheep of the Lake District'). Our aim is thereby to make all of our lives a little 'less forlorn', using stories that capture our imagination, delight or inspire us, make us think, or move us to tears or laughter.

Some – but far from all – of the Cape Rebel stories come from books we have published, and every story is available in both English and Afrikaans, these being the languages we speak at home.

The name Cape Rebel is invariably associated with the Anglo-Boer War (1899-1902), so a few comments on this subject are warranted.

During the Anglo-Boer War, in some respects South Africa's 'civil war', the word 'joiner' was used to signify a Boer combatant who had gone over to the other side, and 'joined' the enemy – in the sense of actively assisting against the Boers. Such persons were, understandably, regarded as traitors.

A joiner was different to a *'hensopper'*, a combatant who had surrendered. It was one thing to raise one's hands in surrender, quite another to actively join the enemy against one's own people.

'Cape rebels' were those who, although owing allegiance to the Crown by virtue of their residence in the Cape Colony, actively sided with the Boers against imperialism – and many of them paid the ultimate price for taking this rebel stand.

Although the feelings of subsequent generations concerning Cape rebels, *hensoppers* and joiners might occasionally still run high – and there is no need to read between the lines to discern our sympathies – such distinctions are entirely historical.

In the true spirit of today's Cape Rebel, we invite all readers to become 'joiners' of a different kind – by subscribing to our weekly e-mailed stories. Joining Cape Rebel has no negative connotation. It signifies nothing more than non-partisan interest in South Africa, past and present, and alignment with our core values of truth, courage, integrity and humour.

Some four years down the line, we can say that our stories are not limited to South African sources, although this remains our focus. We promote whatever captures our imaginations and whatever we think will appeal to the broad cross-section of our joiners (which includes people living in many different countries).

In the course of our weekly selections for inclusion in the next Cape Rebel, we have – inevitably – chosen some of Herman Charles Bosman's stories, and it has been nothing short of a delight to rediscover the genius of this South African writer. So it has continued.

It recently occurred to us that there may be an audience for a collection of the Bosman extracts we have selected for inclusion in Cape Rebel over the past four and a half years. At the time of writing, there are some 65 of these – enough to warrant a collection of wonderful stories by the much loved Herman Charles Bosman.

The 'trouble' with many Bosman stories is that, as previously published, they use language that is today considered by many to be offensive, and are for this reason likely to be sidelined by all except diehard Bosman fans and those who readily read between the lines. (The fact that Bosman's use of offensive terms is invariably an instrument for subtle irony may well, in these politically correct times, be lost on some who are unacquainted with his work.)

We are not exponents of political correctness – far from it – but in preparing extracts from Bosman's stories for publication in our Cape Rebel e-mails, we have found that, with very minor adjustments and omissions, Bosman can be presented in ways that still faithfully render his literary art without giving unnecessary offence. We have made such minor adjustments and omissions out of love for Bosman's writing, not from any sense of 'improving' the text. We have also given each extract its own title (always sourced in the text of the story itself), but we also give the name of the story from which it has been extracted, as well as the name of the book in which it was first published, so that purists can easily obtain access to the original stories. We do not believe that, in so doing, we have violated the integrity of Bosman's work.

This book contains 60 stories that we have seen fit to publish in our weekly Cape Rebel e-mails. They represent our 'favourites', and we now publish them in this collection in the hope of reminding Bosman fans – as we ourselves have been reminded – of some of his most delightful stories. (Bosman having died at the age of forty-six, on 14 October 1951, his published work is now in the public domain.) We hope that, by so doing, new readers will be introduced to the dry humour, the enchantment and the deep human resonance to be found in the works of Herman Charles Bosman.

The value and provenance of Bosman's Marico stories can be gleaned from his own words in the following extract from 'Reminiscences', first published in *A Cask of Jereipgo*:

'I was engaged, for a couple of days last week, in going through old files of newspapers and magazines, making a collection of stories I had written over the past fifteen years.

In re-reading some of the Marico Bushveld stories I had written as long ago as the early years of the 1930s, I was surprised to find how intimate was my knowledge of life on the South African farm. I was also astonished at the extent of my familiarity with historical events – and the spirit of the times and the personalities who had featured in them – that had taken place in the *ou* Transvaal.

Anyway, in again perusing those stories, written long ago, I realised where all that local colour came from: I had got it from listening to the talk of elderly farmers in the Marico district who had a whole lot of information that they didn't require for themselves, any more, and that they were glad to bestow on a stranger. It was all information that was, from a scientific point of view, strictly useless.

That was how I learnt all about the First and Second Boer Wars. And about the tribal wars. And about the trouble, in the old days, between the Transvaal and the Orange Free State. And about the Ohrigstad Republic. And about the Stellaland Republic. If any contemporary South African historian would like some fallen-by-the-wayside information about any events in the early days of the South African Republics, I could supply him with all the facts he needs. And, what is more important, with a whole lot of surplus information, outside of just facts.

I regarded them as wonderful storytellers, the old Boers who lived in the Marico district twenty years ago. Most of them had moved into that part of the Transvaal, next to the Bechuanaland Protectorate, in 1917. It was a part of the Transvaal that had remained practically uninhabited since the Anglo-Boer War. I still have very vivid recollections of the Boers who lived in the Marico in those days. I was there as a schoolteacher for a little while. And I can only hope that the information I imparted to the children, in the way of reading, spelling and arithmetic, was – in a minute degree – as significant as the facts that were imparted to me by their parents, whom I went to visit at weekends.

I must have known most of the families living in the Marico Bushveld at that particular time, and some of those farmers had most interesting stories to tell, relating, in a matter-of-fact way, all sorts of unusual circumstances. And my mind absorbed whatever they had to relate, provided that it was of a sufficiently unutilitarian order.'

The Bosman stories collected in this book represent an eclectic collection, selected from week to week without any conscious unifying factor other than that they inspired us to smile, laugh, think, wonder or wander.

We invite all who enjoy these stories to become 'joiners' of Cape Rebel, and thereby to experience something of the soul of South Africa through the many stories still to be told and re-told. There is no cost whatsoever involved.

Nowadays each e-mailed story is accompanied by a podcast, in both English and Afrikaans, accessible by simply clicking on the image above each story. These are available on our website, caperebel.com. Thus joiners can read or listen to each story, or – using two devices – they can do both. (As we have always pledged, we will never share the information of our joiners – who can 'unsubscribe' with a single click.)

Marico Moon, like each issue of Cape Rebel, is a collaborative effort, and I thank Hendrik Jansen, Archie Henderson, David Emslie and Clare Emslie for their unstinting efforts that have culminated in this book. I thank also Marius Roux, our designer, for reliably producing book covers that challenge the adage that you cannot judge a book by its cover, Samantha Reinders, whose photograph was used for the cover of this book, and Ingeborg Pelser, a wonderful breath of fresh air in our lives and a skilled publishing professional, for the inspiration and insight she seems to stimulate so effortlessly.

We hope that readers will enjoy this selection of stories by Herman Charles Bosman, whom we regard as one of South Africa's finest literary talents.

T S Emslie
1 October 2018

Contents

	Introduction	vii
1	The Authentic Stamp of South Africa, from 'Marico Revisited'	1
2	The Gentle Melancholy of the Twilight, from 'Marico Revisited'	4
3	Looking for Strayed Cattle, from 'In the Withaak's Shade'	7
4	Blundering in the Dark, from 'Mafeking Road'	12
5	For the Sake of the Donkeys, from 'Starlight on the Veld'	19
6	The Things that Really Matter, from 'Yellow Moepels'	22
7	Slouching Past in the Dark, from 'Peaches Ripening in the Sun'	24
8	A Peculiar Sort of Smile, from 'The Selons-Rose'	30
9	Juice of the Juba-Berry, from 'The Love Potion'	33
10	More Real than Life, from 'Dream by the Blue Gums'	38
11	Under the Full Moon, from 'Drieka and the Moon'	44
12	Bitter against the English, from 'The Rooinek'	51
13	Too Much Truth, from 'The Rooinek'	55
14	The Wind that Stirs in the Kalahari, from 'The Rooinek'	59
15	When the Moepels are Ripe, from 'Yellow Moepels'	64
16	Cloudy Nights, from 'Starlight on the Veld'	68
17	On the Road to Abjaterskop, from 'Willem Prinsloo's Peach Brandy'	72
18	A Small White Rose, from 'Willem Prinsloo's Peach Brandy'	75
19	Bekkersdal Marathon, from 'A Bekkersdal Marathon'	80
20	An Old Story and an Old Song, from 'The Selons-Rose'	85
21	Stars in their Courses, from 'Stars In Their Courses'	90
22	The Most Wild and the Most Beautiful Thing in the Whole World, from 'Mampoer'	94
23	And in your Heart there are Whisperings, from 'Ox-Wagons on Trek'	102
24	A Very Old Star, from 'Cometh Comet'	108

25	What was in her Heart, from 'Splendours from Ramoutsa'	113
26	As Strange as the African Veld, from 'Unto Dust'	118
27	In Those Days, from 'Border Bad-Man'	124
28	Wanting to Get into History, from 'The Music-Maker'	129
29	Face Downwards, from 'The Affair at Ystespruit'	135
30	The Hoof-beats of a Commando at Full Gallop, from 'A Boer Rip Van Winkel'	140
31	The Look in his Eyes, from 'Veld Maiden'	147
32	For the Transvaal, from 'The Traitor's Wife'	153
33	The Voice of the Drum, from 'The Drum'	158
34	A Time for Sowing, from 'Funeral Earth'	164
35	Like an Orang-Outang, Even, from 'Reminiscences'	168
36	Hiding their Weaknesses, from 'Bushveld Romance'	173
37	Opposite Sides of the Law, from 'Man to Man'	177
38	Nobody Even Interested, from 'Home Town'	181
39	Unchanged, from 'Home Town'	185
40	Psycho-Analysis I, from 'Psycho-Analysis'	189
41	Psycho-Analysis II, from 'Psycho-Analysis'	193
42	When You're a Member of the Family, from 'Secret Agent'	196
43	Real Money, from 'Five-Pound Notes'	201
44	Cattle Thieves and Herdboys, from 'Idle Talk'	207
45	A Pale Wind in a Tall Tree, from 'The Wind in the Tree'	211
46	A Sigh from very Far Away, from 'Potchefstroom Willow'	214
47	A Kind of Sweetness in the Air, from 'Young Man In Love'	218
48	Gutters, from 'Rebuilding Europe's Cities'	222
49	Why Durban is so Uncivilised, from 'Student of Divinity'	226
50	Good Stuff, from 'Street Processions'	229
51	The Awakening of Gigantic Laughter, from 'Humour and Wit'	236
52	With Studied Nonchalance, from 'Paysage de la Highveld'	240
53	A Quality of Granite, from 'The Disappearance of Latin'	244

54 The Poet's Embroidered Lie, from 'Johannesburg'   248
55 A Place for the Soul's Abiding, from 'Universities'   251
56 A Great Tragedy, from 'Writing'   255
57 Too Much like the Real Thing, from
    'Toys in the Shop Window'   259
58 The Dappled Pattern of Shadow and Light, from
    'The Cape Revisited'   265
59 No Crime to be Poor, from 'Easy Circumstances'   271
60 Mountain Retreat of the Smugglers, from 'Rolled Gold'   276
    Glossary   283

1.

The Authentic Stamp of South Africa

From 'Marico Revisited'

In *A Cask of Jerepigo*

A month ago I revisited the Marico Bushveld, a district in the Transvaal to which I was sent, a long time ago, as a schoolteacher, and about which part of the country I have written, in the years that followed, a number of simple stories which I believe, in all modesty, are not without a certain degree of literary merit.

On the train that night on my way back to the Bushveld, I came across a soldier who said to me: 'As soon as I'm out of this uniform, I'm going back to cattle-smuggling.'

These words thrilled me. A number of my stories have dealt with the time-honoured Marico custom of smuggling cattle across the frontier of the Bechuanaland Protectorate. So I asked whether cattle smuggling still went on. 'More than ever,' the soldier informed me. He looked out of the train window into the dark. 'And I'll tell you that at this moment, as I'm sitting here talking to you, there is somebody bringing in cattle through the wire.'

I was very glad to hear this. I was glad to find that the only part of my stories that could have dated had not done so. It is only things indirectly connected with economics that can change. Droughts and human nature don't.

Next morning we were in Mafeking. Mafeking is outside the Transvaal. It is about twenty miles inside the borders of the Northern Cape. And to proceed to Ramoutsa, a village in the Bechuanaland Protectorate which is the nearest point on the railway line to the part of the Groot Marico to which we wanted to go, we first had to get a permit from the immigration official in Mafeking. All this seemed very confusing, somehow. We merely wanted to travel from Johannesburg to an area in the north-western Transvaal, and in order to get there it turned out that we had first to cross into the Cape Province, and that from the Cape we had to travel through the Bechuanaland Protectorate, which is a Crown Colony, and which you can't enter until an immigration official has first telephoned Pretoria about it.

We reached Ramoutsa late in the afternoon.

From there we travelled to the Marico by car. Within the hour we had crossed the border into the Transvaal. We were once more on Transvaal soil, for which we had been, naturally, homesick, having been exiles in foreign parts since early morning. So the moment we crossed the barbed-wire fence separating the Bechuanaland Protectorate from the Marico, we stopped the car and got out onto the veld. We said it was fine to set foot on Transvaal soil once more. And we also said that while it was a good thing to travel through foreign countries, which we had been doing since six o'clock that morning, and that foreign travel had a broadening effect on the mind, we were glad that our heads had not been turned by these experiences, and that we had not permitted ourselves to be influenced by alien modes of life and thought.

We travelled on through the bush over stony paths that were little more than tracks going in between the trees and underneath their branches, the thorns tearing at the windscreen and the hood of the car in the same way as they had done years ago, when I had first visited the Marico. I was glad to find that nothing had changed.

Dusk found us in the shadow of the Dwarsberge, not far from our destination, and we came across a spot on the veld that I recognised. It was one of the stations at which the bi-weekly Government lorry from Zeerust stopped on its way up towards the Limpopo. How the lorry drivers knew that this place was a station, years ago, was through the presence of a large anthill, into the crest of which a pair of kudu antlers had been thrust. That spot had not changed. The anthill was still surmounted by what looked like that same pair of kudu horns. The station had not grown perceptibly in the intervening years. The only sign of progress was that, in addition to the horns on its summit, the anthill was further decorated with a rusty milk-can from which the bottom had been knocked out.

And so I arrived back in that part of the country to which the Transvaal Education Department in its wisdom had sent me years before. There is no other place I know that is so heavy with atmosphere, so strangely and darkly impregnated with that stuff of life that bears the authentic stamp of South Africa.

2.

The Gentle Melancholy of the Twilight

From 'Marico Revisited'

In *A Cask of Jerepigo*

There were features about the Marico Bushveld that were almost too gaudy. That part of the country had been practically derelict since the Anglo-Boer War and the rinderpest. Many of the farms north of the Dwarsberge had been occupied little more than ten years before by farmers who had trekked into the Marico from the Northern Cape and the Western Transvaal. The farmers there were real Boers.

I am told that I have a deep insight into the character of the Afrikaner who lives his life on the *platteland*. I acquired this knowledge in the Marico, where I was sent when my mind was most open to impressions.

Then there was the bush. Thorn-trees. Withaaks and kameeldorings. The kremetart-boom. Swarthaak and blinkblaar and wag-'n-bietjie. Moepels and maroelas. The sun-baked *vlakte* and the thorn tree and South Africa. Trees are more than vegetation and more than symbols and more than pallid sentimentality. Nevertheless, what the oak and the ash and the cypress are to Europe, the thorn-tree is to South Africa. And if laurel and myrtle and bay are for chaplet and wreath, thorns are for a crown.

The bush was populated with kudus and cows and duikers and steenbokkies and oxen and gemsbok and donkeys and occasional leopards. There were also ribbokke in the *krantzes* and green and brown mambas, of which hair-raising stories were told, and mules that were used to pull cars because it was an unhealthy area for horses. Mules were also used for telling hair-raising stories about.

And the sunsets in the Marico Bushveld are incredible things, heavily striped like prison bars and flamboyant like African blankets.

Then there were boreholes, hundreds of feet deep, from which water had to be pumped by hand into the cattle-troughs in times of drought. And there was a Bechuana chief who had once been to London, where he had been received in audience by His Majesty, George V, a former English king; and when, on departing from Buckingham Palace, he had been questioned by the High Commissioner as to what form the conversation had taken, he had replied, very simply, this Bechuana chief: 'We kings know what to discuss.'

There were occasional visits from Dutch Reformed Church *predikants*. And a few meetings of the Dwarsberge *Debatsvereniging*. And there were several local feuds. For I was to find that while the bush was of infinite extent, and the farms very many miles apart, the paths through the thorn-trees were narrow.

It was to this part of the country, the northern section of the Marico Bushveld, where the Transvaal ends and the Bechuanaland Protectorate begins, that I returned for a brief visit after an absence of many years. And I found, what I should have known all along, of course, that it was the present that was haunted, and that the past was not full of ghosts. The phantoms are what you carry around with you, in your head, like you carry dreams under your arm.

And when you revisit old scenes it is yourself, as you were in the past, that you encounter, and if you are in love with yourself – as everybody should be in love with himself, since it is only in that way, as Christ pointed out, that a man can love his neighbour – then there is a sweet sadness in a meeting of this description. There is the gentle melancholy of the twilight, dark eyes in faces upturned in a trancelike pallor. And fragrances. And thoughts like soft rain falling on old tombstones.

When I first went to the Marico it was in that season when the moepels were nearly ripening. And when I returned, years later, it was to find that the moepels in the Marico were beginning to ripen again.

3.

Looking for Strayed Cattle

From 'In the Withaak's Shade'

In *Mafeking Road*

Leopards? – Oom Schalk Lourens said – Oh, yes, there are two varieties on this side of the Limpopo. The chief difference between them is that the one kind of leopard has got a few more spots on it than the other kind. But when you meet a leopard in the veld, unexpectedly, you seldom trouble to count his spots to find out which kind he belongs to. That is unnecessary. Because, whatever kind of leopard it is that you come across in this way, you only do one kind of running. And that is the fastest kind.

I remember the occasion when I came across a leopard unexpectedly, and to this day I cannot tell you how many spots he had, even though I had all the time I needed for studying him. It happened at about midday, when I was out on the far end of my farm, behind a *koppie*, looking for some strayed cattle. I thought the cattle might be there because it is shady under those withaak trees, and there is soft grass that is very pleasant to sit on. After I had looked for the cattle for about an hour in this manner, sitting up against a tree-trunk, it occurred to me that I could look for them just as well, or perhaps even better, if I lay down flat. For even a child knows that cattle aren't so small that you have to stand on stilts or something to see them properly.

So I lay on my back, with my hat tilted over my face, and my legs crossed, and when I closed my eyes slightly the tip of my boot, sticking up into the air, looked just like the peak of Abjaterskop.

Overhead a lonely *aasvoël* wheeled, circling slowly round and round without flapping his wings, and I knew that not even a calf could pass in any part of the sky between the tip of my toe and that *aasvoël* without my observing it immediately. What was more, I could go on lying there under the withaak looking for the cattle like that all day, if necessary.

The more I screwed up my eyes and gazed at the toe of my boot, the more it looked like Abjaterskop. By and by it seemed that it actually was Abjaterskop, and I could see the stones on top of it, and the bushes trying to grow up its sides, and in my ears there was a far-off humming sound, like bees in an orchard on a still day. As I have said, it was very pleasant.

Then a strange thing happened. It was as though a huge cloud, shaped like an animal's head and with spots on it, had settled on top of Abjaterskop. It seemed so funny that I wanted to laugh. But I didn't. Instead, I opened my eyes a little more and felt glad to think that I was only dreaming. Because otherwise I would have to believe that the spotted cloud on Abjaterskop was actually a leopard, and that he was gazing at my boot. Again I wanted to laugh. But then, suddenly, I knew.

And I didn't feel so glad. For it was a leopard, all right – a large-sized, hungry-looking leopard, and he was sniffing suspiciously at my feet. I was uncomfortable. I knew that nothing I could do would ever convince that leopard that my toe was Abjaterskop. I wanted to get up and run for it. But I couldn't. My legs wouldn't work.

Every big-game hunter I have come across has told me the same story about how, at one time or another, he has owed his escape from lions or other wild animals to his cunning in lying down and pretending to be dead, so that the beast of prey loses interest in him and walks off. Now, as I lay there on the grass, with the leopard trying to make up his mind about me, I understood why, in such a situation, the hunter doesn't move.

It's simply that he can't move. That's all. It's not his cunning that keeps him down. It's his legs.

Those were terrible moments. I lay very still, afraid to open my eyes and afraid to breathe. Sniff-sniff, the huge creature went, and his breath swept over my face in hot gasps. You hear of many frightening experiences that a man has in a lifetime. I have also been in quite a few perilous situations. But if you want something to make you suddenly old and to turn your hair white in a few moments, there is nothing to beat a leopard – especially when he is standing over you, with his jaws at your throat, trying to find a good place to bite.

The leopard gave a deep growl, stepped right over my body, knocked off my hat, and growled again. I opened my eyes and saw the animal moving away clumsily. But my relief didn't last long. The leopard didn't move far. Instead, he turned over and lay down next to me.

Yes, there on the grass, in the shade of the withaak, the leopard and I lay down together. The leopard lay half curled up, like a dog, and whenever I tried to move away, he grunted. I am sure that in the whole history of the Groot Marico there have never been two stranger companions engaged in the thankless task of looking for strayed cattle.

Next day, in Fanie Snyman's *voorkamer*, which was used as a post office, I told my story to the farmers of the neighbourhood, while they were drinking coffee and waiting for the motor-lorry from Zeerust.

At first people jested about this leopard. They said it wasn't a real leopard, but a spotted animal that had walked away out of Schalk Lourens's dream, and the upshot of this whole affair was that I too began to have doubts about the existence of the leopard.

But when, a few days later, a huge leopard was seen from the roadside near the *poort*, and then again by Mtosas on the way to Nietverdiend, and again in the turf-lands near the Malopo, matters took a different turn. And when his *spoor* was found at several waterholes, people had no further doubt about the leopard. It was dangerous to walk about in the veld, they said.

Exciting times followed. There was a great deal of shooting at the leopard and a great deal of running away from him. The amount of Martini and Mauser fire I heard in the *krantzes* reminded me of nothing so much as the First Boer War. And the amount of running away reminded me of nothing so much as the Second Boer War.

But always the leopard escaped unharmed. Somehow, I felt sorry for him. The way he had first sniffed at me and then lain down beside me that day under the withaak was a strange thing I couldn't understand. I thought of the Bible, where it is written that the lion shall lie down with the lamb.

I also wondered whether I hadn't dreamt it all. The manner in which these things had befallen me was unearthly, and the leopard began to take up a lot of my thoughts. Also, there was no man I could talk to about it who would be able to help me in any way. Even now, as I'm telling you this story, I'm expecting you to wink at me like Krisjan Lemmer did. (You know that kind of wink. It was to let me know that there was now a new understanding between us, and that we could speak in future as one Marico liar to another.)

Still, I can only tell you the things that happened as I saw them, and what the rest was about only Africa knows.

It was some time before I again walked along the path that leads through the bush to where the withaaks are. But I didn't lie down on the grass again. Because when I reached the place, I found that the leopard had got there before me. He was lying on the same spot, half curled up in the withaak's shade, and his forepaws were folded as a dog's are sometimes. But he lay very still. And even from the distance where I stood I could see the red splash on his breast where a Mauser bullet had gone.

4.

Blundering in the Dark

From 'Mafeking Road'

In *Mafeking Road*

When people ask me, as they often do, how it is that I can tell the best stories of anybody in the Transvaal – Oom Schalk Lourens said, modestly – then I explain to them that I just learn through observing the way that the world has with men and women. When I say this they nod their heads wisely, and say that they understand, and I nod my head wisely also, and that seems to satisfy them. But the thing I say to them is a lie, of course.

For it is not the story that counts. What matters is the way you tell it. The important thing is to know just at what moment you must knock out your pipe on your *veldskoen*, and at what stage of the story you must start talking about the School Committee at Drogevlei. Another necessary thing is to know what part of the story to leave out.

And you can never learn these things.

Look at Floris, the last of the Van Barnevelts. There is no doubt that he had a good story, and he should have been able to get these people to listen to it. Any yet nobody took any notice of him or of the things he had to say. Just because he couldn't tell the story properly.

Accordingly, it made me sad whenever I listened to him talk. For I could tell just where he went wrong. He never knew the moment at which to knock the ash out of his pipe. He always mentioned his opinion of the Drogevlei School Committee in the wrong place. And, what was still worse, he didn't know what part of the story to leave out.

And it was no use my trying to teach him because, as I have said, this is the thing that you can never learn. And so, each time he had told his story, I would see him turn away from me, with a look of doom on his face, and walk slowly down the road, stoop-shouldered, the last of the Van Barnevelts.

~

On the wall of Floris's *voorkamer* is a long family tree of the Van Barnevelts. You can see it there for yourself. It goes back for over two hundred years, to the Van Barnevelts of Amsterdam. At one time it went even further back, but that was before the white ants started on the top part of it and ate away quite a lot of Van Barnevelts. Nevertheless, if you look at this list, you will notice that, at the bottom, under Floris's own name, there is the last entry: 'Stephanus'. And behind the name 'Stephanus', between two bent strokes, you will read the words: '*Obiit* Mafeking'.

At the outbreak of the Second Boer War, Floris van Barnevelt was a widower, with one son, Stephanus, who was aged seventeen. The commando from our part of the Transvaal set off very cheerfully. We made a fine show with our horses and our wide hats, and our bandoliers, and with the sun shining on the barrels of our Mausers.

Young Stephanus van Barnevelt was the gayest of us all. But he said there was one thing he didn't like about the war, and that was that, in the end, we would have to go over the sea. He said that, after we had invaded the whole of the Cape, our commando would have to go on a ship and invade England also.

But we didn't go overseas, just then. Instead, our *veldkornet* told us that the burghers from our part had been ordered to join the big commando that was lying at Mafeking. We had to go and shoot a man there called Baden-Powell.

We rode steadily on into the west. After a while we noticed that our *veldkornet* frequently got off his horse and engaged in conversation with passing tribesmen, leading them some distance from the roadside and speaking earnestly to them. Of course, it was right that our *veldkornet* should explain to the Shangaans that it was wartime now, and that the Republic expected every tribesman to stop smoking so much *dagga* and to think seriously about what was going on. But we noticed that each time at the end of the conversation the Shangaan would point towards something, and that our *veldkornet* would take great pains to follow the direction of the tribesman's finger.

Of course, we understood then what it was all about. Our *veldkornet* was a young fellow, and he was shy to let us see that he didn't know the way to Mafeking.

Somehow, after that, we didn't have so much confidence in our *veldkornet*.

~

After a few days we got to Mafeking. We stayed there a long while, until the English troops came and relieved the place. Then we left. We left quickly. The English troops had brought a lot of artillery with them. And if we had had difficulty finding the road to Mafeking, we had no difficulty finding the road away from Mafeking. And this time our *veldkornet* did not need a Shangaan, either, to point with his finger where we had to go. Even though we did a lot of travelling in the night.

Long afterwards, I spoke to an Englishman about this. He said it gave him a queer feeling to hear about the other side of the story of Mafeking. He said that there had been great rejoicing in England when Mafeking was relieved, and that it was strange to think of the other aspect of it – of a defeated country, and of broken commandos blundering in the dark.

I remember many things that happened on the way back from Mafeking. There was no moon. And the stars shone down fitfully on the road that was full of guns, and frightened horses, and desperate men. The veld throbbed with the hoofbeats of baffled commandos. The stars looked down on scenes that told sombrely of a nation's ruin; they looked on the muzzles of Mausers that had failed the Transvaal for the first time.

Of course, as a burgher of the Republic, I knew what my duty was. It was to get as far away as I could from the place where, in the sunset, I had last seen the English artillery. The other burghers also knew their duty. Our commandants and *veldkornets* had to give very few orders. Nevertheless, although I rode very fast, there was one young man who rode faster. He kept ahead of me all the time. He rode as a burgher should ride when there may be stray bullets flying – with his head well down, and with his arms almost round the horse's neck.

He was Stephanus, the young son of Floris van Barnevelt.

There was much grumbling and dissatisfaction some time afterwards, when our leaders started making an effort to get the commandos in order again. In the end, they managed to get us to halt. But most of us felt that this was a foolish thing to do. Especially as there was still a lot of firing going on all over the place, in a haphazard fashion, and we couldn't tell how far the English had followed us in the dark. Furthermore, the commandos had scattered in so many different directions that it seemed hopeless to try and get them together again, until after the war. Stephanus and I dismounted and stood by our horses. Soon there was a large body of men around us. Their figures looked strange and shadowy in the starlight. Some of them stood by their horses. Others sat on the grass by the roadside. '*Vas staan, burgers, vas staan,*' came the commands of our officers. And all the time, we could still hear what sounded like a lot of lyddite.

'The next thing they'll want,' Stephanus van Barnevelt said, 'is for us to go back to Mafeking. Perhaps our commandant has left his tobacco pouch behind there.'

Some of us laughed at this remark, but Floris, who had not dismounted, said that Stephanus ought to be ashamed of himself for talking like that. From what we could see of Floris in the gloom, he looked quite impressive, sitting very straight in the saddle, with the stars shining on his beard and rifle.

'If the *veldkornet* told me to go back to Mafeking,' Floris said, 'I would go back.'

'That's how a burgher should talk,' the *veldkornet* said, feeling flattered. For he had had little authority since the time we found out why he was talking to Shangaans on the way to Mafeking.

'I wouldn't go back to Mafeking for anybody,' Stephanus replied, 'except, maybe, to hand myself over to the English.'

'We can shoot you for doing that,' the *veldkornet* said. 'It's contrary to military law.'

'I wish I knew something about military law,' Stephanus answered. 'Then I would draw up a peace treaty between Stephanus van Barnevelt and England.'

Some of the men laughed again. But Floris shook his head sadly. He said the Van Barnevelts had fought bravely against Spain, in a war that lasted 80 years.

~

Suddenly, out of the darkness, there came a sharp rattle of musketry, and our men started getting uneasy again. But the sound of the firing decided Stephanus. He jumped on his horse quickly.

'I'm turning back,' he said. 'I'm going to hands-up to the English.'

'No, don't go,' the *veldkornet* called to him lamely, 'or at least, wait until the morning. They may shoot you in the dark by mistake.'

As I have said, the *veldkornet* had very little authority.

~

Two days passed before we again saw Floris van Barnevelt. He was in a very worn and troubled state, and he said that it had been very hard for him to find his way back to us.

'You should have asked a Shangaan,' one of our number said, with a laugh. 'All the Mshangaans know our *veldkornet*.'

But Floris did not speak about what had happened that night, when we saw him riding out under the starlight, following after his son and shouting to him to be a man, and to fight for his country. And Floris did not mention Stephanus again – his son was not worthy to be a Van Barnevelt.

~

After that we got separated. Our *veldkornet* was the first to be taken prisoner. And I often felt that he must feel very lonely on St Helena – because there was no Shangaan there, from whom he could ask the way out of the barbed-wire camp.

Then, at last, our leaders came together at Vereeniging, and peace was made. And we returned to our farms, relieved that the war was over, but with heavy hearts at the thought that it had all been for nothing, and that over the Transvaal the Vierkleur would wave no more.

And Floris van Barnevelt put back in its place, on the wall of the *voorkamer*, the copy of his family tree that had been carried with him in his knapsack throughout the war. Then a new schoolmaster came to this part of the Marico, and after a long talk with Floris, the schoolmaster wrote behind Stephanus's name, between two curved lines, the two words that you can still read there: '*Obiit* Mafeking'.

~

Consequently, if you ask any person hereabouts what '*obiit*' means, he is able to tell you right away that it is a foreign word, and that it means to ride up to the English, holding your Mauser in the air, with a white flag tied to it – near the muzzle.

It was long afterwards that Floris van Barnevelt began telling his story.

But then, no one took any notice of him. And they wouldn't allow him to be nominated for the Drogevlei School Committee – on the grounds that a man must be wrong in the head to talk in such an irresponsible fashion.

But I knew that Floris had a good story, and that its only fault was that he told it badly. He mentioned the Drogevlei School Committee too soon. And he knocked the ash out of his pipe in the wrong place. And he always insisted on telling that part of the story that he should have left out.

5.

For the Sake of the Donkeys

From 'Starlight on the Veld'

In *Mafeking Road*

It was a cold night – Oom Schalk Lourens said – and the stars shone with that frosty sort of light that you see on the wet grass some mornings, when you forget that it is winter and you get up early, by mistake. The wind was like a girl sobbing out her story of betrayal to the stars.

Jan Ockerse and I had been to Derdepoort by donkey-cart. We came back in the evening. And Jan Ockerse told me of a road round the foot of a *koppie* that would be a short cut back to Drogevlei. Thus it was that we were sitting on the veld, close to the fire, waiting for the morning. We would then be able to ask a Shangaan to tell us a short cut back to the foot of that *koppie*.

'But I know that was the right road,' Jan Ockerse insisted, flinging another armful of wood on the fire.

'Then it must have been the wrong *koppie*,' I answered, 'or the wrong donkey-cart. Unless you also want me to believe that I am at this moment sitting at home in my *voorkamer*.'

The light from the flames danced frostily on the spokes of a cart-wheel, and I was glad to think that Jan Ockerse must be feeling as cold as I was.

'It's a funny sort of night,' Jan Ockerse said, 'and I'm very miserable and hungry.'

I was glad of that, too. I had begun to fear that he was enjoying himself.

'Do you know how high up the stars are?' Jan asked me next.

'No, not from here,' I said, 'but I worked it all out once, when I had a pencil. That was on the Highveld, though. But from where we are now, in the Lowveld, the stars are further away. You can see that they look smaller, too.'

'Yes, I expect so,' Jan Ockerse answered, 'but a schoolteacher told me a different thing in the bar at Zeerust. He said that the stargazers work out how far away a star is by the number of years that it takes them to find it in their telescopes. This schoolteacher dipped his finger in the brandy and drew a lot of pictures and things on the bar counter, to show me how it was done. But one part of his drawings always dried up on the counter before he had finished doing the other part with his finger. He said that was the worst of that dry sort of brandy. Yet, he didn't finish his explanation, because the barmaid came and wiped it all off with a rag. Then the schoolteacher told me to come with him and he would use the blackboard in the other classroom. But the barmaid wouldn't allow us to take our glasses into the private bar, and the schoolteacher fell down just about then, too.'

'He seems to be one of that new kind of schoolteacher,' I said, 'the kind that teaches the children that the earth turns round the sun. I'm surprised they didn't sack him.'

'Yes,' Jan Ockerse answered, 'they did.'

I was glad to hear that also.

It seemed that there was a waterhole near where we were outspanned. For a couple of jackals started howling mournfully. Jan Ockerse jumped up and piled more wood on the fire.

'I don't like these wild animal noises,' he said.

'They're only jackals, Jan,' I said.

'I know,' he answered, 'but I was thinking of our donkeys. I don't want our donkeys to get frightened.'

Suddenly a deep growl came to us from out of the dark

bush. And it didn't sound like a particularly mournful growl, either. Jan Ockerse worked very fast then with the wood.

'Perhaps it would be even better if we made two fires, and lay down between them,' Jan Ockerse said. 'Our donkeys will feel less frightened if they see that you and I are safe. You know how a donkey's mind works.'

The light of the fire shone dimly on the skeletons of the tall trees that the white ants had eaten, and we soon had two fires going. By the time that the second deep roar from the bush reached us, I had made an even bigger fire than Jan Ockerse, for the sake of the donkeys.

Afterwards it got quiet again. There was only the stirring of the wind in the thorn branches, and the rustling movement of things that you hear in the bushveld at night.

Jan Ockerse lay on his back and put his hands under his head, and once more looked up at the stars.

6.

The Things that Really Matter

From 'Yellow Moepels'

In *Mafeking Road*

If ever you spoke to my father about witchdoctors – Oom Schalk Lourens said – he would always relate one story. And at the end of it he would explain that, while a witchdoctor could foretell the future for you, from the bones, at the same time he could only tell you the things that didn't matter. My father used to say that the important things were as much hidden from the witchdoctor as from the man who listened to his prophecy.

My father said that when he was sixteen he went with his friend, Paul, a stripling of about his own age, to a black witchdoctor. They had heard that this witchdoctor was very good at throwing the bones.

This witchdoctor lived alone in a mud hut. While they were still on the way to the hut, the two youths laughed and jested; but as soon as they got inside, they felt different. They were impressed. The witchdoctor was very old and very wrinkled. He had on a queer headdress made up from the tails of different wild animals.

You could tell that the boys were overawed as they sat there on the floor in the dark. Because my father, who had meant to hand the witchdoctor only a plug of Boer tobacco, gave him a whole roll. And Paul, who had said, when they were outside, that he was going to give him nothing at all, actually handed over his hunting knife.

Then the witchdoctor threw the bones. He threw first for

my father, and told him many things. He told him that he would grow up to be a good burgher, and that he would one day be very prosperous. He would have a big farm and many cattle and two ox-waggons.

But what the witchdoctor did not tell my father was that in years to come he would have a son, Schalk, who would tell better stories than any man in the Marico.

Then the witchdoctor threw the bones for Paul. For a long while he was silent. He looked from the bones to Paul, and back to the bones, in a strange way. Then he spoke.

'I can see you go far away, my *kleinbaas*,' he said, 'very far away over the great waters. Away from your own land, my *kleinbaas*.'

'And the veld?' Paul asked, 'and the *krantzes* and the *vlaktes*?'

'And away from your own people,' the witchdoctor said.

'And will I ... will I ...'

'No, my *kleinbasie*,' the witchdoctor answered, 'you will not come back. You will die there.'

My father said that when they came out of that hut, Paul Kruger's face was very white.

That was why my father used to say that, while a witchdoctor could tell you true things, he could not tell you the things that really mattered.

And my father was right.

7.

Slouching Past in the Dark

From 'Peaches Ripening in the Sun'

In *Unto Dust*

The way Ben Myburg lost his memory – Oom Schalk Lourens said – made a deep impression on us all. We reasoned that that was the sort of thing that a sudden shock could do to you. There were those in our small *seksie* of General Du Toit's commando who could recall similar stories of how people, in a moment, could forget everything about the past, just because of a single dreadful happening.

A shock like that can have the same effect on you even if you are prepared for it. Maybe it can be worse, even. And in this connection I often think of what it says in the Good Book, about that which you most feared having now at last caught up with you.

~

Our commando went as far as the border by train. And when the engine came to a stop on a piece of open veld, and it wasn't for water, this time, and the engine-driver and fireman didn't step down with spanners and use bad language, then we understood that the train stopping there was the beginning of the Second Boer War.

We were wearing new clothes and we had new equipment, and the sun was shining on the barrels of our Mausers. Our new clothes had been requisitioned for us by our *veldkornets* at stores along the way. All the *veldkornet* had to do was to sign his name on a piece of paper for whatever his men purchased.

In most cases, after we had patronised a store in this manner, the shopkeeper would close his shutters for the day. And three years would pass, and the Boer War would be over, before the shopkeeper would display any sort of inclination to open his shutters again.

Maybe he should have closed them before we came.

Only one *seksie* of General Du Toit's commando entered Natal looking considerably dilapidated. This *seksie* looked as though it was already the end of the Boer War, and not just the beginning. Afterwards we found out that their *veldkornet* had never learnt to write his name.

~

'You don't seem to remember me, Schalk,' a young fellow came up and said to me. I admitted that I didn't recognise him, straight away, as Ben Myburg. He did look different in those smart light-green riding pants and that new hat with the ostrich feather stuck in it. You could see that he had patronised some mine concession store before the owner had closed his shutters.

'But I would know you anywhere, Schalk,' Ben Myburg went on. 'Just from the quick way you hid that soap under your saddle a couple of minutes ago. I remembered where I had last seen something so quick. It was two years ago, at the *Nagmaal* in Nylstroom.'

I told Ben Myburg that if it was that jar of brandy he meant, then he must realise that there had also been a good deal of misunderstanding about it. Moreover, it wasn't even a full jar, I said.

But I congratulated him on his powers of memory, which I said I was sure would yet stand the Republic in good stead.

And I was right. For afterwards, when the war of the big commandos was over, and we were in constant retreat, it would be Ben Myburg who, next day, would lead us back to the donga in which we had hidden some mealie-meal and a tin of cooking fat. And if the tin of cooking fat was empty, he would be able to tell us right away if it was humans or baboons. A human had a different way of eating cooking fat out of a tin from a baboon, Ben Myburg said.

Ben Myburg had been recently married to Mimi van Blerk, who came from Schweitzer-Reneke, a district that was known as far as the Limpopo for its attractive girls. I remembered Mimi van Blerk well. She had full red lips and thick yellow hair. Ben Myburg always looked forward very eagerly to getting letters from his pretty young wife. He would also read out to us extracts from her letters, in which she encouraged us to drive the English into the blue grass – which was the name we gave to the sea in those days. For the English, we had other names.

~

Eighteen months later saw the armed forces of the Republic in a worse case than I should imagine any army has ever been in, and that army still fighting. We were spread all over the country in small groups. We were in rags.

Many burghers had been taken prisoner. Others had yielded themselves up to British magistrates, holding not their rifles in their hands but their hats. There were a number of Boers, also, who had gone over and joined the English.

For the Transvaal Republic it was near the end of a tale that you tell, sitting around the kitchen fire on a cold night. The story of the Transvaal Republic was at that place where you clear your throat before saying which of the two men the girl finally married. Or whether it was the cattle-smuggler or the Sunday school superintendant who stole the money. Or whether it was a real ghost or just her uncle with a sheet around him that Lettie van Zyl saw at the drift.

~

By the following evening we had crossed the *rant* and arrived at Ben Myburg's farm. We camped among the smoke-blackened walls of his former homestead, erecting a rough shelter with some sheets of corrugated iron that we could still use. And although he must have known only too well what to expect, what Ben Myburg saw there came as so much of a shock to his senses that, from that moment on, all he could remember from the past vanished forever.

It was pitiful to see the change that came over him. If his farm had been laid to ruins, the devastation that took place in Ben Myburg's mind was no less dreadful.

Perhaps it was that, in truth, there was nothing more left in the past to remember.

We noticed, also, that in singular ways, certain fragments of the by-gone would come into Ben Myburg's mind; and that he would almost – but not quite – succeed in fitting these pieces together.

We observed that almost immediately. For instance, we remained camped on his farm for several days. And one morning, when the fire for our mealie-*pap* was crackling under one of the few remaining fruit-trees that had once been an orchard, Ben Myburg reached up and picked a peach that was, in advance of its season, ripe and yellow.

'It's funny,' Ben Myburg said, 'but I seem to remember, from long ago, reaching up and picking a yellow peach, just like this one. I don't quite remember where.'

We did not tell him.

Some time later our *seksie* was captured in a night attack.

For us the Boer War was over. We were going to St Helena. We were driven to Nylstroom, the nearest railhead, in a mule-wagon. It was a strange experience for us to be driving along the main road, in broad daylight, for all the world to see us. From years of wartime habit, our eyes still went to the horison. A bitter thing about our captivity was that among our guards were men of our own people.

Outside Nylstroom we alighted from the mule-wagon and the English sergeant in charge of our escort got us to form fours by the roadside. It was queer – our having to learn to be soldiers at the end of a war instead of at the beginning.

Eventually we got into some sort of formation, the *veldkornet*, Jurie Bekker, Ben Myburg and I making up the first four. It was already evening. From a distance we could see the lights in the town. The way to the main street of Nylstroom led by the cemetery. Although it was dark, we could yet distinguish several rows of newly made mounds. We did not need to be told that they were concentration camp graves. We took off our battered hats and tramped on in a great silence.

Soon we were in the main street. We saw, then, what those lights were. There was a dance at the hotel. Paraffin lamps were hanging under the hotel's low, wide verandah. There was much laughter. We saw girls and English officers. In our unaccustomed fours, we slouched past in the dark.

Several of the girls went inside then. But a few of the women-folk remained on the verandah, not looking in our direction. Among them I noticed in particular a girl leaning on an English officer's shoulder. She looked very pretty, with the light from a paraffin lamp shining on her full lips and yellow hair.

When we had turned the corner, and the darkness was

wrapping us round again, I heard Ben Myburg speak.

'It's funny,' I heard Ben Myburg say, 'but I seem to remember, from long ago, a girl with yellow hair, just like that one. I don't quite remember where.'

And this time, too, we did not tell him.

8.

A Peculiar Sort of Smile

From 'The Selons-Rose'

In *Unto Dust*

Any story – Oom Schalk Lourens said – about that half-red flower, the selons-rose, must be an old story. It is the flower that a Marico girl most often pins in her hair to attract her lover. The selons-rose is also the flower that here, in the Marico, we customarily plant upon a grave.

One thing that certain thoughtless people sometimes hint at about my stories is that nothing ever seems to happen in them. Then there is another kind of person who goes even further, and says that the stories I tell are all stories he has heard before, somewhere long ago – he can't remember when exactly, but somewhere at the back of his mind he knows it is not a new story.

I have heard that remark passed quite often – which is not surprising, seeing that I really don't know any new stories. But the funny part of it is that these very people will come around, say, ten years later, and ask me to tell them another story. And they will say, then, because of what they have learnt of life in between, that the older the story, the better.

Anyway, I have come to the conclusion that with an old story, it is like with an old song. People tire of a new song readily.

I remember how it was when Marie du Preez came back to the Bushveld after her parents had sent her overseas to learn singing, because they had found diamonds on their farm, and because Marie's teacher had said that she had a nice singing voice. Then, when Marie came back from Europe – through the diamonds on the Du Preez farm having given out suddenly – we on this side of the Dwarsberge were keen to have Marie sing for us.

There was a large attendance, that night, when Marie du Preez gave a concert in the Drogedal schoolroom. She sang what she called arias from Italian opera. And at first things did not go at all well. We didn't care much for those new songs in Italian. One song was about the dawn being near, goodbye beloved, and about being under somebody's window – that was what Marie's mother told us, in quick whispers, it was. Marie du Preez's mother came from the Cape and had studied at the Wellington seminary. Another song was about mother see these tears. The Hollander schoolmaster told me the meaning of that one. But I don't know if it was Marie's mother that was meant.

We didn't actually dislike those songs that Marie du Preez sang. It was only that we weren't moved by them.

Accordingly, after the interval, when Marie was again stepping up onto the low platform before the blackboard on which the teacher wrote sums on school-days, Philippus Bonthuys, a farmer who had come all the way from Nietverdiend to attend the concert, got up and stood beside Marie du Preez. And because he was so tall and broad it seemed almost as though he stood half in front of her, elbowing her a little, even.

Philippus Bonthuys said he was just a plain Dopper. And we all cheered. Then Philippus Bonthuys said that his grandfather was also just a plain Dopper, who wore his pipe and his tobacco-bag on a piece of string fastened at the side of his trousers. We cheered a lot more, then. Philippus Bonthuys went on to say that he liked the old songs best. They could keep those new songs about laugh because somebody has stolen your clown. We gathered from that that Marie's mother had been explaining to Philippus Bonthuys, also in quick whispers, the meanings of some of Marie's songs.

And before we knew where we were, the whole crowd in the schoolroom was singing, with Philippus Bonthuys beating time, *My oupa was 'n Dopper, en 'n Dopper was hy*. You have no idea how stirring that old song sounded, with Philippus Bonthuys beating time, in the night, under the thatch of that Marico schoolroom, and with Marie du Preez looking slightly bewildered but joining in all the same – since it was her concert, after all – and not singing in Italian, either.

We sang many songs, after that, and they were all old songs. We sang *Die vaal hare en die blou oge* and *Daar waar die son en die maan ondergaan* and *Vat jou goed en trek, Ferreira* and *Met my rooi rok voor jou deur*. It was very beautiful.

We sang until late into the night. Afterwards, when we congratulated Marie du Preez's mother, who had arranged it all, on the success of her daughter's concert, *Mevrou* Du Preez said it was nothing, and she smiled.

But it was a peculiar sort of a smile.

9.

Juice of the Juba-Berry

From 'The Love Potion'

In *Mafeking Road*

You mention the juba-plant – Oom Schalk Lourens said – oh, yes, everybody in the Marico knows about the juba-plant. It grows high up on the *krantzes*, and they say you must pick off one of its little red berries at midnight, under the full moon. Then, if you are a young man, and you are anxious for a girl to fall in love with you, all you have to do is squeeze the juice of the juba-berry into her coffee.

They say that after the girl has drunk the juba-juice, she begins to forget all sorts of things. She forgets that your forehead is rather low, and that your ears stick out, and that your mouth is too big. She even forgets having told you, the week before last, that she wouldn't marry you if you were the only man in the Transvaal.

All she knows is that the man she gazes at, over her empty coffee cup, has grown remarkably handsome. You can see from this that the plant must be very potent in its effects. I mean, if you consider what some of the men in the Marico look like.

~

One night I was out shooting in the veld with a lamp fastened on my hat. You know that kind of shooting – in the glare of the lamplight you can only see the eyes of the thing you are aiming at, and you get three months if you are caught.

They made it illegal to hunt by lamplight since the time a policeman got shot in the foot, this way, when he was out tracking cattle-smugglers on the Bechuanaland border.

The magistrate at Zeerust, who did not know the ways of the cattle-smugglers, found that the shooting was an accident. This verdict satisfied everybody except the policeman, whose foot was still bandaged when he came into court. But the men in the *Volksraad*, some of whom had been cattle-smugglers themselves, knew better than the magistrate did as to how the policeman came to have a couple of buckshot in the soft part of his foot, and accordingly they brought in this new law.

Therefore I walked very quietly that night on the *krantz*. Frequently I put out my hand and stood very still among the trees, and waited long moments to make sure I was not being followed. Ordinarily, there would have been little to fear, but a couple of days before two policemen had been seen disappearing into the bush. By their looks they seemed young policemen, anxious for promotion, who didn't know that it is more becoming for a policeman to drink an honest farmer's peach brandy than to arrest him for hunting by lamplight.

I was walking along, turning the light from side to side, when suddenly, about a hundred paces from me, in the full brightness of the lamp, I saw a pair of eyes. When I also saw, above the eyes, a policeman's khaki helmet, I remembered that a moonlight night, such as that was, was not so good for finding buck.

So I went home.

I took the shortest way, too, which was over the side of the *krantz* – the steep side – and on my way down I clutched at a variety of branches, tree-roots, stone ledges and tufts of grass. Later on, at the foot of the *krantz*, when I came to and was able to sit up, there was that policeman bending over me.

'Oom Schalk,' he said, 'I was wondering if you would lend

me your lamp.'

I looked up. It was Gideon van der Merwe, a young policeman who had been stationed for some time at Derdepoort. I had met him on several occasions, and had found him very likeable.

'You can have my lamp,' I answered, 'but you must be very careful. It's worse for a policeman to get caught breaking the law than for an ordinary man.'

Gideon van der Merwe shook his head.

'No, I don't want to go shooting with the lamp', he said, 'I want to …'.

And then he paused.

He laughed nervously.

'It seems silly to say it, Oom Schalk,' he said, 'but perhaps you'll understand. I've come to look for a juba-plant. I need it for my studies. For my third-class sergeant's exam. And it'll soon be midnight, and I can't find one of those plants anywhere.'

I felt sorry for Gideon. It struck me that he would never make a good policeman. If he couldn't find a juba-plant, of which there were thousands on the *krantz*, it would be much harder for him to find the *spoor* of a cattle smuggler.'

So I handed him my lamp and explained where he had to go and look. Gideon thanked me and walked off.

Half an hour later he was back.

He took a red berry out of his tunic pocket and showed it to me.

For fear that he should tell any more lies about needing that juba-berry for his studies, I spoke first.

'Lettie Cordier?' I asked.

Gideon nodded. He was very shy, though, and wouldn't talk much at the start. But I had guessed long ago that Gideon van der Merwe was not calling at Krisjan Cordier's house so often just to hear Krisjan relate the story of his life.

~

Next morning I rode over to Krisjan Cordier's farm to remind him about a tin of sheep-dip that he still owed me from the last dipping season. When Lettie came in with the coffee, I made a casual remark to her father about Gideon van der Merwe.

I didn't take much notice of Krisjan's remarks, however. Instead, I looked carefully at Lettie when I mentioned Gideon's name. She didn't give much away, but I am quick at these things, and I saw enough. The colour that crept into her cheeks. The light that came in her eyes.

On my way back I encountered Lettie. She was standing under a thorn-tree. With her brown arms and her sweet, quiet face and her full bosom, she was a very pretty picture. There was no doubt that Lettie Cordier would make a fine wife for any man. It wasn't hard to understand Gideon's feelings about her.

'Lettie,' I asked, 'do you love him?'

'I love him, Oom Schalk,' she answered.

It was as simple as that.

~

When I saw Gideon some time afterwards, he was elated, as I had expected he would be.

'So the juba-plant worked?' I enquired.

'It was wonderful, Oom Schalk,' Gideon answered, 'and the funny part of it is that Lettie's father wasn't there, either, when I put that juba-juice into her coffee. Lettie had brought him a message, just before then, that he was wanted in the mealie-lands.'

'And was the juba-juice all they claim for it?'

'You'd be surprised how quickly it acted,' he said. 'Lettie just took one sip at the coffee, and then jumped straight onto my lap.'

But then Gideon van der Merwe winked in a way that made me believe that he was not so very simple, after all.

'I was pretty certain that the juba-juice would work, Oom Schalk,' he said, 'after Lettie's father told me that you had visited there that morning.'

10.

More Real than Life

From 'Dream by the Blue Gums'

In *Mafeking Road*

In the heat of the midday – Oom Schalk Lourens said – Adrian Naudé and I were glad to be resting there, shaded by the tall bluegums that stood in a clump by the side of the road.

I sat on the grass with my head and shoulders supported against a large stone. Adrian Naudé, who had begun by leaning against a tree-trunk with his legs crossed and his fingers interlaced behind his head and his elbows out, lowered himself to the ground by degrees. For a short while he remained seated on his haunches, then he sighed and slid forward, very carefully, until he was lying stretched out at full length, with his face in the grass.

~

'It's not so bad for you, *Neef* Schalk,' Adrian Naudé went on, yawning. 'You've got a big comfortable stone to rest your head and shoulders against. Whereas I've got to lie down flat on the dry grass, with all the sharp points sticking into me. You're always like that, *Neef* Schalk. You always pick the best for yourself.'

By the unreasonable nature of his remarks, I could tell that Adrian Naudé was being overtaken by a spell of drowsiness.

'You're always like that,' Adrian went on. 'It's one of the low traits of your character. Always picking the best for yourself. There was that time in Zeerust, for instance. People always mention that – when they want to talk about how low a man can be …'

I could see that the heat of the day and his condition of being half asleep might lead Adrian to say things that he would no doubt be very sorry for, afterwards. So I interrupted him, speaking very earnestly for his own good.

'It's quite true, *Neef* Adrian,' I said, 'that this stone against which I am lying is the only one in the vicinity. But I can't help that any more than I can help this clump of bluegums being here. It's funny about these bluegums, now, growing like this by the side of the road, when the rest of the veld around here is bare. I wonder who planted them. As for this stone, *Neef* Adrian, it's not my fault that I saw it first. It was just luck. But you can knock out your pipe against it whenever you want to.'

This offer seemed to satisfy Adrian. At all events, he didn't pursue the argument. I noticed that his breathing had become very slow and deep and regular, and the last remark he made was so muffled as to be almost unintelligible. It was: 'To think that a man can fall so low.'

From that I judged that Adrian Naudé was dreaming about something.

It was very pleasant there, on the yellow grass, by the roadside, underneath the bluegums, whose shadows slowly lengthened as midday passed into afternoon. Nowhere was there sound or movement. The whole world was at rest, with the silence of the dust on the deserted road, and with the peace of the bluegums' shadows. My companion's measured breathing seemed to come from very far away.

Then it was that a strange thing happened.

What is in the first place remarkable about what I am now going to relate to you is that it shows you clearly how short a dream is. And how much you can dream in just a few moments. In the second place, as you'll see when I get to the end of it, this story proves how, right in broad daylight, a queer thing can take place – almost in front of your eyes, as it were – and you may wonder about it forever afterwards, and you will never understand it.

Well, as I was saying, what with Adrian Naudé lying asleep within a few feet of me, and everything being so still, I was on the point of also dropping off to sleep, when, in the distance – so small that I could barely distinguish its outlines – I caught sight of the mule-cart whose return Adrian and I were awaiting. From where I lay, with my head on the stone, I had a clear view of the road all the way up to where it disappeared over the *bult*.

But as I gazed, I felt my eyelids getting heavy. I told myself that, with the glare of the sun on the road, I would not be able to keep my eyes open much longer. I remember thinking how foolish it would be to fall asleep, then, with the mule-cart only a short distance away. It would pull up almost immediately, and I would have to wake up again. I told myself I was being foolish – and, of course, I fell asleep.

It was while I was still telling myself that in a few moments the mule-cart would be coming to a stop in the shadow of the bluegums, that my eyes closed and I fell asleep. And I started to dream. And from this you can tell how swift a thing a dream is, and how much you can dream in just a few moments.

For I know the exact moment in which I started to dream. It was when I was looking very intently at the driver of the mule-cart and I suddenly saw, to my amazement, that the driver was no longer Jonas, but Adrian Naudé. And seated beside Adrian Naudé was a girl in a white frock. She had yellow hair that hung far down over her shoulders, and her name was Francina. The next minute the mule-cart drew up, and Jonas jumped off and tied the reins to a wheel.

So it was between those flying moments that I dreamt about Adrian Naudé and Francina.

'It's difficult to believe, Francina,' Adrian Naudé was saying, nodding his head in my direction. 'It's difficult to believe a man can sink so low. If I tell you what happened in Zeerust …'

I was getting annoyed now. After all, Francina was a complete stranger, and Adrian had no right to slander me in that fashion. What was more, I had a very simple explanation for the Zeerust incident. I felt that, if only I could be alone with Francina for a few minutes, I would be able to convince her that what had happened in Zeerust was not to my discredit at all.

But even as I started talking to Francina, I realised that there was no need for me to say anything. She put her hand on my arm and looked at me. And the sun was on her hair, and the shadows of the bluegums were in her eyes. And by the way she smiled at me, I knew that nothing Adrian could say about me would ever make any difference to her.

Moreover, Adrian Naudé had gone. You know how it is in a dream.

~

Then it all changed, suddenly. I seemed to know that it was only a dream, and that I wasn't really standing up under the trees with Francina. I seemed to know that I was actually lying on the grass, with my head and shoulders resting against a stone. I even heard the mule-cart jolting over the rough part of the road.

But the next instant I was dreaming again.

I dreamt that Francina was explaining to me, in gentle and sorrowful tones, that she could not stay any longer. And that she had put her hand on my arm for the last time, in farewell. She said I was not to follow her, but that I had to close my eyes when she turned away, for no one was to know where she had come from.

~

It was a vivid dream. Part of it seemed more real than life, as is frequently the case with a dream on the veld, dreamt fleetingly, in the heat of the noonday.

I asked Francina where she lived.

'Not far from here,' she answered, 'no, not far. But you may not follow me. None may go back with me.'

She still smiled, in that way in which women smiled long ago, but as she spoke there came into her eyes a look of such intense sorrow that I was afraid to ask why I could not accompany her. And when she told me to close my eyes, I had no power to protest.

And, of course, I didn't close my eyes. Instead, I opened them, just as Jonas was jumping down from the mule-cart to fasten the reins onto a wheel.

Adrian Naudé woke up about the same time that I did, and asked Jonas why he had been away so long. And I got up from the grass, and stretched my limbs, and wondered about dreams. It seemed incredible that I could have dreamed so much in such a few moments.

And there was a strange sadness in my heart because the dream had gone. My mind was filled with a deep sense of loss. I told myself that it was foolish to have feelings like that about a dream, even though it was a particularly vivid dream and part of it seemed more real than life.

Then, when we were ready to go, Adrian Naudé took out his pipe. Before filling it, he stooped down as though to knock the ash out of it – as I had invited him to do before we fell asleep. But it so happened that Adrian Naudé did not ever knock his pipe out against that stone.

'That's funny,' I heard Adrian say, as he bent forward.

I saw what he was about, so I knelt down and helped him. When we had cleared away the accumulation of yellow grass and dead leaves at the foot of the stone, we found that the inscription on it, though battered, was quite legible. It was very simply worded. Just a date chiselled into the stone. And below the date, a name: Francina Malherbe.

11.

Under the Full Moon

From 'Drieka and the Moon'

In *Mafeking Road*

There is a queer witchery about the moon when it is full – Oom Schalk Lourens remarked – especially the moon that hangs over the valley of the Dwarsberge in the summertime. It does strange things to your mind, the Marico moon, and in your heart are wild and fragrant fancies, and your thoughts go very far away. Then, if you have been sitting on your front stoep, thinking these thoughts, you sigh and murmer something about the way of the world, and carry your chair inside.

I have seen the moon in other places besides the Marico. But it is not the same there.

Braam Venter, the man who fell off the Government lorry once, near Nietverdiend, says that the Marico moon is like a woman laying green flowers on a grave. Braam Venter often says things like that. Particularly since the time he fell off the lorry. He fell on his head, they say.

Always when the moon shines full like that, it does something to our hearts that we wonder very much about and that we never understand. Always it awakens memories. And it is singular how different these memories are with each one of us.

Johannes Oberholtzer says that the full moon always reminds him of one occasion when he was smuggling cattle over the Bechuanaland border. He says he never sees a full moon without thinking of the way it shone on the steel wire-cutters that he was holding in his hand when two mounted policemen rode up to him. And the next night Johannes Oberholtzer again had a good view of the full moon; he saw it through the window of the place he was in. He says the moon was very large and very yellow, except for the black stripes in front of it.

And it was in the light of the full moon that hung over the thorn-trees that I saw Drieka Breytenbach.

Drieka was tall and slender. She had fair hair and blue eyes, and lots of people considered that she was the prettiest woman in the Marico. I thought so, too, that night I met her under the full moon by the thorn-trees. She had not been in the Bushveld very long. Her husband, Petrus Breytenbach, had met her and married her in the Schweizer-Reneke district, where he had trekked with his cattle for a while during the big drought.

Afterwards, when Petrus Breytenbach was shot dead with his own Mauser by a worker on his farm, Drieka went back to Schweizer-Reneke, leaving the Marico as strangely and as silently as she had come to it.

And it seemed to me that the Marico was a different place because Drieka Breytenbach had gone. And I thought of the moon, and the tricks it plays with your senses, and the stormy witchery that it flings at your soul. And I remembered what Braam Venter had said, that the full moon is like a woman laying green flowers on a grave. And it seemed to me that Braam Venter's words were not so much nonsense, after all, and that worse things could happen to a man than that he should fall off a lorry on his head. And I thought of other matters.

But all this happened only afterwards.

When I saw Drieka that night she was leaning against a thorn-tree beside the road where it goes down to the drift. But I didn't recognise her at first. All I saw was a figure dressed in white with long hair hanging down loose over its shoulders. It seemed very unusual that a figure should be there like that at such a time of night. I remembered certain stories I had heard about white ghosts. I also remembered that a few miles back I had seen a boulder lying in the middle of the road. It was a fair-sized boulder and it might be dangerous for passing mule-carts. So I decided to turn back at once and move it out of the way.

I decided very quickly about the boulder. And I made up my mind so firmly that the saddle-girth broke, from the sudden way in which I jerked my horse back on his haunches. Then the figure came forward and spoke, and I saw that it was Drieka Breytenbach.

'Good evening,' I said, in answer to her greeting, 'I was just going back because I had remembered about something.'

'About ghosts?' she asked.

'No,' I replied truthfully, 'about a stone in the road.'

Drieka laughed at that. So I laughed too. And then Drieka laughed again. And then I laughed. In fact, we did quite a lot of laughing between us. I got off my horse and stood beside Drieka in the moonlight. And if somebody had come along at that moment and said that the *predikant*'s mule-cart had been capsised by the boulder in the road, I would have laughed still more.

That is the sort of thing the moon in the Marico does to you, when it is full.

I didn't think of asking Drieka how she came to be there, or why her hair was hanging down loose, or who it was that she had been waiting for under the thorn-tree. It was enough that the moon was there, big and yellow over the veld, and that the wind blew softly through the trees, and across the grass, and against Drieka's white dress, and against the mad singing of the stars.

~

Before I knew what was happening we were seated on the grass under the thorn-tree whose branches leant over the road. And I remember that for quite a while we remained there without talking, sitting side by side on the grass with our feet in the soft sand. And Drieka smiled at me with a misty sort of look in her eyes, and I saw that she was lovely.

I felt that it was not enough that we should go on sitting there in silence. I knew that a woman – even a moon-woman like Drieka – expected a man to be more than just good-humoured and honest. I knew that a woman wanted a man to be an entertaining companion for her. So I beguiled the passing moments for Drieka with interesting conversation.

I explained to her how, a few days before, a pebble had worked itself into my *veldskoen* and had rubbed some skin off the top of one of my toes. I took off my *veldskoen* and showed her the place. I also told her about the rinderpest and about the way two of my cows had died of the *miltsiekte*. I also knew a lot about blue-tongue in sheep, and about *gallansiekte* and the *haarwurm*, and I talked to her airily about these things, just as easily as I am talking to you now.

But, of course, it was the moonlight that did it. I never knew before that I was so good in this idle, butterfly kind of talk. And the whole thing was so innocent, too. I felt that if Drieka Breytenbach's husband, Petrus, were to come along and find us sitting there side by side, he would not be able to say much about it. At least, not very much.

~

After a while I stopped talking.
Drieka put her hand in mine.

'Oh, Schalk,' she whispered, and the moon and that misty look were in her blue eyes. 'Do tell me some more.'

I shook my head.

'I'm sorry, Drieka,' I answered. 'I don't know any more.'

'But you must, Schalk,' she said very softly. 'Talk to me about – about other things.'

I thought steadily for some moments.

'Yes, Drieka,' I said at length. 'I have remembered something. There is one more thing I haven't told you about the blue-tongue in sheep …'

'No, no, not that,' she interrupted, 'talk to me about other things. About the moon, say.'

So I told her two things that Braam Venter has said about the moon. I told her the green flower one and another one.

'Braam Venter knows lots more things like that about the moon,' I explained. 'You'll see him next time you go to Zeerust for the *Nagmaal*. He's a short fellow with a bump on his head, from where he fell …'

'Oh, no, Schalk,' Drieka said again, shaking her head, so that a wisp of her fair hair brushed against my face, 'I don't want to know about Braam Venter. Only about you. You think out something on your own about the moon and tell it to me.'

I understood what she meant.

'Well, Drieka,' I said thoughtfully. ' The moon – the moon is all right.'

'Oh, Schalk!' Drieka cried. 'That's much finer than anything Braam Venter could ever say – even with that bump on his head.'

Of course, I told her that it was nothing and that I could perhaps say something even better if I tried. But I was very proud, all the same. And somehow it seemed that my words brought us close together. I felt that a handful of words, spoken under the full moon, had made a new and witch thing come into the life of Drieka and me.

~

We were holding hands then, sitting on the grass with our feet in the road, and Drieka lent her head on my shoulder, and her long hair stirred softly against my face, but I looked only at her feet. And I thought for a moment that I loved her. And I did not love her because her body was beautiful, or because she had red lips, or because her eyes were blue. In that moment, I did not understand about her body, or her lips, or her eyes. I loved her for her feet, and because her feet were in the road next to mine.

And yet all the time I felt, far away at the back of my mind, that it was the moon that was doing these things to me.

'You have got good feet for walking on,' I said to Drieka.

'Braam Venter would have said that I have good feet for dancing on,' Drieka answered, laughing. And I began to grow jealous of Braam Venter.

The next thing I knew was that Drieka had thrown herself into my arms.

'Do you think I am very beautiful, Schalk?' Drieka asked.

'You are very beautiful, Drieka,' I answered slowly, 'very beautiful.'

'Will you do something for me, Schalk?' Drieka asked again, and her red lips were very close to my cheek. 'Will you do something for me, if I love you very much?'

'What do yo want me to do, Drieka?'

She drew my head down to her lips and whispered hot words in my ear.

And so it came that I thrust her from me, suddenly. I jumped unsteadily to my feet; I found my horse and rode away. I left Drieka Breytenbach where I had found her, under the thorn-tree by the roadside, with her hot whisperings still ringing in my ears, and before I reached home, the moon had set behind the Dwarsberge.

~

Well, there is not much left for me to tell you. In the days that followed, Drieka Breytenbach was always in my thoughts. Her long, loose hair, and her lips, and her feet that had been in the roadside sand with mine. But if she really was the ghost that I had at first taken her to be, I could not have been more afraid of her.

And it seemed singular that, while it had been my words, spoken in the moonlight, that had helped to bring Drieka and me closer together, it was Drieka's hot breath, whispering wild words in my ear, that had sent me so suddenly from her side.

Once or twice I even felt sorry for having left her in that fashion.

And later on, when I heard that Drieka Breytenbach had gone back to Schweizer-Reneke, and that her husband had been shot dead with his own Mauser by one of his own farm workers, I was not surprised. In fact, I had expected it. Only it did not seem right, somehow, that Drieka should have got a farm worker to do the thing that I had refused to do.

12.

Bitter against the English

From 'The Rooinek'

In *Mafeking Road*

*R*ooineks – Oom Schalk Lourens said – are queer. For instance, there was that day when my nephew Hannes and I had dealings with a couple of Englishmen near Dewetsdorp. It was shortly after Sanna's Post, and Hannes and I were lying behind a rock, watching the road. Hannes spent moments like that in what he called a useful way. He would file the points of his Mauser cartridges on a piece of stone until the lead showed through the steel, in that way making them into dum-dum bullets.

I often spoke to my nephew Hannes about that.

'Hannes,' I used to say, 'that is a sin. The Lord is looking at you.'

'That's all right,' Hannes replied, 'the Lord knows that this is the Anglo-Boer War, and in wartime He will always forgive a little foolishness like this, especially as the English are so many.'

Anyway, as we lay behind that rock, we saw, far down the road, two horsemen come galloping up. We remained perfectly still and let them approach to within four hundred paces. They were English officers. They were mounted on first-rate horses, and their uniforms looked very fine and smart. They were the most stylish-looking men I had seen for some time, and I felt quite ashamed of my own ragged trousers and *veldskoens*. I was glad that I was behind a rock and that they couldn't see me. Especially as my jacket was also torn all the way down the back, as a result of my having had, three days before, to get through a barbed-wire fence rather quickly. I got through just in time, too. The *veldkornet*, who was a fat man and couldn't run so fast, was about twenty yards behind me. And he remained on the wire with a bullet through him. All through the Anglo-Boer War, I was pleased that I was thin and never troubled with corns.

Hannes and I fired at about the same time. One of the officers fell off his horse. He struck the road with his shoulders and rolled over twice, kicking up the red dust as he turned. Then the other soldier did a queer thing. He drew up his horse and got off. He gave just one look in our direction. Then he led his horse up to where the other man was twisting and struggling on the ground. It took him a little while to lift him onto his horse, for it is no easy matter to pick up a man like that, when he is helpless. And he did all this slowly and calmly, as though he was not concerned about the fact that the men who had just shot his friend were lying only a few hundred yards away. He managed in some way to support the wounded man across the saddle, and walked on beside the horse. After going a few yards, he stopped and seemed to remember something. He turned round and waved at the spot where he imagined we were hiding, as though inviting us to shoot. During all that time I had simply lain watching him, astonished at his coolness.

But when he waved his hand, I thrust another cartridge into the breach of my Martini, and aimed. I aimed very carefully, and was just on the point of pulling the trigger when Hannes put his hand on the barrel, and pushed up my rifle.

'Don't shoot, Oom Schalk,' he said. 'That's a brave man.'

I looked at Hannes in surprise. His face was very white. I said nothing, and allowed my rifle to sink down onto the grass, but I couldn't understand what had come over my nephew.

It seemed that not only was that Englishman queer, but that Hannes was also queer. That's all nonsense, not killing a man just because he's brave. If he's a brave man and he's fighting on the wrong side, that's all the more reason to shoot him.

I was with my nephew Hannes for another few months after that. Then one day, in a skirmish near the Vaal River, Hannes, with a few dozen other burghers, was cut off from the commando, and had to surrender. That was the last I ever saw of him. I heard later on that, after taking him prisoner, the English searched Hannes and found dum-dum bullets in his possession. They shot him for that. I was very much grieved when I heard of Hannes's death. He had always been full of life and high spirits. Perhaps Hannes was right in saying that the Lord didn't mind about a little foolishness like dum-dum bullets. But the mistake he made was in forgetting that the English did mind.

I was in the veld until they made peace.

Then we laid down our rifles and went home. What I knew my farm by was the hole under the *koppie* where I had quarried slate stones for the threshing-floor. That was about all that remained as I had left it. Everything else was gone. My home was burnt down. My lands were laid waste. My cattle and sheep were slaughtered. Even the stones I had piled for the *kraals* were pulled down.

My wife came out of the concentration camp and we went together to look at our old farm. My wife had gone into the concentration camp with our two children, but she came out alone. And when I saw her again and noticed the way she had changed, I knew that I, who had been through all the fighting, had not seen the Anglo-Boer War.

Neither Sannie nor I had the heart to go on farming again, on that same place. It would be different without the children playing about the house and getting into mischief. We got paid out some money by the new Government for part of our losses. So I bought a wagon and oxen, and we left the Free State, which was not even the Free State any longer. It was now called the Orange River Colony.

We trekked right through the Transvaal into the northern part of the Marico Bushveld. Years ago, as a boy, I had trekked through that same country with my parents. Now, when I went there again, I felt that it was still good country. It was on the far side of the Dwarsberge, near Derdepoort, that we got a Government farm. Afterwards other farmers trekked in there as well. One or two of them had also come from the Free State, and I knew them. There were also a few Cape rebels whom I had seen on commando. All of us had lost relatives in the war. Some had died in the concentration camps, some on the battlefield. Others had been shot for going into rebellion.

So, taken all in all, we who trekked into that part of the Marico that lay nearest the Bechuanaland border were bitter against the English.

13.

Too Much Truth

From 'The Rooinek'

In *Mafeking Road*

It was in the first year of our having settled around Derdepoort that we heard that an Englishman had bought a farm next to Gerhardus Grobbelaar. This was when we were sitting in the *voorkamer* of Willem Odendaal's house, which was used as a post office.

Once a week the post-cart came up with letters from Zeerust, and we gathered at Willem Odendaal's house and talked and smoked and drank coffee. Very few of us ever got letters, and then it was mostly demands to pay for the boreholes that had been drilled on our farms, or for cement and fencing materials. But every week, regularly, we went for the post. Sometimes the post-cart didn't come, because the Groen River was in flood, and most of us would have gone home without noticing it if somebody hadn't spoken about it.

When Koos Steyn heard that an Englishman was coming to live among us, he got up from the *riempiesbank*.

'Nee kêrels,' he said, 'always when the Englishman comes, it means that a little later the Boer has got to shift. I'll pack my wagon and make coffee, and just trek first thing tomorrow morning.'

Most of us laughed then. Koos Steyn often said funny things like that. But some didn't laugh. Somehow, there seemed to be too much truth in Koos Steyn's words.

We discussed the matter and decided that, if we Boers in the Marico could help it, the *rooinek* would not stay among us too long. About half an hour later, one of Willem Odendaal's children came in and said that there was a strange wagon coming along the big road. We went to the door and looked out. As the wagon came nearer, we saw that it was piled up with all kinds of furniture, and also sheets of iron and farming implements. There was so much stuff on the wagon that the tent had been taken off to get everything on.

The wagon rolled along and came to a stop in front of the house. With the wagon there was a man who walked up to where we were standing. He was dressed just as we were, in shirt and trousers and *veldskoens*, and he had dust all over him. But when he stepped over a thorn-bush we saw that he had socks on too. Therefore we knew that he was an Englishman.

Koos Steyn was standing in front of the door.

The Englishman went up to him and held out his hand.

'Good afternoon,' he said in Afrikaans. 'My name is Webber.'

Koos shook hands with him.

'My name is Prince Lord Alfred Milner,' Koos Steyn said.

That was when Lord Milner was Governor of the Transvaal, and we all laughed. The *rooinek* also laughed.

'Well, Lord Prince,' he said, 'I can speak your language a little, and I hope that later on I'll be able to speak it better. I'm coming to live here, and I hope that we'll all be friends.'

He then came round to all of us, but the others turned away and refused to shake hands with him. He came up to me last of all. I felt sorry for him, for although his nation had dealt unjustly with my nation, and I had lost both my children in the concentration camp, still it was not so much the fault of this Englishman. It was the fault of the English Government, who wanted our gold mines. And it was also the fault of Queen Victoria, who didn't like Oom Paul Kruger, because they say that when he went over to London Oom Paul spoke to her for only a few minutes. Oom Paul said that he was a married man and that he was afraid of widows.

When the Englishman Webber went back to his wagon, Koos Steyn and I walked with him.

~

Webber and Koos Steyn became very friendly. Koos Steyn's wife had had a baby just a few weeks before Webber arrived. It was the first child they had had after being married for seven years, and they were very proud of it. It was a girl. Koos Steyn had said that he would sooner it had been a boy, but that, even so, it was better than nothing. Right from the first, Webber had taken a liking to that child, who was christened Jemima – after her mother. Often when I passed Koos Steyn's house, I saw the Englishman sitting on the front stoep with the child on his knee.

In the meantime, the other farmers around there became annoyed on account of Koos Steyn's friendship with the *rooinek*. They said that Koos was a *hensopper* and a traitor to his country. He was intimate with a man who had helped to bring about the downfall of the Afrikaner nation.

Yet it was not fair to call Koos a *hensopper*. Koos had lived in the Graaff-Reinet district when the war broke out, so that he was a Cape Boer and need not have fought. Nevertheless, he joined up with a Free State commando and remained until peace was made; and if at any time the English had caught him, they would have shot him as a rebel, in the same way they shot Scheepers and others.

Gerhardus Grobbelaar spoke about this once when we were in Willem Odendaal's post office.

'You are not doing right,' Gerhardus said. 'Boer and Englishman have been enemies since after Slagtersnek.

We've lost this war, but someday we'll win. It's the duty we owe to our children's children to stand against the *rooineks*. Remember the concentration camps.'

There seemed to me to be truth in what Gerhardus said.

'But the English are here now, and we've got to live with them,' Koos answered. 'When we get to understand one another, perhaps we won't need to fight any more. This Englishman Webber is learning Afrikaans very well, and someday he might almost be one of us. The only thing I can't understand about him is that he has a bath every morning. But if he stops that, and if he doesn't brush his teeth any more, you'll hardly be able to tell him from a Boer.'

Although he made a joke about it, I felt that there was also truth in what Koos Steyn said.

14.

The Wind that Stirs in the Kalahari

From 'The Rooinek'

In *Mafeking Road*

Then, the year after the drought, the *miltsiekte* broke out. We all became very discouraged. Nearly all of us in that part of the Marico had started farming again on what the Government had given us. Now that the stock had died, we had nothing. We couldn't even sow mielies because, at the rate at which the cattle were dying, in a short while we would have no oxen left to pull the plough.

It was then that somebody got hold of the idea of trekking. In a few days we were talking of nothing else. Somebody mentioned German West Africa.

'The blight of the English is over South Africa,' Gerhardus Grobbelaar said. 'We'll remain here only to die. We must go away somewhere where there is not the Englishman's flag.'

In a few weeks' time we had arranged everything. We were going to trek across the Kalahari into German territory. Everything we had, we loaded up. We drove the cattle ahead and followed behind on our wagons. There were five families: the Steyns, the Grobbelaars, the Odendaals, the Ferreiras, and Sannie and I. Webber also came with us. I think it was not so much that he was anxious to leave as that he and Koos Steyn had become very much attached to one another, and the Englishman did not wish to remain behind alone.

The youngest person in our trek was Koos Steyn's daughter, Jemima, who was then about eighteen months old. Being the baby, she was a favourite with all of us.

Webber sold his wagon and went with Koos Steyn's trek.

~

We had got so far into the desert that we began telling one another that we must be near the end. Although we knew that German West Africa was far away, and that in the way we had been travelling we had got little more than into the beginning of the Kalahari, yet we tried to tell one another lies about how near water was likely to be. But, of course, we only told those to one another. Each man in his own heart knew what the real truth was.

~

After a while there was no more weeping in our camp. Some of the women who lived through the dreadful things of the days that came after, and got safely back to the Transvaal, never again wept. What they had seen appeared to have hardened them. In this respect they had become as men. I think it is the saddest thing that ever happens in this world, when women pass through great suffering that makes them become as men.

~

So far we had followed Gerhardus through all things, and our faith in him had been great. But now that he had decided to turn back, we lost our belief in him. We lost it suddenly, too. We knew that it was best to turn back, and that to continue would mean that we would all die in the Kalahari. And yet, if Gerhardus had said we must still go on, we would have done so. We would have gone through with him right to the end.

But now that he had as much as said that he was beaten by the desert, we had no more faith in Gerhardus.

That is why Paul Kruger was a greater man than Gerhardus. Paul Kruger was that kind of man whom we still worshipped even when he decided to retreat. If it had been Paul Kruger who had told us that we had to go back, we would have returned with strong hearts. We would have retained exactly the same love for our leader, even if we had known that he was beaten. But from the moment that Gerhardus said we must go back, we all knew that he was no longer our leader. Gerhardus knew that also.

~

Then we saw that Koos Steyn had become mad. For he refused to return. He inspanned his oxen, and got ready to trek on.

'But, man,' Gerhardus Grobbelaar said to him, 'you've got no water to drink.'

'I'll drink coffee then,' Koos Steyn answered, laughing as always, and took up the whip and walked away beside the wagon. And Webber went off with him, just because Koos Steyn had been good to him, I suppose. That's why I have said that Englishmen are queer. Webber must have known that if Koos Steyn had not actually gone wrong in the head, still what he was doing now was madness, and yet he stayed with him.

We separated. Our wagons went slowly back to Malopolole. Koos Steyn's wagon went deeper into the desert. I looked back at the Steyns. At that moment Webber also looked round. He saw me and waved his hand. It reminded me of that day in the Anglo-Boer War when that other Englishman, whose companion we had shot, also turned round and waved.

Eventually we got back to Malopolole with two wagons and a handful of cattle. We had abandoned the other wagons. Awful things had happened in the desert. A number of children had died. Gerhardus Grobbelaar's wagon was in front of me. Once I saw a bundle being dropped through the side of the wagon-tent. I knew what it was. Gerhardus would not trouble to bury his dead child, and his wife lay in the tent too weak to move. So I got off the wagon and scraped a small heap of sand over the body. All I remember of the rest of the journey to Malopolole is the sun and the sand. And the thirst.

Until today I am not sure how many days we were on our way back, unless I sit down and work it all out, and even then I suppose I would get it wrong. We got back to Malopolole and water. We said we would never go away from there again. I don't think that even those parents who had lost children grieved about them then. They were stunned with what they had gone through. But I knew that, later on, it would all come back again. Then they would remember things about shallow graves in the sand, and Gerhardus Grobbelaar and his wife would think of a little bundle lying out in the Kalahari. And I knew how they would feel.

Afterwards we fitted out a wagon with fresh oxen; we took an abundant supply of water and went back into the desert to look for the Steyn family. With the help of some Bechuanas, who could see tracks that we could not see, we found the wagon. The oxen had been outspanned; a few lay dead beside the wagon. The Bechuanas pointed out to us footprints in the sand, which showed which way those two men and that woman had gone.

In the end we found them.

Koos Steyn and his wife lay side by side in the sand. The woman's head rested on the man's shoulder. Her long hair had become loosened, and blew softly in the wind. A great deal of fine sand had drifted over their bodies. We never found the baby Jemima. She must have died somewhere along the way, and Koos Steyn must have buried her.

But we agreed that the Englishman Webber must have passed through terrible things. He could not even have had any understanding left as to what the Steyns had done with their baby. He probably thought, up to the moment when he died, that he was carrying the child. For, when we lifted his body, we found, still clasped in his dead and rigid arms, a few old rags and a child's clothes.

It seemed to us that the wind, that always stirs in the Kalahari, blew very quietly and softly that morning.

Yes, the wind blew very gently.

15.

When the Moepels are Ripe

From 'Yellow Moepels'

In *Mafeking Road*

I shall never forget the scene of our departure, in front of the *veldkornet*'s house, in the early morning, when there were still shadows on the *rante*, and a thin wind blew through the grass. We had no *predikant* there, but an *ouderling*, with two bandoliers slung across his body, and a Martini in his hand, said a few words. He was a strong and simple man, with no great gifts of oratory. But when he spoke about the Transvaal, we could feel what was in his heart.

And we took off our hats in silence.

It was not long afterwards that I again took off my hat in much the same way. Then it was at Majuba Hill. It was after the battle, and the *ouderling* still had the two bandoliers around him when we buried him at the foot of the *koppie*.

But what impressed me most was the prayer that followed the *ouderling's* brief address. In front of the *veldkornet's* house we knelt, each burgher with a rifle at his side. And the womenfolk knelt down with us. And the wind seemed very gentle as it stirred the tall grass-blades, very gentle as it swept over the bared heads of the men, and fluttered the *kappies* and skirts of the women, very gentle as it carried the prayers of our nation across the veld.

After that we stood up and sang a hymn. The ceremony was over. The *agterryers* brought us our horses. And, dry-eyed and tight-lipped, each woman sent her man forth to war. There was no weeping.

Then, in accordance with Boer custom, we fired a volley into the air.

'*Voorwaarts, burgers,*' came the *veldkornet*'s order, and we cantered down the road in twos.

Before we left, I had overheard Neels Potgieter saying something to Martha Rossouw as he lent out of the saddle and kissed her. My sister Annie, standing beside my horse, also heard this.

'When the moepels are ripe, Martha,' he said, 'I will come to you again.'

Annie and I looked at each other, and smiled. It was a pretty thing Neels had said. But then Martha was also pretty. More pretty, even, than the veld trees that bore those yellow moepels, I reflected – and more wild, even, too.

I was still thinking of this when our commando passed over the *bult*, in a long line, on our way south, towards Natal, and the other commandos, and Majuba.

~

All the time I was on commando, I received only one letter. It came from Annie, my sister. Annie said, at the end of her letter, that she and Martha Rossouw had been to see a witchdoctor. They had gone to find out about Neels Potgieter and me.

If I had been at home, I would not have permitted Annie to indulge in this nonsense. Especially as the witchdoctor had said to her, 'Yes, missus, I can see *Baas* Schalk Lourens. He will come back safe. He is very clever, *Baas* Schalk. He lies behind a big stone, with a dirty brown blanket pulled over his head. And he stays behind the stone until the fighting is finished – quite finished.'

According to Annie's letter the witchdoctor had told her

a few other things about me, too. I won't bother to repeat them now. I think I've said enough to show you what sort of scoundrel that old witchdoctor was. He took advantage of the credulity of a simple girl, but he also tried to be funny at the expense of a young man who was fighting for his country's freedom.

What was more, Annie said she had recognised that it was me right away, just from the witchdoctor's description of that blanket.

To Martha Rossouw the witchdoctor had said, '*Baas* Neels Potgieter will come back to you, missus, when the moepels are ripe again. At sundown, he will come.'

That was all he had said about Neels, and there wasn't very much in that, anyway, seeing that Neels himself – except for the bit about sundown – had made the very same prophecy the day the commando had set out. I suppose the witchdoctor had been too busy thinking out foolish and spiteful things about me, to be able to give any proper attention to Neels Potgieter's affairs.

I didn't mention Annie's letter to Neels. He might have wanted to know more than I was willing to tell him. More, even, than Martha was willing to tell him – Martha of the wild heart.

~

Then, at last, the war ended, and over the Transvaal the Vierkleur waved again. The commandos went home by their different ways. And our leaders revived their old quarrels as to who should be President. And everywhere, except for a number of lonely graves on hillside and *vlakte*, things were as they had been before Sir Theophilus Shepstone had come.

It was getting on towards evening when our small band

rode over the *bult*, and once more came to a halt at the *veldkornet*'s house. A messenger had been sent in advance to announce our coming, and women and children and old men had gathered from afar, to welcome their victorious burghers home from the war. And there were tears in many eyes when we sang, '*Hef, Burgers, Hef*'.

And the moepels were ripe and yellow on the trees.

And in the dusk Neels Potgieter found Martha Rossouw, and kissed her. At sundown, as the witchdoctor had said. But there was one important thing that the witchdoctor had not said. It was something that Neels Potgieter did not know, either, just then.

It was that Martha did not want him anymore.

16.

Cloudy Nights

From 'Starlight on the Veld'

In *Mafeking Road*

When the fires were piled high with wood, Jan Ockerse again said that it was a funny night, and once more started talking about the stars.

'What do you think sailors do at sea, Schalk,' he said, 'if they don't know the way and there aren't any other ships around from which they can ask?'

'They've got it all written down on a piece of paper with a lot of red and blue on it,' I answered. 'And there are black lines that show you the way from Cape Town to St Helena. And figures to tell you how many miles down the ship will go if it sinks. I went to St Helena during the Anglo-Boer War.

'You can live in a ship just like an ox-waggon. Only, a ship isn't so comfortable, of course. And it's further between outspans.'

'I heard, somewhere, that sailors find their way by the stars,' Jan Ockerse said. 'I wonder what people want to tell me things like that for.'

He lay silent for a while, looking up at the stars, and thinking.

'I remember one night when I stood on Annie Steyn's stoep, and spoke to her about the stars,' Jan Ockerse said later. 'I was going to trek with the cattle to the Limpopo because of the drought. I told Annie that I would be away until the rains came, and I told her that every night when I was gone, she had to look at a certain star and think of me. I showed her which star. Those three stars there, that are close together in a straight line. She had to remember me by the middle one, I said.

'But Annie explained that Willem Mostert, who had trekked to the Limpopo about a week before, had already picked that middle star for her to remember him by.

'So I said, all right, the top star would do.

'But Annie said that one already belonged to Stoffel Brink.

'In the end I agreed that she could remember me by the bottom star, and Annie was still saying that she would look at the lowest one of those three stars every night and think of me, when her father, who seemed to have been listening behind the door, came onto the stoep and said: "What about cloudy nights?" in what he supposed was a clever sort of way.'

'What happened then?' I asked Jan Ockerse.

'Annie was very annoyed,' he replied. 'She told her father that he was always spoiling things. She told him that he wasn't a bit funny, really, especially as I was the third young man to whom he had said the same thing. She said that no matter how foolish a young man might be, her father had no right to make jokes like that in front of him.

'It was good to hear the way Annie stood up for me. Anyway, what followed was a long story.

'I came across Willem Mostert and Stoffel Brink by the Limpopo. And we remained together there for several months. It must have been an unusual sight for a stranger to see three young men sitting around the campfire, every night, looking up at the stars.

'We got friendly, after a while, and when the rains came, the three of us trekked back to the Marico. And I found, then, that Annie's father had been right. About the cloudy nights, I mean.

'For I understood that it was on just such a sort of night that Annie had run off to Johannesburg with a *bywoner* who was going to look for work on the mines.'

Jan Ockerse sighed, and returned to his thinking.

But with all the time we had spent talking and sleeping, most of the night had slipped away. We kept only one fire going now, and Jan Ockerse and I took turns in putting on the wood.

It gets very cold just before dawn, and we were both shivering.

'Anyway,' Jan Ockerse said after a while, 'now you know why I am interested in the stars. I was a young man when this happened. And I have told very few people about it. About seventeen people, I should say. The others wouldn't listen.

'But always, on a clear night, when I see those bright stars in a row, I look for a long time at the lowest star, and there seems to be something very friendly about the way it shines. It seems to be my star, and its light is different from the light of the other stars ... and you know, Schalk, Annie Steyn had such red lips. And such long, soft hair, Schalk. And there was that smile of hers.'

Afterwards the stars grew pale, and we started rounding up the donkeys and got ready to go. And I wondered what Annie Steyn would have thought of it, if she had known that, during all those years, there was this man looking up at the stars on nights when the sky was clear, dreaming about her lips and her hair and her smile. But as soon as I reflected about it, I knew what the answer was also. Of course, Annie Steyn would think nothing of Jan Ockerse. Nothing at all. And, no doubt, Annie Steyn was right.

But it was strange to think that we had passed a whole night talking about the stars. And I did not know, until then, that it was all on account of a love story of long ago.

We climbed onto the cart and set off to look for the way home.

'I know that schoolteacher in the Zeerust bar was all wrong,' Jan Ockerse said finally, 'when he tried to explain how far away the stars are. The lower of those three stars – ah, it has just faded – is very near to me. Yes, it is near.'

17.

On the Road to Abjaterskop

From 'Willem Prinsloo's Peach Brandy'

In *Mafeking Road*

No – Oom Schalk Lourens said – you don't get flowers in the Groot Marico. It's not a bad district for mealies, and I once grew quite good onions in a small garden I made next to the dam, but what you can really call flowers are rare things here. Perhaps it's the heat. Or the drought.

Yet, whenever I talk about flowers, I think of Willem Prinsloo's farm on Abjaterskop, where the dance was, and I think of Fritz Pretorius, sitting pale and sick by the roadside, and I think of the white rose that I wore in my hat, jauntily. But most of all, I think of Grieta.

If you walk over my farm to the *hoogte*, and look towards the north-west, you can see Abjaterskop behind the ridge of the Dwarsberge. People will tell you that there are ghosts on Abjaterskop, and that it was once the home of witches. I can believe that. I was at Abjaterskop only once. That was many years ago. And I never went there again. Still, it wasn't ghosts that kept me away, nor was it witches.

Grieta Prinsloo was due to come back from the finishing school at Zeerust, where she had gone to learn English manners and dictation and other high-class subjects. Therefore Willem Prinsloo, her father, arranged a big dance on his farm at Abjaterskop, to celebrate Grieta's return.

I was invited to the party. So was Fritz Pretorius. And so was every person in the district, from Derdepoort to Ramoutsa. What was more, practically everybody went. Of course, we were all somewhat nervous about meeting Grieta. With all the superior things she had learnt at the finishing school, we wouldn't be able to talk to her in a chatty sort of way, just as though she were an ordinary Boer girl. But what fetched us all to Abjaterskop, in the end, was our knowledge that Willem Prinsloo made the best peach brandy in the district.

Fritz Pretorius spoke to me of the difficulty brought about by Grieta's learning.

'Yes, *jong*,' he said, 'I'm feeling pretty shaky about talking to her, I can tell you. I've been rubbing up my education a bit, though. Yesterday I took out my old slate that I last used when I left school seventeen years ago, and I did a few sums. I did some addition and subtraction. I tried a little multipliation, too. But I've forgotten how that's done.'

I told Fritz that I would have liked to help him, but that I had never learnt as far as multiplication.

The day of the dance arrived. The post-cart bearing Grieta to her father's house passed through Drogedal in the morning. In the afternoon I got dressed. I wore a black jacket, fawn trousers, and a pink shirt. I also put on the brown boots I had bought about a year before, and that I'd never had occasion to wear. For I would have looked silly walking about the farm in a pair of shop boots, when everybody else wore home-made *veldskoens*.

I believed, as I got on my horse, and set off down the Government road, with my hat rakishly on one side, that I would easily be the best-dressed young man at that dance.

It was getting on towards sunset when I arrived at the foot of Abjaterskop, which I had to skirt in order to reach Willem Prinsloo's farm, nestling in a hollow behind the hills. I felt, as I rode, that it was stupid for a man to live in a part that was reputed to be haunted. The trees grew taller and denser, as they always do on rising ground. And they also got a lot darker.

All over the place were queer, heavy shadows. I didn't like the look of them. I remembered stories I had heard of the witches of Abjaterskop, and what they did to travellers who lost their way in the dark. It seemed an easy thing to lose your way among those tall trees. Accordingly, I spurred my horse on to a gallop, to get out of this gloomy region as quickly as possible. After all, a horse is sensitive about things like ghosts and witches, and it was my duty to see that my horse was not frightened unnecessarily. Especially as a cold wind suddenly sprang up through the *poort*, and once or twice it sounded as though an evil voice were calling my name. I started riding fast then. But a few moments later I looked round and realised the position. It was Fritz Pretorius galloping along behind me.

'What's your hurry?' Fritz asked, when I slowed down to allow him to overtake me.

'I wanted to get through those trees before it was too dark,' I answered. 'I didn't want my horse to get frightened.'

'I suppose that's why you were riding with your arms around his neck,' Fritz observed. 'To soothe him.'

I did not reply. But what I did notice was that Fritz was also very stylishly dressed. True, I beat him as far as the shirt and the boots went, but he was dressed in a new grey suit, with his socks pulled up over the bottoms of his trousers. He also had a handkerchief which he ostentatiously took out of his pocket several times.

Of course, I couldn't be jealous of a person like Fritz Pretorius. I was only annoyed at the thought that he was making himself ridiculous by going to a party with an outlandish thing like a handkerchief.

18.

A Small White Rose

From 'Willem Prinsloo's Peach Brandy'

In *Mafeking Road*

We arrived at Willem Prinsloo's house. There were so many ox-wagons drawn up on the veld that the place looked like a *laager*. Prinsloo met us at the door.

'Go right through, *kêrels*,' he said, 'the dancing is in the *voorhuis*. The peach brandy is in the kitchen.'

Although the *voorhuis* was big, it was so crowded as to make it almost impossible to dance. But it was not as crowded as the kitchen. Nor was the music in the *voorhuis* – which was provided by a number of men with guitars and concertinas – as loud as the music in the kitchen, where there was no band, but each man sang for himself.

We knew from these signs that the party was a success.

When I had been in the kitchen for about half an hour, I decided to go into the *voorhuis*. It seemed a long way, now, from the kitchen to the *voorhuis*, and I had to lean against the wall several times, to think. I passed a number of other men who were also leaning against the wall like that, thinking. One man even found that he could think best by sitting on the floor with his head on his arms.

You could see that Willem Prinsloo made good peach brandy.

Then I saw Fritz Pretorius, and the sight of him brought me to my senses right away. Airily flapping his white handkerhief in time to the music, he was talking to a girl who smiled at him with bright eyes and red lips and small white teeth.

I knew at once that it was Grieta.

She was tall and slender and very pretty, and her dark hair was braided with a wreath of white roses that you could see had been picked that same morning in Zeerust. And she didn't look the sort of girl, either, in whose presence you had to appear clever and educated. In fact, I felt that I wouldn't really need the twelve times table I had torn off the back of a school writing book, and thrust into my jacket pocket before leaving home.

You can imagine that it was not too easy for me to get a word in with Grieta while Fritz was hanging around. But I managed it eventually, and while I was talking to her I had the satisfaction of seeing, out of the corner of my eye, the direction that Fritz took. He went into the kitchen, flapping his handkerchief behind him – into the kitchen, where the laughter was, and the singing, and Willem Prinsloo's peach brandy.

I told Grieta that I was Schalk Lourens.

'Oh yes, I have heard of you,' she answered, 'from Fritz Pretorius.'

I knew what that meant. So I told her that Fritz was known all over the Marico for his lies. I also told her other things about Fritz. Ten minutes later, when I was still talking about him, Grieta smiled and said that I could tell her the rest some other night.

'But I must tell you one more thing now,' I insisted. 'When he knew that he would be meeting you here at the dance, Fritz started doing homework.'

I told her about the slate and the sums, and Grieta laughed softly. It struck me again how pretty she was. And her eyes were radiant in the candlelight. And the roses looked very white against her dark hair. And all this time the dancers whirled around us, and the band in the *voorhuis* played lively dance tunes, and from the kitchen there issued weird sounds of jubilation.

The rest happened very quickly.

I can't even remember how it all came about. But what I do know is that when we were outside, under the tall trees, with the stars over us, I could easily believe that Grieta was not a girl at all, but one of the witches of Abjaterskop who wove strange spells.

Yet by listening to my talk, nobody would have guessed the wild, thrilling things that were in my heart.

I told Grieta about last year's drought, and about the difficulty of keeping the white ants from eating through the door and window frames, and about the way my new brown boots tended to take the skin off my toes if I walked quickly.

Then I moved closer to her.

'Grieta,' I said, taking her hand. 'Grieta, there is something I want to tell you.'

She pulled her hand away. She did it gently, though. Sorrowfully, almost.

'I know what you want to say,' she answered.

I was surprised at that.

'How do you know, Grieta?' I asked.

'Oh, I know lots of things,' she replied, laughing again. 'I haven't been to finishing school for nothing.'

'I don't mean that,' I answered at once. 'I wasn't going to talk about spelling or arithmetic. I was going to tell you that …'

'Please don't say it, Schalk,' Grieta interrupted me. 'I – I don't know whether I'm worthy of hearing it. I don't know, even …'

'But you are so lovely,' I exclaimed. 'I've got to tell you how lovely you are.'

But at the very moment I stepped forward, she retreated

swiftly, eluding me. I couldn't understand how she had timed it so well. For, try as I might, I couldn't catch her. She sped lightly and gracefully among the trees, and I followed her as best I could.

It was not only my want of learning that handicapped me. There was also my new boots. And Willem Prinsloo's peach brandy. And the shaft of a mule-cart – the lower end of the shaft, where it rests on the grass.

I didn't fall very hard, though. The grass was long and thick there. But even as I fell, a great happiness came into my heart. And I didn't care about anything else in the world.

Grieta had stopped running. She turned around. For an instant her body, slender and misty in the shadows, swayed towards me. Then her hand flew to her hair. Her fingers pulled at the wreath. And the next thing I knew was that there lay, within reach of my hand, a small white rose.

I shall always remember the thrill with which I picked up that rose, and how I trembled when I stuck it in my hat. I shall always remember the stir that I caused when I walked into the kitchen. Everybody stopped drinking to look at the rose in my hat. The young men made jokes about it. The older men winked slyly, and patted me on the back.

Although Fritz Pretorius was not in the kitchen to witness my triumph, I knew that he would get to hear of it somehow. That would make him realise that it was imprudent for a fellow like him to set up as Schalk Lourens's rival.

During the rest of the night I was a hero.

The men in the kitchen made me sit on the table. They plied me with brandy, and they drank to my health. Afterwards, when a dozen of them carried me outside, onto an ox-wagon, for fresh air, they fell with me only once.

At daybreak I was still on that wagon.

I woke up feeling very sick – until I remembered about

Grieta's rose. There was that white rose, still stuck in my hat, for the whole world to know that Grieta Prinsloo had chosen me before all other men.

But what I didn't want people to know was that I had remained asleep on that ox-wagon hours after the other guests had gone. So I rode away very quietly, glad that nobody was astir to see me go.

My head was dizzy as I rode back, but in my heart it felt like green wings beating; and although it was day now, there was the same soft wind in the grass that had been there when Grieta had flung the rose at me, standing under the stars.

I rode slowly through the trees on the slopes of Abjaterskop, and reached the place where the path turns south There I saw something that made me wonder whether those fashionable schools did not perhaps teach the girls too much.

First I saw Fritz Pretorius's horse by the roadside.

Then I saw Fritz. He was sitting up against a thorn-tree, with his chin resting on his knees. He looked very pale and sick. But what made me wonder a great deal about those finishing schools was that in Fritz's hat, which had fallen to the ground some distance away from him, there was a small white rose.

19.

Bekkersdal Marathon

From 'A Bekkersdal Marathon'

In *A Bekkersdal Marathon*

It all happened through *Dominee* Welthagen one Sunday morning going into a trance in the pulpit. And we did not realise that he was in a trance. It was an illness that overtook him in a strange and sudden fashion.

At each service the *predikant*, after reading a passage from the Bible, would lean forward with his hand on the pulpit rail and give out the number of the hymn we had to sing. For years his manner of conducting the service had been exactly the same. He would say, for instance, 'We will now sing Psalm 82, verses 1 to 4.' Then he would allow his head to sink forward onto his chest and he would remain rigid, as though in prayer, until the last notes of the hymn died away in the church.

Now, on that particular morning, just after he had announced the number of the psalm, without mentioning which verses, *Dominee* Welthagen again took a firm grip on the pulpit rail, and allowed his head to sink forward onto his breast. We did not realise that he had fallen into a trance of a peculiar character that kept his body standing upright while his mind was blank. We only learned that later.

In the meantime, while the organ was playing the opening bars, we began to realise that *Dominee* Welthagen had not indicated how many verses we had to sing. But he would discover his mistake, we thought, after we had been singing for a few minutes.

All the same, one or two of the younger members of the

congregation did titter, slightly, when they took up their hymn-books. For *Dominee* Welthagen had announced Psalm 119. And everybody knows that Psalm 119 has 176 verses.

That was a church service that will never be forgotten in Bekkersdal.

We sang the first verse, and then the second, and then the third. When we got to about the sixth verse, and the minister still gave no sign that it would be the last, we assumed that he wished us to sing the first eight verses. For, if you open your hymn-book, you will see that Psalm 119 is divided into sets of eight verses, each ending with the word '*Pouse*'.

We ended the last notes of verse eight with more than an ordinary number of turns and twirls, confident that at any moment *Dominee* Welthagen would raise his head and let us know that we could sing 'Amen'.

It was when the organ started up very slowly and solemnly with the music for verse nine that a real feeling of disquiet overcame the congregation. But, of course, we gave no sign of what went on in our minds. We held *Dominee* Welthagen in too much veneration.

Nevertheless, I would rather not say too much about our feelings, when verse followed verse, and *Pouse* succeeded *Pouse*, and still *Dominee* Welthagen made no sign that we had sung long enough, or that there was anything unusual about what he was demanding of us.

After they had recovered from their first surprise, the members of the church council conducted themselves in a most exemplary manner. Elders and deacons tiptoed up and down the aisles, whispering words of reassurance to such members of the congregation, men as well as women, who gave signs of wanting to panic.

At one stage it looked as though we were going to have trouble from the organist. That was when Billy Robertse, at the end of the 34th verse, held up his black bottle and signalled quietly to the elders to indicate that his medicine had finished. At the end of the 35th verse he made signals of a less quiet character, and again at the end of the 36th verse. That was when Elder Landsman tiptoed out of the church and went round to the *Konsistorie*, where the *Nagmaal* wine was kept. When Elder Landsman came back into the church, he had a long black bottle half-hidden under his *manel*. He took the bottle up to the organist's gallery, still walking on tiptoe.

At verse 61 there was almost a breakdown. That was when a message came from the back of the organ, where *Koster* Claassen and the assistant verger, whose task it was to turn the handle that kept the organ supplied with wind, were in a state close to exhaustion. So it was Deacon Cronje's turn to go tiptoeing out of the church. Deacon Cronje was head-warder at the local gaol. When he came back it was with three burly convicts in striped jerseys, who also went through the church on tiptoe. They arrived just in time to take over the handle from *Koster* Claassen and the assistant verger.

At verse 98 the organist again started making signals about his medicine. Once more Elder Landsman went round to the *Konsistorie*. This time he was accompanied by another elder and a deacon, and they stayed away somewhat longer than the previous time when Elder Landsman had gone on his own. On their return, the deacon bumped into a small hymn-book table at the back of the church. Perhaps it was because the deacon was a fat, red-faced man, not used to tiptoeing.

At verse 124 the organist signalled again, and the same three members of the church council filed out to the *Konsistorie*, the deacon walking in front this time.

It was about then that the pastor of the Full Gospel Apostolic Faith Church, about whom *Dominee* Welthagen had in the past used language almost as strong as that he had used about the Pope, came up to the front gate of the church to see what was afoot. He lived near our church and, having heard the same hymn tune being played over and over for about eight hours, he was a very amazed man. Then he saw the door of the *Konsistorie* open, and two elders and a deacon coming out, walking on tiptoe – they having apparently forgotten that they were not in the church just then. When the pastor saw one of the elders hiding a black bottle under his *manel*, a look of understanding came over his features. The pastor walked off, shaking his head.

At verse 152 the organist signalled again. This time Elder Landsman and the other elder went out alone. The deacon stayed behind in the deacon's bench, apparently deep in thought. The organist signalled again, for the last time, at verse 169. So you can imagine how many visits the two elders made to the *Konsistorie* altogether.

Eventually the last verse came, and the last line of the last verse. This time it had to be Amen. Nothing could stop it.

I would rather not describe the state that the congregation was in. And by then the three convicts, red stripes and all, were – in the Bakhatla tongue – threatening mutiny.

'Aa-m-e-e-n' came from what sounded like less than a score of voices, hoarse with singing. The organ music died away.

Maybe it was the sudden silence that at last brought *Dominee* Welthagen out of his long trance. He raised his head, and looked slowly about him. His gaze travelled over the congregation; and then, looking at the window, he saw that it was night. We then understood right away what was going on in *Dominee* Welthagen's mind. He thought he had just come into the pulpit, and that this was the beginning of the evening service. We realised that, during all the time we had been singing, the *predikant* had been in a state of unconsciousness.

Once again *Dominee* Welthagen took a firm grip on the pulpit rail. His head again started drooping forward onto his breast, but before he went into a trance for the second time, he gave the hymn for the evening service.

'We will,' announced *Dominee* Welthagen, 'sing Psalm 119.'

20.

An Old Story and an Old Song

From 'The Selons-Rose'

In *Unto Dust*

Marie du Preez – Oom Schalk Lourens said – had not been away from the Marico for very long, but her overseas visit had made her restive.

That, of course, was something I could not understand. I had also been to foreign parts. During the Boer War I had been a prisoner on St Helena. And twice I had been in Johannesburg.

One thing about St Helena was that there were no *Uitlanders* on it. There were just Boers and English and Coloureds and Indians, like you come across here in the Marico. There were none of those all-sorts that you have to push past on the pavements of Johannesburg.

And each time I got back to my own farm, and I could sit on my stoep and fill my pipe with honest Magaliesberg tobacco, I was pleased to think that I was away from all that sin that you read about in the Bible.

But with Marie du Preez it was different.

Marie du Preez, after she came back from Europe, spoke a great deal about how unhappy a person with a sensitive nature could be about certain aspects of life in the Marico.

We were not unwilling to agree with her.

'When I woke up that morning at Nietverdiend,' Willie Prinsloo said to Marie during a party at the Du Preez homestead, 'and I found that I couldn't inspan my oxen because my trek-chain had been stolen – well, to a person with a sensitive nature, I can tell you how unhappy I felt about the Marico.'

Marie said that that was the sort of thing that made her ill, almost.

~

Shortly afterwards Marie du Preez made a remark that hurt me, a little.

'People here in the Marico say all the same things, over and over again,' Marie announced. 'Nobody ever says anything new. You all talk just like the people in Oom Schalk Lourens's stories. Whenever we have visitors, it's always the same thing. If it's a husband and wife, the man will always start talking first. And he'll say that his Afrikaner cattle are in a bad way with the heart-water. Even though he drives his cattle straight out onto the veld with the first frost, and even though he keeps to regular seven-day dipping, he just can't get rid of the heart-water ticks.'

Marie du Preez paused. None of us said anything, at first. I only know what I was thinking. I thought to myself that, even though I only dip my cattle when the Government inspector from Onderstepoort is in the neighbourhood, still I lose just as many Afrikaner beasts from the heart-water as any of the farmers hereabouts who go in for the seven-day dipping.

'They should dip the Onderstepoort inspector every seven days,' Jurie Bekker called out suddenly, expressing all of our feelings.

'And they should drive the Onderstepoort inspector straight out into the veld with the first frost,' Willie Prinsloo added.

We got pretty well worked up, I can tell you.

'And it's the same with the women,' Marie du Preez went

on. 'Do they ever discuss books or fashion or music? No. They also talk just like those simple Boer women that Oom Schalk Lourens's head is so full of. They talk about the amount of Kalahari sand that the Indian in the store at Ramoutsa mixed with the last bag of yellow sugar they bought from him. You know, I've heard the same thing so often, I'm surprised there's any sand at all left in the Kalahari desert, the way that Indian uses it all up.'

Those of us who were in the Du Preez *voorkamer* that evening, in spite of our amusement, also felt sad at the thought of how Marie du Preez had changed from her old natural self, like a seedling that has been transplanted too often in different kinds of soil.

'One thing I'm glad about, though,' Marie said, after a pause, 'is that since my return from Europe I've not yet come across a Marico girl who wears a selons-rose in her hair to make herself look more attractive to a young man – as happens, time after time, in Oom Schalk's stories.'

This remark of Marie's gave a new turn to the conversation, and I felt relieved. For a moment I had feared that Marie du Preez was also becoming addicted to the kind of Bushveld conversation she complained about, and that she, too, was beginning to say the same thing over and over again.

Several women started talking, after that, about how hard it was to get flowers to grow in the Marico, on account of the prolonged droughts. The most they could hope for was to keep a bush of selons-roses alive near the kitchen door. It was a flower that seemed, if anything, to thrive on harsh sunlight, soapy dish-water and Marico earth, the women said.

~

Some time later Theunis du Preez engaged a young fellow, Joachem Bonthuys, to come and work on his farm as a *bywoner*. Joachem was a nephew of Philippus Bonthuys, and I was at the post office when he arrived at Drogedal, on the lorry from Zeerust – with Theunis du Preez and his daughter, Marie, there to meet him.

Joachem Bonthuys's appearance was not very prepossessing, I thought. He shook hands somewhat awkwardly with the farmers who had come to meet the lorry to collect their milk cans. Joachem did not seem to have much to say for himself, either, until Theunis du Preez, his new employer, asked him what his journey up from Zeerust had been like.

'The veld is dry all the way,' he replied. 'And I've never seen so much heart-water in the Afrikaner herds. They should dip their cattle every seven days,' he said.

Joachem Bonthuys spoke at great length, then, and I could not help smiling to myself when I saw Marie du Preez turn away. In that moment, my feelings grew warmer towards Joachem. I felt that, at all events, he was not the kind of young man who would go and sing foreign songs under a respectable Boer girl's window.

All this brings me back to what I was saying about an old song and an old story. For it was quite a while before I again had occasion to visit the Du Preez farm. And when I sat smoking on the stoep with Theunis du Preez, it was just like an old story, hearing him talk about his rheumatism.

Marie came out onto the stoep with a tray to bring us our coffee. – Yes, you've heard all that before, the same sort of thing. The same stoep. The same tray. – And for that reason, when she held out the glass bowl towards me, Marie du Preez apologised about the yellow sugar.

'It's full of Kalahari sand, Oom Schalk,' she said. 'It's that Indian at Ramoutsa.'

And when she turned to go back into the kitchen, leaving two old men to their stories, it was not difficult for me to guess who the young man was for whom she was wearing a half-red flower in her hair.

21.

Stars in their Courses

From 'Stars in their Courses'

In *A Bekkersdal Marathon*

'It said over the wireless,' At Naudé announced, 'that the American astronomers are moving out of Johannesburg. They are taking their telescopes, and the things they have been studying the stars with, to Australia. There's too much smoke in Johannesburg for them to be able to see the stars properly.'

He paused, as though inviting comment. But none of us had anything to say. We weren't much interested in the Americans and their stars. Or in Australia, either, for that matter.

'The American astronomers have been in Johannesburg for many years,' At Naudé went on, wistfully, as though the impending removal of the astronomical research station was a matter of personal regret to him. 'They have been here for years, and now they are going because of the smoke. It gets into their eyes – just when they've nearly seen a new star in their telescopes, I suppose. Well, smoke is like that, of course. It gets into your eyes just at the wrong time.'

What At Naudé had said now was something we could all understand. It was something we had all experienced. It was different from what he had been saying before. Getting smoke in your eyes, at an inconvenient moment, was something everybody in the Marico understood.

Immediately, Chris Welman started telling us about the time he was asked by Koos Nienaber, as a favour, to stand on a *rant* of the Dwarsberge, from where he was able to see the Derdepoort police post very clearly. Koos Nienaber, it would seem, had private business with a chief near Ramoutsa, which had to do with bringing a somewhat large herd of cattle with long horns across the border.

'I could see the police post very well from there,' Chris Welman said. 'I was standing near a Mtosa hut. When the Mtosa woman lifted a petrol tin onto her head and went down in the direction of the *spruit*, for water, I moved over to an iron pot that a fire had been burning underneath all afternoon.'

He could still see those two policemen – dealing out the cards to each other and taking turns to drink out of a black bottle – quite distinctly, Chris Welman said, when he lifted the lid of the iron pot. He wasn't in the least bit worried about those two policemen, then. Actually, he admitted, he was, if anything, more concerned lest the Mtosa woman should suddenly come back to the hut, with the petrol tin on her head, having forgotten something. And it had to be at that moment, just when he was lifting the lid, that smoke from the fire crackling underneath the pot got into his eyes. It was the most awful kind of stabbing smoke that you could ever imagine, Chris Welman said. What the Mtosa woman had made that fire with, he had no idea. Cow dung and *bitter-bessie*, he knew. That was a kind of fuel that received some countenance, still, in the less frequented areas along the Malopo. And it made a kind of smoke which, if it got into your eyes, could blind you temporarily for up to at least a quarter of an hour.

Chris Welman went on to say that he was also not unfamiliar with the effects of the smoke of the renosterbos, in view of the fact that he retained many childhood memories of a farm in the Eastern Province, where it was still quite usual to find a house with an old-fashioned abba-kitchen.

Chris Welman sighed deeply. Partly, we felt, that sigh had its roots in a nostalgia for the past. His next words showed, however, that it was linked with a grimmer sort of reality.

'When I got back to the top of that *rant*,' Chris Welman declared simply, 'the two policemen weren't there, at the police post, anymore. And Koos Nienaber had been fined so often before that this time the magistrate would not let him off with a fine. Koos Nienaber took it like a man when the magistrate gave him six months,' Chris Welman concluded.

More than one of us, sitting in Jurie Steyn's *voorkamer*, sighed, too, then. We also knew what it was to get smoke in your eyes at the wrong moment. And we also knew what it was to hold a sudden and unexpected conversation with a policeman on border patrol, while you were nervously shifting a pair of wire-cutters from one hand to the other.

Gysbert van Tonder brought the discussion back to the subject of the stars.

'If the American astronomers are leaving South Africa because they can't stand our sort of smoke,' Gysbert van Tonder declared, 'well, I suppose there's nothing we can do about it. I didn't think that an astronomer, watching the stars at night through a telescope, would worry very much about smoke – or about cinders from looking out of a train window, either, for that matter – getting into his eyes. I imagined somehow that an astronomer would be above that sort of thing.

Young Vermaak, the schoolteacher, was able to put Gysbert van Tonder right then. 'It isn't the smoke that gets into their eyes,' he explained. 'It's the smoke in the atmosphere that interferes with the observations and the mathematical calculations that astronomers have to make to get a knowledge of the movement of the heavenly bodies.'

We looked at each other, then, with feelings of awe. In

general, of course, we'd never had much respect for the schoolteacher, seeing that all he had was book-learning, but what did give us pause for reflection on this occasion was the thought that just in his brain – just inside his head, that didn't seem very much different from any one of our heads – the young schoolmaster should have so much knowledge.

Only Jurie Steyn was not taken out of his depth.

'It's like that book my wife used to study a great deal before we got married,' Jurie Steyn said. 'I've told you about it before. It's called *Napoleon's Dream Book*. Well, that's a lot like what young Vermaak has been talking about now. At the back of the *Napoleon Dream Book*, it's got 'What the Stars Foretell' for every day of the year. It says that on Wednesdays you must wear green, and on some other day you must write a letter to a relative you haven't seen since I don't know when. Anyway, I suppose that's why those American star-gazers are leaving Johannesburg. It's something they saw in the stars, I expect.'

Chris Welman said he wondered whether what the American astronomers had been seeing through their telescope was that the star of the American nation was going up, or that it was going down.

'Perhaps Jurie Steyn's wife can work it out from the dream book,' Gysbert van Tonder said.

22.

The Most Wild and the Most Beautiful Thing in the Whole World

From 'Mampoer'

In *Mafeking Road*

The berries of the karee-*boom* – Oom Schalk Lourens said, nodding his head in the direction of the tall tree whose shadows were creeping towards the edge of the stoep – may not make the best kind of mampoer that there is. What I mean is that karee brandy is not as potent as the brandy you distil from moepels or maroelas. Even peach brandy, they say, can make you forget the rust in the corn quicker than the mampoer you make from karee berries.

But karee-mampoer is white and soft to look at, and the smoke that comes from it when you pull the cork out of the bottle is pale and rises up in slow curves. And in a time of drought, when you have been standing at the borehole all day, pumping water for the cattle, so that by evening the water has a bitter taste for you, then it is very soothing to sit on the front stoep, like now, and to get somebody to pull the cork out of a bottle of this kind of mampoer. Your hands will be sore and stiff from the pump-handle, so that if you try and pull it out, the cork will seem as deep down in the bottle as the water in the borehole.

~

The Most Wild and the Most Beautiful Thing in the Whole World

Many years ago, when I was a young man, and I sat here, on the front stoep, and I saw that white smoke floating away slowly and gracefully from the mouth of the bottle, and with a far-off fragrance, I used to think that the smoke looked like a young girl walking veiled under the stars. And now that I have grown old, and I look at that white smoke, I imagine that it is a young girl walking under the stars, and still veiled. I have never found out who she is.

Hans Kriel and I were in the same party that had gone from this section of the Groot Marico to Zeerust for the *Nagmaal*. And it was a few evenings after our arrival, when we were on a visit to Chris Wilman's house on the outskirts of the town, that I learnt something of the first half of Hans Kriel's love story – that half at which I laughed. The knowledge of the second half came a little later, and I didn't laugh then.

We were sitting on Krisjan Wilman's stoep and looking out in the direction of Sephton's Nek. In the setting sun, the *koppies* were red on one side; on the other side, their shadows were lengthening rapidly over the *vlakte*. Krisjan Wilman had already poured out the mampoer, and the glasses were going round.

'That big shadow there is rushing through the thorn trees just like a black elephant,' Adrian Bekker said. 'In a few minutes' time it will be at Groot Marico station.'

'The shorter the days are, the longer the shadows get,' Frikkie Marais said. 'I learnt that at school. There are also lucky and unlucky shadows.'

'You are talking about ghosts, now, not shadows,' Adrian Bekker interrupted him, learnedly. 'Ghosts are all the same length, I think, more or less.'

'No, it is the ghost stories that are all the same length,' Krisjan Wilman said. 'The kind you tell.'

It was good mampoer, made from karee berries that were

plucked when they were still green and full of thick sap, just before they had begun to whiten, and we said things that contained much wisdom.

~

'It was like the shadow of a flower on her left cheek,' I heard Hans Kriel say, and immediately I sat up to listen, for I could guess of whom it was that he was talking.

'Is it on the lower part of the cheek?' I asked. 'Two small purple marks?'

Because in that case I would know for sure that he was talking about the new waitress in the Zeerust café. I had seen her only once, through the plate-glass window, and because I had liked her looks, I had gone up to the counter and asked for a roll of Boer tobacco, which she said they did not stock. When she said they didn't stock kudu biltong, either, I had felt too embarrassed to ask for anything else. Only afterwards did I remember that I could have sat down and ordered a cup of coffee and some *harde beskuit*. But it was too late then. By that time I felt that she could see that I came from this part of the Marico, even though I was wearing my hat well back on my head.

'Did you – did you speak to her?' I asked Hans Kriel after a while.

'Yes,' he said, 'I went in and asked her for a roll of Boer tobacco. But she said they didn't sell tobacco by the roll, or kudu biltong either. She said this last with a sort of a sneer. I thought it was funny, seeing that I hadn't asked for kudu biltong. So I sat down in front of a little table and ordered some *harde beskuit* and a cup of coffee. She brought me a number of little dry, flat cakes with letters on them I couldn't read very well. Her name is Marie Rossouw.'

'You must have said quite a lot to her to have found out her name,' I said, with something in my voice that must have made Hans Kriel suspicious.

'How do you know who I'm talking about?' he demanded suddenly.

'Oh, never mind,' I answered, 'let's ask Krisjan Wilman to refill our glasses.'

I winked at the others and we all laughed, because by that time Hans Kriel was sitting half sideways on the *riempie* bench, with his shoulders drawn up very high and his whole body seeming to be kept up by one elbow. It wasn't long after that that he moved his elbow, so that we had to pick him up from the floor and carry him into the *voorkamer*, where we laid him in a corner on some leopard skins.

But before that he had spoken more about Marie Roussouw, the new waitress in the café. He said he had passed by and had seen her through the plate-glass window, and there had been a vase of purple flowers on the counter, and he had noticed those two marks on her cheek, and those marks had looked very pretty to him, like two small shadows from those purple flowers.

'She is very beautiful,' Hans Kriel had said. 'Her eyes have got deep things in them, like those dark pools behind Abjaterskop. And when she smiled at me once – by mistake, I think – I felt as though my heart was rushing over the *vlaktes* like that shadow we saw in the sunset.'

'You must be careful of those dark pools behind Abjaterskop,' I had warned him. 'We know those pools have got witches in them.'

I felt it was a pity that we had had to carry him inside, shortly afterwards. For the mampoer had begun to make Hans Kriel talk rather well.

As it happened, Hans Kriel was not the only one, that

night, who encountered difficulties with the *riempie* bench. Several more of us were carried inside. And when I look back on that *Nagmaal* my most vivid memories are not of what the *predikant* said at the church service, or of Krisjan Wilman's mampoer, even, but of how very round the black spots were on the pale yellow of the leopard skin. They were so round that every time I looked at them they were turning.

In the morning Krisjan Wilman's wife woke us up and brought us coffee. Hans Kriel and I sat up side by side on the leopard skins, and in between drinking his coffee, Hans Kriel said strange things. He was still talking about Marie Roussouw.

'Just after dark I got up from the front stoep and went to see her in the café,' Hans Kriel said.

'You may have got up from the front stoep,' I answered, 'but you never got up from these leopard skins. Not from the moment we carried you here. That's the truth.'

'I went to the café,' Hans Kriel said, ignoring my interruption, 'and it was very dark. She was there alone. I wanted to find out how she had got those marks on her cheek. I think she is very pretty even without them. But with those marks, Marie Roussouw is the most wild and the most beautiful thing in the whole world.'

'I suppose her cheek got cut there when she was a child,' I suggested. 'Perhaps when a bottle of her father's mampoer exploded.'

'No,' Hans Kriel replied, very earnestly. 'No. It was something else. I asked her there, in the café, when we were alone together, and it suddenly seemed as though the whole place was awash with moonlight, and there was no counter between us any more, and there was a strange laughter in her eyes when she brought her face very close to mine. And she said: "I know you won't believe me. But that is where the devil kissed me. Satan kissed me there when we were behind Abjaterskop. Shall I show you?"

'That was what she said to me,' Hans Kriel continued, 'and I knew, then, that she was a witch. And that it was a very sinful thing to be in love with a witch. And so I caught her up, in my arms, and I whispered, trembling all the time: "Show me," and our heads rose up very tall through the shadows. And everything moved very fast, faster than the shadows move from Abjaterskop in the setting of the sun. And I knew that we were behind Abjaterskop, and that her eyes were indeed the dark pools there, with the tall reeds growing on the edges. And then I saw Satan come in between us. And he had hooves and a forked tail. And there were flames coming out of him. And he stooped down and kissed Marie Roussouw on her cheek, where those marks were. And she laughed. And her eyes danced with merriment. And I found that it was all the time I who was kissing her. Now, what do you make of this, Schalk?'

I said, of course, that it was the mampoer. And that I knew, now, why I had been sleeping in such discomfort. It wasn't because the spots on the leopard were turning like round wheels, but because I had Satan sleeping next to me all night. And I said that this discovery wasn't new, either. I had always suspected something like that about him.

But I got an idea. And while the others were at breakfast, I went out, on the pretext that I had to go and help Manie Burghers with his oxen at the church square outspan. But instead, I went into the café, and because I knew her name was Marie Roussouw, when the waitress came for my order I could ask her whether she was related to the Roussouws of Rysmierbult, and I could tell her that I was distantly related to that family, also.

In the daylight, there was about that café none of the

queerness that Hans Kriel had spoken about. It was all very ordinary. Even those purple flowers were still on the counter. They looked slightly faded.

And then, suddenly, while we were talking, I asked her the thing I was burning to know.

'That mark on your cheek, *juffrou*,' I said, 'will you tell me where you got it from?'

Marie Roussouw brought her face very close to mine, and her eyes were like dark pools with dancing light in them.

'I know you won't believe me,' she said, 'but that is where Satan kissed me. When we were at the back of Abjaterskop together. Shall I show you?'

~

It was broad daylight. The morning lay yellow on the world and the sun shone in brightly through the plate-glass window, and there were quite a number of people in the street. And yet, as I walked out of the café quickly and along the pavement, I was shivering.

With one thing and another, I did not come across Hans Kriel again until three or four days later, when the *Nagmaal* was over and we were trekking to the other side of the Dwarsberge once more.

We spoke of a number of things, and then, trying to make my voice sound natural, I made mention of Marie Rossouw.

'That was a queer sort of dream you had,' I said.

'Yes,' he answered, 'it was queer.'

'And did you find out,' I asked, again trying to sound casual, 'about those marks on her cheek?'

'Yes,' Hans Kriel answered, 'I asked Marie and she told me. She said that when she was a child a bottle of mampoer burst in the *voorkamer*. Her cheek got cut by a splinter of glass. She is an unusual kind of girl, Marie Rossouw.'

'Yes,' I agreed, moving away. 'Oh, yes.'

But I also thought that there are things about mampoer that you cannot understand very easily.

23.

And in your Heart there are Whisperings

From 'Ox-wagons on Trek'

In *Mafeking Road*

When I see the rain beating white on the thorn-trees, as it does now – Oom Schalk Lourens said – I remember another time when it rained. And there was a girl in an ox-wagon who dreamed. And in answer to her dreaming, a lover came galloping to her side from out of the veld. But he tarried only a short while, this lover who had come to her from the mist of the rain and the warmth of her dreams.

And yet, when he had gone, there was a slow look in her eyes that must have puzzled her lover very much – for it was a look of satisfaction, almost.

~

We had been to Zeerust for the *Nagmaal* church service, which we attended once a year.

You know what it is with these *Nagmaals*.

The Lord spreads these festivities over so many days that you have time, not only to go to church, but also to go to the bioscope. Sometimes you can even go to the bar, but then you must go in the back way, through the dark alley next to the draper's shop.

Zeerust is a small place, and if you are seen going into the bar during *Nagmaal*, people are liable to talk. I can still remember how surprised I was one morning when I went into that dark alley next to the draper's shop, and found the *predikant* there, wiping his mouth. The *predikant* looked at me and shook his head solemnly, and I felt very guilty.

So I went to the bioscope instead.

~

A few days later, five ox-wagons, full of people who had been to the Zeerust *Nagmaal*, were trekking along the road that led back to the Groot Marico. Inside the wagon-tents sat the women and children, listening to the rain pelting against the canvas. The drivers walked by the side of the oxen, cracking their long whips while the rain beat in their faces.

Overhead everything was black, except for the frequent flashes of lightening that tore across the sky.

After I had walked in this manner for some time, I began to get lonely. So I handed the whip to my *voorloper*, and went on ahead to Adriaan Brand's wagon. For some distance I walked in silence beside Adriaan. He had his trousers rolled up to his knees, and he had much trouble brandishing his whip and, at the same time, keeping the rain out of his pipe.

'It's Minnie,' Adriaan Brand said suddenly, referring to his nineteen-year-old daughter. 'There's one place in Zeerust where Minnie shouldn't go. And every *Nagmaal*, to my sorrow, I find that she's been there. And it all goes to her head.'

'Oh yes,' I answered. 'It always does.'

All the same, I was somewhat startled at Adriaan's remarks. Minnie didn't strike me as the sort of girl who would go and spend her father's money drinking peach brandy in the bar. I started wondering if she'd seen me in the draper's alley. Then Adriaan went on talking, and I felt more at ease.

'The place where they show those moving pictures,' he explained. 'Every time Minnie goes there, she comes back with ideas that are useless for a farmer's daughter. But this time it has made her quite impossible. For one thing, she says she won't marry Frans du Toit any more. She says Frans is too honest.'

'Well, that needn't be a difficulty, Adriaan,' I said. 'You can teach Frans du Toit a few of the things you've done. That'll make him dishonest enough. Like the way you put your brand on those oxen that strayed into your *kraal*. Or the way you altered the figures on the compensation forms after the rinderpest. Or the way ...'.

Adriaan looked at me with some disfavour.

'It isn't that,' he interrupted me, while I was still trying to call to mind a lot of other things he was able to teach Frans du Toit. 'Minnie wants a mysterious sort of man. She wants a man who's dishonest, but who's got foreign manners and a good heart. She saw a man like that at the picture place she went to, and since then ...'.

~

We both looked round together.

Through the mist of the white rain, a horseman came galloping up towards our wagons. He rode fast. Adriaan Brand and I stood and watched him.

By this time our wagons were some distance behind the others.

The horseman came thundering along at full galop until he was abreast of us. Then he pulled up sharply, jerking his horse onto his hind legs.

The stranger told us that his name was Koos Fichardt, and that he was on his way to the Bechuanaland Protectorate. Adriaan Brand and I introduced ourselves, and shortly afterwards Fichardt accepted our invitation to spend the night with us.

We outspanned a mile or so further on, drawing the five wagons up close together and getting what shelter we could by spreading bucksails.

Next morning there was no more rain. By that time, Koos Fichardt had seen Adriaan Brand's daughter, Minnie. So he decided to stay with us longer.

We trekked on again and, from where I walked beside my oxen, I could see Koos Fichardt and Minnie. They sat at the back of Adriaan Brand's wagon, hatless, with their legs hanging down and the morning breeze blowing through their hair, and it was evident that Minnie was fascinated by the stranger. Also, he seemed to be very much interested in her.

You do get like that, when there is suddenly a bright morning after long rains, and a low wind stirs the wet grass, and you feel, for a little while, that you know the same thing that the veld knows, and in your heart there are whisperings.

Most of the time they sat holding hands, Fichardt talking a great deal and Minnie nodding her pretty head at intervals, encouraging him to continue. They were all lies he told her, I suppose, as only a young man in love can tell lies.

Fichardt was tall and dark and well-dressed. He walked with a swagger. He had easy and engaging manners, and we all liked him.

~

That night, when we outspanned next to the Groen River, it was very pleasant. We all gathered around the campfire, and roasted meat and cooked crushed mielies. We sang songs and told ghost stories. And I wondered what Frans du Toit – the honest youth whom Minnie had discarded in Zeerust –

would have thought if he could see Minnie Brand and Koos Fichardt sitting unashamedly in each other's arms, for all the world to see their love, while the light of the campfire cast a rich glow over the thrill that was on their faces.

And although I knew how wonderful were the passing moments for these two, yet somehow, somehow, because I had seen so much of the world, I also felt sorry for them.

The next day we did not trek.

The Groen River was in flood from the heavy rains, and Oupa van Tonder, who had lived a long time in the Cape and was well versed in the ways of rivers – and who even knew how to swim – told us that it would not be safe to cross the drift for another twenty-four hours. Accordingly, we decided to remain camped out where we were until the next morning.

At first Koos Fichardt was much disturbed by this news, explaining how necessary it was for him to get into the Bechuanaland Protectorate by a certain day. After a while, however, he seemed to grow more reconciled to the necessity of waiting until the river had gone down.

But I noticed that he frequently gazed out over the veld, in the direction from which we had come. He gazed out rather anxiously, I thought.

~

Night came, and the occupants of the five wagons again gathered around the blazing fire. In some ways, that night was even grander than the one before. The songs we sang were more rousing. The stories we told seemed to have more power in them.

There was much excitement the following morning by the time the wagons were ready to go through the drift. And the excitement did not lie only in the bustle of inspanning the oxen.

For when we crossed the river, it was without Koos Fichardt, and there was a slow look in Minnie's eyes.

The wagons creaked and splashed in the water, and we saw Koos Fichardt for the last time, sitting on his horse, with a uniformed horseman on either side of him. And when he took off his hat in farewell, he had to use both hands, because of the cuffs that held his wrists together.

What I will always remember, however, is the slow look in Minnie's eyes. It was a kind of satisfaction, almost, at the thought that all the things that had come to the girl she had seen in the picture, had now come to her too.

24.

A Very Old Star

From 'Cometh Comet'

In *Unto Dust*

Hans Engelbrecht – Oom Schalk Lourens said – was the first farmer in the Schweizer-Reneke district to trek. With his wife and his daughter, and what was left of his cattle, he moved away to the northern slopes of the Dwarsberge, where the drought was less severe.

~

We trekked away in different directions. Four or five families eventually came to a halt at the foot of the Dwarsberge, near the place where Hans Engelbrecht was outspanned. In a vast area of the Schweizer-Reneke district, only one man had chosen to stay behind. He was Ocker Gieljan, a young *bywoner*, who had worked for Hans Engelbrecht since his boyhood.

Hans Engelbrecht was only partly surprised when, on the morning that the ox-wagon was loaded, and the long line of oxen, that were skin and bone, started stumbling along the road to the north, Ocker Gieljan had made it clear that he was not leaving the farm. The *voorloper* had already gone to the head of the *span*, and Hans Engelbrecht's wife, and his eighteen-year-old daughter, Maria, were seated on the wagon, under the tent-sail, when Ocker Gieljan suddenly declared that he had decided to stay behind on the farm, to 'look after things here'.

Hans Engelbrecht was in no mood to argue with a *bywoner*. Accordingly, half a sack of mealie-meal and a quantity of biltong were unloaded in front of Ocker Gieljan's mud-walled room.

~

The time came, also, when Hans Engelbrecht was brought to understand that the Lord had visited still more trouble on himself and his family. A little while before we had trekked away from our farms, a young insurance agent had left the district – suddenly – for Cape Town. That was a long distance to run away, especially when you think of how bad the roads were in those days.

It became commonplace, after a while, for Maria Engelbrecht to be seen seated in the grass, beside her father's wagon, weeping. Few pitied her. She must have sat in the grass, too often, with that insurance agent, Lettie Grobler said to some of the women – forgetting that there had been no grass left in the Schweizer-Reneke veld at the time when Hans Engelbrecht's daughter was being courted.

It was easy for Maria to wipe the tears from her face, another woman said. Easier than to wipe away her shame, the woman meant.

~

Now and again, from some traveller who had passed through Schweizer-Reneke, we who had trekked out of that stricken region would hear a few useless things about it. Ocker Gieljan was still on the Engelbrecht farm, we heard. And the only other living creature in the whole district was a solitary crow. A passing traveller had seen Ocker Gieljan at the borehole. He was pumping water into a trough for the crow, the traveller said.

'When his mealie-meal gives out, Ocker will find his way here, right enough,' Hans Engelbrecht growled impatiently.

~

Then the night came when, from our encampment beside the Malopo, we first saw the comet, in the place above the Dwarsberge *rante* where the sun had gone down. We all began to wonder what the new star with the long tail meant. Would it bring rain? We didn't know. We could see, of course, that the star was an omen. But we didn't know what sort of omen it was.

We knew many things about the veld and the sky and the seasons. But even the oldest Free State farmer among us did not know what effect a comet would have on a mealie crop.

Hans Engelbrecht said that we should send for the Reverend Losper, the missionary who ministered to the Bechuanas at Ramoutsa, but the rest of us ignored this suggestion.

During the nights that followed, the comet became more clearly visible.

~

The appearance of the comet caused consternation among the Bechuanas in the village of Ramoutsa, where the mission station was. It did not take long for some of their stories about the star to reach our encampment on the other side of the Malopo.

Soon afterwards, a number of other stories started to come out of the wilder parts of the Bushveld. It seemed that the farther a tribe lived away from civilisation, the more detailed and dependable was the information about the comet.

I know that I began to feel that Hans Engelbrecht had made the right suggestion in the first place when he had said that we should send for the missionary. I sensed that a number of others in our camp shared my feelings, but no one wanted to make this admission openly.

Lettie Grobler said that the Lord was coming down to punish all of us for the sins of Maria Engelbrecht. This thought disturbed us greatly, and we began to resent Maria's presence in our midst. It was then that Hans Engelbrecht sent for the missionary.

~

Meanwhile, the Reverend Losper had his hands full with the Bechuanas at Ramoutsa, who seemed on the point of panicking in earnest. The latest story about the comet had just reached them, and because it had come from somewhere in the deepest part of Africa, thumped out on the tom-toms, it was the most terrifying story of all.

Consequently, because of the tumult at Ramoutsa, it happened that Ocker Gieljan arrived at the encampment before the Reverend Losper got there.

~

Ocker Gieljan looked very tired and dusty on that afternoon when he walked up to Hans Engelbrecht's wagon. He took off his hat and, smiling somewhat, sat down – without speaking – in the shade of the veld-tent, inside which Maria Engelbrecht lay on a matress. Neither Hans Engelbrecht nor his wife asked Ocker Gieljan anything about his journey from the farm. They knew he would have nothing to tell.

Shortly afterwards, Ocker Gieljan made a communication to Hans Engelbrecht, speaking diffidently. Thereupon Hans Engelbrecht went into the tent and spoke to his wife and daughter. A few minutes later he came out, looking pleased with himself.

'Sit down here on the *riempiesstoel*, Ocker,' Hans Engelbrecht said to his prospective son-in-law, 'and tell me how you came to leave the farm.'

'I got lonely,' Ocker Gieljan answered, thoughtfully. 'You see, the crow flew away. I was alone, after that. The crow was then already weak. He didn't fly straight, as crows do. His wings wobbled.'

When he told me about this, years later, Hans Engelbrecht said that something in Ocker Gieljan's tone brought him a sudden vision of the way his daughter, Maria, had also left the Schweizer-Reneke district. With broken wings.

I thought that the Reverend Losper looked relieved to find, on his arrival at the camp, some time later, that all that was required of him, now, was the performance of a marriage ceremony.

On the next night but one, Maria Engelbrecht's child was born. All of the adults in our little trekker community came in the night and in the rain – which had been falling steadily for several hours – with gifts for Maria and her child.

And when I saw the star again, during a temporary break in the rain clouds, it seemed to me that it was not such a new star, after all. It was, indeed, a very old star.

25.

What was in her Heart

From 'Splendours from Ramoutsa'

In *Mafeking Road*

No – Oom Schalk Lourens said – I don't know why it is that people always ask me to tell them stories. Even though they all know that I can tell better stories than anybody else. Much better. What I mean is, I wonder why people listen to stories. Of course, it is easy to understand why a man should ask me to tell him a story when there's a drought in the Marico. Because then he can sit on the stoep and smoke his pipe and drink coffee, while I'm talking, so that my story keeps him from having to go to the borehole, in the hot sun, to pump water for his cattle.

By the earnest manner in which the farmers of the Marico ask me for stories at certain periods, I am always able to tell that there is no breeze to drive the windmill, and that the pump-handle is heavy, and that the water is very far down. And at such times I have often observed the look of sorrow that comes into a man's eyes, when he knows that I am near the end of my story and that he will shortly have to reach for his hat.

And when I have finished the story, he says: 'Yes, Oom Schalk. That's the way of the world. Yes, that story is very deep.'

But I know that all the time he is really thinking of how deep the water is in the borehole.

As I have said, it is when people have other reasons for asking me to tell them a story that I start wondering as I do now. When they ask me at those times when there is no ploughing to be done and there are no barbed-wire fences to be put up in the heat of the day. And I think that these reasons are deeper than any stories and deeper than the water in the boreholes when there is a drought.

There was young Krisjan Geel, for instance. He once listened to a story. It was foolish of him to have listened, of course, especially as I hadn't told it to him. He had heard it from the Indian behind the counter of the shop in Ramoutsa. Krisjan Geel related this story to me, and I told him straight out that I didn't think much of it. I said anybody could guess, right from the start, why the princess was sitting beside the well. Anybody could see that she hadn't come there just because she was thirsty. I also said that the story was too long, and that even if I was thinking of something else, I would still have told it in such a way that people would have wanted to hear it to the end. I pointed out lots of other details like that.

Krisjan Geel said he had no doubt that I was right, but that the man who had told him the story was an Indian, after all, and that for an Indian, perhaps, it wasn't too bad. He also said that there were quite a number of customers in the place, and that that made it more difficult for the Indian to tell the story properly, because he had to stand at such an awkward angle, all the time, weighing out things with his foot on the scale.

By his tone, it sounded as though Krisjan Geel was quite sorry for the Indian.

So I spoke to him very firmly.

'The Indian in the store at Ramoutsa,' I said, 'has told me much better stories than that before today. He once told me that there were no burnt mealies mixed with the coffee beans he sold me. Another one that was almost as good was when he said …'

'And to think that the princess went and waited by the

well,' Krisjan Geel interrupted me, 'just because once she had seen the young man there.'

'Another good one,' I insisted, 'was when he said there was no Kalahari sand in the sack of yellow sugar I bought from him.'

'And she had only seen him once,' Krisjan Geel went on, 'and she was a princess.'

'And I had to give most of that sugar to the pigs,' I said. 'It didn't melt or sweeten the coffee. It just stayed like mud at the bottom of the cup.'

'She waited by the well because she was in love with him,' Krisjan Geel ended up, lamely.

'I just mixed it in with the pigs' mealie-meal,' I said. 'They ate it very fast. It's funny how fast a pig eats.'

Krisjan Geel didn't say any more after that one. No doubt he realised that I wasn't going to allow him to impress me with a story told by an Indian, and not very well told either. I could see what the Indian's idea was. Just because I had stopped buying from his shop after that unpleasantness about the coffee beans and the sugar – which were only burnt mealies and Kalahari sand, as I explained to a number of my neighbours – he had hit on this uncalled-for way of paying me back. He was setting up as my rival. He was also going to tell stories.

And on account of the long start I had on him, he was using all sorts of unfair methods. Like putting princesses in his stories. And palaces. And elephants that were all dressed up with yellow and red hangings and that were trained to trample on the king's enemies at the word of command. Whereas the only kind of elephants I could talk about were those that didn't wear red hangings or gold bangles, and that didn't worry about whether or not you were the king's enemy: they just trampled on you first, anyhow, and without any sort of training, either.

At first I felt it was very unfair of the Indian to come along with stories like that. I couldn't compete. But when I thought it over carefully, I knew that it didn't matter. The Indian could tell all the stories he liked about a princess riding around on an elephant. For there was one thing I knew I could always do better than the Indian. In just a few words, and without even talking about the princess, I would be able to let people know, subtly, what was in her heart. And this was more important than all the palaces and temples and elephants with gold ornaments on their feet.

Perhaps the Indian realised the truth of what I am saying now. At all events, after a while he stopped wasting the time of his customers with stories of emperors. In between telling them that the price of sheep-dip and axle-grease had gone up. Or perhaps his customers grew tired of listening to him.

~

The days passed, and the drought came, and the farmers of the Marico put in much of their time at the boreholes, pushing the heavy pump-handles up and down. The Indian's brief period of storytelling was almost forgotten. Even Krisjan Geel came to admit that there was such a thing as overdoing these stories of magnificence.

'All these things he says about temples, and so on,' Krisjan Geel said, 'with white floors and shining red stones in them. And rajahs. Do you know what a rajah is, Oom Schalk? No, I don't know, either. You can have too much of that. It was only that one story of his that was any good. The one about the princess. She had rich stones in her hair, and pearls sewn on to her dress. And so the young man never guessed why she had come there. He didn't guess that she loved him. But perhaps I didn't tell you the story properly the first time, Oom Schalk.

Perhaps I should tell it to you again. I've already told it to many people.'

But I declined this offer hurriedly. I replied that there was no need for him to go over all that again. I said that I remembered the story very well, and that if it was all the same to him, I should prefer not to hear it a second time. He might just spoil it in telling it all over again.

'Why you're so interested in that story,' I said, 'is because you like to imagine yourself as that young man.'

Krisjan Geel agreed with me that this was the reason why the Indian's story had appealed to him so much. And he went on to say that a young man had no chance, really, in the Marico. What with the droughts, and the cattle getting the *miltsiekte*, and the mosquitoes buzzing around so that you couldn't sleep at night.

And when Krisjan Geel left me, I could see – very clearly – how much he envied the young man in the Indian's story.

As I have said before, there are some strange things about stories, and about the people who listen to them. I thought so particularly on a hot afternoon, a few weeks later, when I saw Lettie Viljoen. The sun shone on her upturned face, and on her bright yellow hair. She sat with one hand pressed in the dry grass of last summer, and I thought of what a graceful figure she was, and how slender her wrists were.

And because Lettie Viljoen hadn't come there riding on an elephant with orange trappings and gold bangles, and because she wasn't wearing a string of red stones at her throat, Krisjan Geel knew, of course, that she wasn't a princess.

And I suppose this was the reason why, during all the time he was talking to her, telling her the story about the princess at the well, Krisjan Geel never guessed about Lettie Viljoen, and what it was that had brought her there, in the heat of the sun, to the borehole.

26.

As Strange as the African Veld

From 'Unto Dust'

In *Unto Dust*

I have noticed that when a young man or woman dies, people get the feeling that there is something beautiful and touching in the event, and that it is different from the death of an old person. In the thought, say, of a girl of twenty sinking into an untimely grave, there is a sweet wistfulness that makes people talk all kinds of romantic words. She died, they say, young, she that was so full of life and so fair. She was a flower that withered before it bloomed, they say, and it all seems so fitting and beautiful that there is a good deal of resentment, at the funeral, over the crude questions that a couple of men in plain clothes from the *landdrost*'s office are asking about cattle-dip.

But when you've grown old, nobody is very much interested in the manner of your dying. Nobody except you yourself, that is. And I think that your past life has got a lot to do with the way you feel when you get near the end of your days. I remember how, when he was lying on his deathbed, Andries Wessels kept on telling us that it was because of the blameless path he had trodden from his earliest years that he could compose himself in peace to lay down his burdens. And I certainly never saw a man breathe his last more tranquilly, seeing that right up to the end he kept on murmuring to us how happy he was, with heavenly hosts and invisible choirs of angels all around him.

Just before he died, he told us that the angels had even

become visible. They were medium-sized angels, he said, and they had cloven hoofs and carried forks. It was obvious that Andries Wessels's ideas were getting a bit confused by then, but all the same I never saw a man die in a more hallowed sort of calm.

~

Once, during the malaria season in the Eastern Transvaal, it seemed to me, when I was in a high fever and like to die, that the whole world was a big burial ground. I thought it was the earth itself that was a graveyard, and not just those little fenced-in bits of land dotted wth tombstones, in the shade of a Western Province oak tree or by the side of a Transvaal *koppie*. This was a nightmare that worried me a great deal, and so I was very glad, when I recovered from the fever, to think that we Boers had properly marked out places on our farms for people to be laid to rest in, in a civilised Christian way, instead of having to be buried just anyhow, along with a dead wild cat, maybe, or a Bushman with a clay-pot, and things.

When I mentioned this to my friend, Stoffel Oosthuizen, who was in the Low Country with me at the time, he agreed whole-heartedly. There were people who talked in a high-flown way of death as the great leveller, he said, and those high-flown people also declared that everyone was made kin by death. He would still like to see those things proved, Stoffel Oosthuizen said. After all, that was one of the reasons why the Boers trekked away into the Transvaal and the Free State, he said – because the British government wanted to give the vote to any Cape Coloured person walking about.

The first time he heard that sort of talk about death coming to all of us alike, and making us all equal, Stoffel Oosthuizen's suspicions were aroused. It sounded like something out of a speech made by one of those liberal Cape politicians, he explained.

I found something very comforting in Stoffel Oosthuizen's words.

Then, to illustrate his contention, Stoffel Oosthuizen told me a story about an incident that took place in a bygone Transvaal tribal war. I don't know whether he told the story incorrectly, or whether it was just that kind of story, but, by the time he had finished, all my uncertainties had, I discovered, come back to me.

~

'You can go and look at Hans Welman's tombstone any time you are at Nietverdiend,' Stoffel Oosthuizen said. 'The slab of red sandstone is weathered by now, of course, seeing how long ago it all happened. But the inscription is still legible. I was with Hans Welman on that morning when he fell. Our commando had been ambushed by the tribe, and was retreating. I could do nothing for Hans Welman. Once, when I looked round, I saw a tall warrior bending over him and plunging an assegaai into him. Shortly afterwards I saw the warrior stripping the clothes off Hans Welman. A yellow dog was yelping excitedly around his black master. Although I was in grave danger myself, with several dozen warriors making straight for me on foot through the bush, the fury I felt at the sight of what that tall warrior was doing made me hazard a last shot. Reining in my horse, and taking what aim I could under the circumstances, I pressed the trigger. My luck was in. I saw the warrior fall forward beside the naked body of Hans Welman. Then I set spurs to my horse and galloped off at full speed, with the foremost of my pursuers already almost upon me. The last I saw was that yellow dog bounding up to his master – whom I had wounded mortally, as we were to discover later.

'As you know, that tribal war dragged on for a long time. There were few pitched battles. Mainly, what took place were bush skirmishes like the one in which Hans Welman lost his life.

'After about six months, quiet of a sort was restored to the Marico and the Zoutpansberg districts. Then the day came when I went out, in the company of a handful of other burghers, to fetch in the remains of Hans Welman, at his widow's request, for burial in the little cemetery plot on the farm. We took a coffin with us on a Cape cart.

'We located the scene of the skirmish without difficulty. Indeed, Hans Welman had been killed not very far from his own farm, which had been temporarily abandoned, along with the other farms in that part, during the time that the trouble lasted. We went to the spot where I remembered having seen Hans Welman lying dead on the ground, with the tall warrior next to him. From a distance I again saw that yellow dog. At our approach he slipped away into the bush. I could not help feeling that there was something rather stirring about that beast's fidelity, even though it was bestowed on a dead warrior.

'We were now confronted with a queer situation. We found that what was left of Hans Welman and the warrior consisted of little more than pieces of sun-dried flesh and the dismembered fragments of bleached skeletons. The sun and the wild animals and the birds of prey had done their work. There was a heap of human bones, with here and there leathery strips of blackened flesh. But we could not tell which was the white man and which was the black man. To make it still more confusing, a lot of bones were missing altogether, having no doubt been dragged away by wild animals into their bushveld lairs. Another thing was that Hans Welman and that warrior had been just about the same size.'

~

Stoffel Oosthuizen paused in his narrative, and I let my imagination dwell for a moment on the situation. I realised just how those Boers must have felt about it: about the thought of bringing the remains of a Transvaal burgher home to his widow for a Christian burial, and perhaps having a lot of the warrior's bones mixed up with those of the burgher, lying in the same tomb, on which the mauve petals from the oleander overhead would fall.

~

'I remember one of our party saying that that was the worst of these tribal skirmishes,' Stoffel Oosthuizen continued. 'If it had been a war against the English, and part of a dead Englishman had got lifted into that coffin by mistake, it wouldn't have mattered so much,' he said.

There seemed to me, in this story, to be something as strange as the African veld. Stoffel Oosthuizen said that the party of Boers spent almost a whole afternoon with the remains in order to try and get the white man sorted out from the black man. By evening they had laid all they could find of what seemed like Hans Welman's bones in the coffin in the Cape cart. The rest of the bones and the flesh they buried on the spot.

Stoffel Oosthuizen added that, no matter what the difference in the colour of their skin had been, it was impossible to say that the warrior's sun-dried flesh was any blacker than the white man's. Alive, you couldn't go wrong in distinguishing between a white man and a black man. Dead, you had great difficulty in telling them apart.

~

'Naturally, we burghers felt very bitter about this whole affair,' Stoffel Oosthuizen said, 'and our resentment was something we couldn't quite explain. Afterwards, several other men who were there that day told me that they had the same feelings of suppressed anger that I did. They wanted somebody – just once – to make a remark such as "in death they were not divided". Then you would have seen an outburst all right. Nobody did say anything like that, however. We all knew better.

'Two days later, a funeral service was conducted in the little cemetery on the Welman farm, and shortly afterwards the sandstone memorial that you can still see there was erected.'

~

That was the story Stoffel Oosthuizen told me, after I had recovered from my fever. It was a story that, as I have said, had in it features as strange as the African veld. But it brought me no peace, in my broodings, after that attack of malaria. Especially when Stoffel Oosthuizen spoke of how he had had occasion, one clear night when the stars were shining bright, to pass that quiet graveyard on the Welman farm. Something leapt up from the mound beside the sandstone slab, Stoffel Oosthuizen said, and it gave him quite a turn.

It was that same yellow dog.

27.

In Those Days

From 'Border Bad-Man'

In *Jurie Steyn's Post Office*

Oupa Bekker mentioned another occasion on which a border patrolman came and assumed duty in the Marico, for the first time.

'Of course, I'm talking of very long ago, now,' Oupa Bekker said. 'The patrolman's name was Duvenhage, and we could see that they had explained to him in Pretoria that his most important work would be to put down the awful cattle-smuggling that was going on here, in those days.'

'Oh yes, in those days, of course,' Gysbert van Tonder said, quickly.

Jurie Steyn challenged Gysbert van Tonder at once.

'What do you mean by saying "in those days", like that?' Jurie Steyn asked. 'What about the bunch of cattle with wide horns and all colours that you've got in the camp by the *kloof*, there, right now? I suppose you'll tell us next that you bought them on the Johannesburg market.'

'And I expect that why you keep that herd in the *kloof*,' Chris Welman observed to Gysbert van Tonder, sarcastically, 'is because they're the sort of cows and oxen that don't like people to come prying into their affairs.'

'Especially when they've still got Bechuanaland Protectorate clay between their hoofs,' Jurie Steyn remarked. 'Turf clay.'

So Gysbert van Tonder said that they would have to prove it. And so Jurie Steyn told us what he would have done if he had been a border patrol policeman, instead of a postmaster. And then Gysbert said that if Jurie Steyn sorted out hoofprints in the dust like he sorted letters in his post office, then you could bring Bechuanaland cattle across the Convention line in broad daylight.

Thereupon Oupa Bekker said what a queer thing it was that there should be so much jealousy among Marico farmers.

'I mean, there isn't one of us who wouldn't smuggle in a few head of cattle if he got the chance,' Oupa Bekker said, 'and yet, when you hear of your neighbour doing it – and you yourself didn't do it, that time – and you picture to yourself a herd of all sorts of cattle crowded against the barbed-wire fence on one side of your neighbour's farm, sniffing the wind from the Protectorate, and lowing, why, you get pretty mad about it. It's almost like you're also pawing the *polgras* with your hoofs, sniffing the wind that blows from Bechuanaland.'

We couldn't but admit that there was much truth in Oupa Bekker's words. At the same time – as Chris Welman pointed out, then – there was such a thing as overdoing this cattle-smuggling business. And it was people that overdid it who gave all the Marico farmers a bad name, he said.

Gysbert van Tonder sniffed. It was a different type of sniff from the kind Oupa Bekker had been talking about.

'A bad name!' Gysbert van Tonder said, his lip curling. 'Well, there are some people sitting here in this *voorkamer*, now, that would give any district they stayed in a bad name, just by living in it. Even if they lived in the Cape Peninsula, it would get a bad name – and you can't tell me there's any cattle-smuggling going on in the Cape Peninsula. Unless you can smuggle in cattle off ships.'

Gysbert van Tonder grew thoughtful after that last remark. It was as though he was considering the possibilities.

~

'Wasn't Duvenhage the patrolman that was caught smuggling quite a big herd of cattle across the border?' Chris Welman asked. 'With his police boys helping him? I seem to remember something about it. The police boys were singing Bechuana cattle songs, with the patrolman joining in.'

'Yes, the same,' Oupa Bekker replied, 'and I still remember my first meeting with him. He asked me where their hangout was. And when I said I didn't know what he meant, he said the cattle-smuggling kings. The heads in the game, he explained. He wanted to know where they sat, talking and drinking.'

Oupa Bekker said that he could see, from that, that Patrolman Duvenhage's training on the Illicit Diamond staff in Kimberley had been of such a nature as to leave him somewhat out of touch with conditions in the Groot Marico Bushveld.

'I mean, I couldn't go and tell him that there wasn't such a thing as a gang of foreign cattle-smugglers working in these parts,' Oupa Bekker said. 'After all, we all know that if there is such a thing as a few head of cattle being brought across the line on a night when there isn't much of a moon, well, then we know it can be almost any Marico farmer trying to do a bit of good for himself.

'And we know that there is no particular place where that Marico farmer will go and sit, and drink, and talk about it, afterwards.

'The only place where a Marico farmer might have a drink would be in the Zeerust bar during *Nagmaal*. And then he would only talk about the crops, or about the *Dominee*'s sermon, or about how he's got the laziest *bywoner* on this side of the Dwarsberge, and how that *bywoner* has the impudence to be making eyes at his daughter.'

Oupa Bekker went on to explain the details of a piece of strategy he and his partner, Japie Krige, had thought up, to get Patrolman Duvenhage out of the way on a night when they were going to smuggle cattle into the Transvaal.

~

'But that evening,' Oupa Bekker said, 'when it was not a Bechuana from Japie Krige that came to my door, but Patrolman Duvenhage, then I knew there was something wrong.'

All the same, Oupa Bekker said, he could tell by Patrolman Duvenhage's manner that he had not come to arrest him.

'Duvenhage walked straight into my *voorkamer* and didn't even take his helmet off,' Oupa Bekker said. 'And when my little yellow *brak* pup snapped at him, Patrolman Duvenhage landed one with his boot that sent the yellow *brak* pup flying through the door, and then it travelled about a hundred yards up the road before it turned round to let out a yelp. I could tell from these signs that Patrolman Duvenhage didn't have a case against me.'

So Gysbert van Tonder said, yes, he knew. It was when a border patrolman came to your house, and was polite, that you had to watch out. It was when the patrolman patted your youngest son on the head, and asked him what class he was in – professing surprise that he should be so far advanced with his education – that the next thing the patrolman would say to you was to get your jacket.

Oupa Bekker said Patrolman Duvenhage had come pretty straight to the point, but it was when Patrolman Duvenhage started talking about how much there would be in it for himself, that an unhappy note crept into the conversation. For Patrolman Duvenhage had spoken, very emphatically, about what he called a rake-off, a word Oupa Bekker had not heard of until then.

'When Japie Krige arrived at about midnight, with the herd of smuggled cattle, the drovers singing their chorus of a Bechuana cattle song,' Oupa Bekker went on, 'he came into my *voorkamer* prepared to be very indignant, because I had not assisted him at the fence.

'But when he saw who it was sitting opposite me at the table, Japie Krige turned white. And I have never seen a man hide a pair of wire-cutters behind his back quicker than Japie Krige did then. But Patrolman Duvenhage did not even bother to look up from the figures he was working out on a piece of paper.

'One thing I'll say is that Japie Krige and I never brought any more cattle over the line while Duvenhage was the patrolman. We just couldn't, I mean. Patrolman Duvenhage's percentage rake-off, that he worked out for us on paper, was too high. In the end, the only man left in the business was Patrolman Duvenhage himself.

'I often wonder how he came to be transferred from his post in Kimberley.'

28.

Wanting to Get into History

From 'The Music-Maker'

In *Mafeking Road*

Of course, I know about history – Oom Schalk Lourens said – it's the stuff children learn in school. Only the other day, at Thys Lemmer's post office, Thys's little son, Stoffel, started reading out of his history book, about a man called Vasco da Gama, who visited the Cape. At once, Dirk Snyman started telling young Stoffel about the time when he himself had visited the Cape, but young Stoffel didn't take much notice of him. So Dirk Snyman said that that just showed you.

~

Yes, it's a queer thing about wanting to get into history. Take the case of Manie Kruger, for instance.

Manie Kruger was one of the best farmers in the Marico. He knew just how much peach brandy to pour out for the tax collector, to make sure that he would nod dreamily at everything Manie said. And at a time of drought, Manie Kruger could run to the Government for help much quicker than any man I ever knew.

Then, one day, Manie Kruger read an article in the *Kerkbode* about a musician who said that he knew more about music than Napoleon did. After that – having first read another article, to find out who Napoleon was – Manie Kruger was a changed man. He could talk of nothing but his place in history, and of his musical career.

Of course, everybody knew that no man in the Marico could be counted in the same class with Manie Kruger, when it came to playing the concertina.

No Bushveld dance was complete without Manie Kruger's concertina. When he played a *vastrap*, you couldn't keep your feet still. But after he had decided to become the sort of musician that gets into history books, it was strange the way that Manie Kruger altered. For one thing, he said he would never again play at a dance. We all felt sad about that. There would be the peach brandy in the kitchen; in the *voorkamer* the feet of the dancers would go through the steps of schottische and the polka and the waltz and the mazurka, but on the *riempies* bench in the corner, where the musicians sat, there would be no Manie Kruger. And they would play *Die vaal hare en die blou oge* and *Vat jou goed en trek, Ferreira*, but it would be another's fingers that swept over the concertina keys. And when, with the dancing and the peach brandy, the young men called out '*dagbreek toe*,' it would not be Manie Kruger's head that bowed down to the applause.

It was sad to think about all this.

For so long, at the Bushveld dances, Manie Kruger had been the chief musician.

And of all those who mourned this change that had come over Manie, we could see that there was no one more grieved than Letta Steyn.

And Manie said such queer things at times. Once he said that what he had to do to get into history was to die of consumption in the arms of a princess, like another musician he had read about. Only it was hard to get consumption in the Marico, because the climate was so healthy.

Although Manie stopped playing his concertina at dances, he played a great deal in another way. He started giving what he called recitals. I went to several of them. They were very impressive.

At the first recital I went to, I found that the front part of Manie's *voorkamer* was taken up by rows of benches and chairs that he had borrowed from those of his neighbours who didn't mind having to eat their meals on candle-boxes and upturned buckets. At the far end of the *voorkamer*, a wide green curtain was hung on a piece of string. When I came in, the place was full. I managed to squeeze in, on a bench between Jan Terblanche and a young woman in a blue *kappie*. Jan Terblanche had been trying to hold this young woman's hand.

Manie Kruger was sitting behind the green curtain. He was already there when I came in. I knew it was Manie by his *veldskoens*, which were sticking out from underneath the curtain. Letta Steyn sat in front of me. Now and again, when she turned round, I saw that there was a flush on her face, and a look of dark excitement in her eyes.

At last everything was ready, and Joel – the farm labourer to whom Manie had given this job – slowly drew the green curtain aside. A few of the younger men called out '*Middag, ou Manie*,' and Jan Terblanche asked if it wasn't very close and suffocating, sitting there like that behind that piece of green curtain.

Then he started to play.

And we all knew that it was the most wonderful concertina music we had ever listened to. It was Manie Kruger at his best. He had practised a long time for that recital; his fingers flew over the keys; the notes of the concertina swept into our hearts; and the music of Manie Kruger lifted us right out of that *voorkamer* and into a strange, rich and dazzling world.

It was fine.

The applause right through was terrific. At the end of each

piece, Joel closed the curtain in front of Manie, and we sat waiting for a few minutes until the curtain was drawn aside again. But after that first time, there was no more laughter about this procedure. The recital lasted for about an hour and a half, and the applause at the end was even greater than at the start. And during those ninety minutes, Manie left his seat only once. That was when there was some trouble with the curtain, and he got up to kick Joel.

At the end of the recital, Manie did not come forward and shake hands with us, as we had expected. Instead, he slipped through, behind the green curtain, into the kitchen, and sent word that we could come and see him round the back. At first we thought this a bit queer, but Letta Steyn said it was all right. She explained that in other countries, the great musicians and stage performers all received their admirers at the back. Jan Terblanche said that if these actors used their kitchens for entertaining their visitors in, he wondered where they did their cooking.

Nevertheless, most of us went round to the kitchen, and we had a good time congratulating Manie Kruger and shaking hands with him; and Manie spoke much of his musical future, and of the triumphs that would come to him in the great cities of the world, when he would stand before the curtain and bow to the applause.

Manie gave a number of other recitals, after that. They were all equally fine. Only, as he had to practise all day, he couldn't pay much attention to his farming. The result was that his farm went to pieces, and he got into debt. The court messengers came and attached half his cattle while he was busy practising for his fourth recital. And he was practising for his seventh recital when they took away his ox-waggon and mule-cart.

Eventually, when Manie Kruger's musical career reached

that stage when they took away his plough and the last of his oxen, he sold up what remained of his possessions and left the Bushveld, on his way to those great cities he had so often talked about. It was very grand, the send-off that the Marico gave him. The *predikant* and the *Volksraad* member both made speeches about how proud the Transvaal was of her great son. Then Manie replied. Instead of thanking his audience, however, he started abusing us left and right, calling us a mob of hooligans, and soulless Philistines, and saying how much he despised us.

Naturally, we were very much surprised at this outburst, as we had always been kind to Manie Kruger, and had encouraged him all we could. But Letta Steyn explained that Manie didn't really mean the things he said. She said it was just that every great artist was expected to talk in that way about the place he came from.

So we knew it was all right, and the more offensive the things were that Manie said about us, the louder we shouted '*Hoor, hoor vir Manie.*' There was a particularly enthusiastic round of applause when he said that we knew as much about art as a *boomslang*. His language was hotter than anything I had ever heard – except once. And that was when De Wet said what he thought of Cronje's surrender to the English at Paardeberg. We could feel that Manie's speech was the real thing. We cheered ourselves hoarse that day.

And so Manie Kruger went. We received one letter to say that he had reached Pretoria. But after that, we heard no more of him.

Yet always, when Letta Steyn spoke of Manie, it was as a child speaks of a dream, half-wistfully; and, always, with the voice of a wistful child, she would tell me how one day, one day he would return. And often, when it was dusk, I would see her sitting on the stoep, gazing out across the veld into the evening, down the dusty road that led between the thorn-trees and beyond the Dwarsberge, waiting for the lover who would come to her no more.

It was a long time before I again saw Manie Kruger. And then it was in Pretoria. I had gone there to interview the *Volksraad* member about an election promise. It was quite by accident that I saw Manie. And he was playing the concertina – playing as well as ever, I thought. I went away quickly.

But what affected me very strangely was just that one glimpse I had of the green curtain of the bar in front of which Manie Kruger played.

29.

Face Downwards

From 'The Affair at Ysterspruit'

In *Unto Dust*

When the talk came round to the old days, leading up to and including the Second Boer War, I was always interested when they had a photograph that I could examine, at some farmhouse, in that part of the Groot Marico District that faces towards the Kalahari. And when they showed me, hanging framed against a wall of the *voorkamer* – or having brought it from an adjoining room – a photograph of a burgher of the South African Republic, father or son or husband or lover, then it was always with a thrill of pride in my land and my people that I looked on a likeness of a hero of the Boer War.

I was a schoolteacher, many years ago, at a little school in the Marico bushveld, near the border of the Bechuanaland Protectorate. The Transvaal Education Department expected me to visit the parents of the schoolchildren in the area at intervals. But even if this *huisbesoek* were not part of my after-school duties, I would have gone and visited the parents in any case. And when I discovered, after one or two casual calls, that the older parents were a fund of first-class story material, that they could hold the listener enthralled with tales of the past, with embroidered reminiscences of Transvaal life in the old days, then I became very conscientious about *huisbesoek*.

'What happened after that, Oom?' I would say, calling on a parent for about the third week in succession, 'when you were trekking through the *kloof* that night, I mean, and you had muzzled both the black calf with the dappled belly and your daughter, so that Mojaja's men would not be able to hear anything?'

And then the Oom would knock out the ash from his pipe on to his *veldskoen* and he would proceed to relate – his words had a slow and steady rumble, with the red dust of the road in their sound, almost – a tale of terror or of high romance or of soft laughter.

~

It was quite by accident that I came across Ouma Engelbrecht in a two-roomed, mud-walled dwelling some little distance off the Government Road and a few hundred yards away from the homestead of her son-in-law, Stoffel Brink, on whom I had called earlier in the afternoon. I had not been in the Marico very long, then, and my interview with Stoffel Brink had been, on the whole, unsatisfactory. I wanted to know how deep the Boer trenches were dug into the foot of the *koppies* at Magersfontein, where Stoffel Brink had fought. Stoffel Brink, on the other hand, was anxious to learn whether, in regard to what I taught the children, I would follow the guidance of the local school committee, of which he was chairman, or whether I was one of that new kind of schoolteacher who went by a little printed book of subjects supplied by the Education Department. He added that this latter class of schoolmaster was causing a lot of unpleasantness in the Bushveld through teaching the children that the earth moved round the sun, and through broaching similar questions of a political nature.

I replied evasively, with the result that Stoffel Brink launched forth for almost an hour on the merits of the old-fashioned Hollander schoolmaster, who could teach the children all he knew himself in eighteen months, because he taught them only facts.

'If a child stays at school longer than that,' Stoffel Brink added, 'then the rest of the time he can only learn lies.'

I left about then, and on my way back, a little distance from the road and half concealed by a tall bush, I found the two-roomed dwelling of Ouma Engelbrecht.

~

I could see that Ouma Engelbrecht did not have much time for her son-in-law, Stoffel Brink. For when I mentioned his references to education, when I had merely sought to learn some details about the Boer trenches at Magersfontein, she said that maybe he could learn all there was to know in eighteen months, but he had not learnt how to be ordinarily courteous to a stranger who came to his door – a stranger, moreover, who was a schoolmaster asking for information about the Boer War.

Then she spoke about her son, Johannes, who didn't have to hide in a Magersfontein trench, but who was sitting straight up on his horse when all those bullets went through him at Ysterspruit, and who died of his wounds some time later. Johannes had always been such a well-behaved boy, Ouma Engelbrecht told me, and he was gentle and kind-hearted.

She told me many stories of his childhood and early youth. She spoke about a time when the span of red Afrikaner oxen got stuck with the wagon in the drift, and her husband and the labourers, with long whip and short sjambok, could not move them – and then Johannes had come along and he had spoken softly to the red Afrikaner oxen, and he had called on each of them by name, and the team had made one last mighty effort, and had pulled the wagon through to the other side.

'And yet they never understood him in these parts,' Ouma Engelbrecht continued. 'They say things about him, and I hardly ever talk of him any more. And when I show them his portrait, they hardly even look at it, and they put the picture away from them, and when they are sitting on that *rusbank* where you are sitting now, they place the portrait of Johannes face downwards beside them.'

I told Ouma Engelbrecht, laughing reassuringly the while, that I stood above the pettiness of local intrigue. I told her that I had already noticed that there were all kinds of queer undercurrents below the placid surface of life in the Groot Marico. There was the example of what had happened that very afternoon, when her son-in-law, Stoffel Brink, had conceived a nameless prejudice against me, simply because I was not prepared to teach the schoolchildren that the earth was flat. I told her that it was ridiculous to imagine that a man in my position, a man of education and wide tolerance, should allow himself to be influenced by local Dwarsberge gossip.

Ouma Engelbrecht spoke freely, then, and the fight at Ysterspruit lived for me again – Kemp and De la Rey and the captured English convoy, the ambush and the booty of a million rounds of ammunition. It was almost as though the affair at Ysterspruit was being related to me, not by a lonely old woman whose son received his death wounds on the *vlaktes* near Klerksdorp, but by a burgher who had taken a prominent part in the battle.

And so, naturally, I wanted to see the photograph of her son, Johannes Engelbrecht.

When it came to the Boer War (although I did not say this to Ouma Engelbrecht), I didn't care if a Boer commander was not very competent or very cunning in his strategy, or if a burgher was not particularly brave. It was enough for me that he had fought. And to me General Snyman, for instance, in spite of the history books' somewhat unflattering assessment of his military qualities, was a hero, none the less. I had seen General Snyman's photograph, somewhere; that face was like Transvaal *blouklip*; those eyes had no fire in them, but a stubborn and elemental strength. You still see Boers in the backveld with that look today.

It was well on towards evening when Ouma Engelbrecht, yielding at last to my cajoleries and entreaties, got up slowly from her chair and went into the adjoining room. She returned with a photograph enclosed in a heavy black frame. I waited, tense with curiosity, to see the portrait of that son of hers who had died of wounds at Ysterspruit, and whose reputation the loose prattle of the neighbourhood had invested with a dishonour as dark as the frame about his photograph.

Flicking a few specks of dust from the portrait, Ouma Engelbrecht handed the picture to me.

And she was still talking about the things that went on in a mother's heart, things of pride and sorrow that the world did not understand, when, in an unconscious reaction, and hardly aware of what I was doing, I placed beside me on the *rusbank*, face downwards, the photograph of a young man whose hat brim was cocked on the right side, jauntily, and whose jacket with narrow lapels was buttoned up high.

With a queer jumble of inarticulate feelings, I realised that, in the affair at Ysterspruit, they were all Mauser bullets that had passed through the youthful body of Johannes Engelbrecht, National Scout.

30.

The Hoof-Beats of a Commando at Full Gallop

From 'A Boer Rip Van Winkel'

In *Unto Dust*

Every writer has got, lying around somewhere in a suitcase or a trunk, various parts of a story that he has worked on from time to time, and that he has never finished, because he hasn't been able to find out how the theme should be handled. Such a story – that I've had lying in a suitcase for many years – centres around the things that happened to Herklaas van Wyk.

The plot of a story has no particular appeal for me. I feel that to sit down and work out a plot does not call for the highest form of literary inspiration. Rather does that form of activity recall the skill of the inventor.

My own stories that I like best are those that have just grown. Some mood, conjured up in half a dozen words, has set me going, and it has often happened to me that, only when I have got to very near the end in the writing of it, has the shape of the story suddenly dawned on me. And more than once I have been surprised to find what a very old tale it was that has kept me from the chimney corner. Agreeably surprised, that is, for I have a preference for old tales.

But my inability to finish writing the story of Herklaas van Wyk is not due to the denouement not having taken some recognisable form in my mind within the last few hundred words. It hasn't been that kind of writer's problem. I didn't put my hand in the hat and a story came out that wouldn't unfold. On the contrary, this story told itself quite all right, in all its main essentials. What is more, within the first few paragraphs, I realised very clearly to what general class of story it belonged. But there were so many hiatuses between the time when Herklaas van Wyk was last seen with the remnants of the Losberg commando, towards the end of the Boer War, in 1902, and the time when he was captured with General Kemp outside Upington in the rebellion of 1914.

If I could fill in that interval of a dozen years satisfactorily, I would still be able to write the story of Herklaas van Wyk. Yet the very fascination of this story is intimately bound up with the nature of that *lacuna*. It is no new thing to have a story of which the end is a mystery – something that the reader must work out for himself, with or without a clue supplied by the author. But when the middle part of a story – which gives atmosphere to the whole sequence of real and imaginery events – is missing, then I feel that I am confronted with an artistic problem of an order that I am not sure it is wise for a writer to tackle.

I don't mind writing a story in which the plot is vague. But when the atmosphere isn't there – the background and the psychology and the interplay of situation and character – then what's left is not my idea of a story.

The events with which Herklaas van Wyk was connected in the early part of 1902 were commonplace enough. There are still a number of Boers alive today who were on commando with him. Kritzinger's invasion of the Cape Colony is an episode that has passed into history. And a considerable body of Boers, members of commandos that kept being split up into ever-smaller groups, succeeded in penetrating to the Atlantic Ocean, and in remaining in the field, deep inside the Cape Colony, long after the main commando had retreated beyond the Vaal.

It was in 1902 that Herklaas van Wyk, then promoted to the rank of *veldkornet*, caught sight, in the blue distance, of the unquiet Atlantic. The small body of men pushed on to the beach. They had come a long way, from the Transvaal and the Free State, and also from the Karoo, where a number of Cape rebels had joined the fighting forces of the Republics. It was a mixed group of burghers that came to a halt on the white sand of the beach south of Okiep.

~

Facing out to sea, Herklaas van Wyk slowly took off his hat.

'It's no good, *kêrels*,' he called out above the roar of the waves and the wind, 'we'll have to go back again. There's no drift around here where we'll be able to get our horses through.'

About Herklaas van Wyk there was a certain measure of grandeur, even in defeat.

And his story, up to that time when the sea-wind was whistling through his black beard, was straightforward enough. In fact, you can read about him in any history book dealing with that period. But it is on his way back to the Transvaal, when he and his men had to elude flying English columns and had to cross barbed-wire fences with blockhouses threaded on to them, that Herklaas van Wyk quits the pages of printed history, complete with dates and place-names, and enters the realm of legend.

It is generally accepted that he was still in the field when the Boer War ended in May 1902. His own story is that he crept into a deserted rondavel at the foot of a *koppie* in the Upington District, and that he fell asleep there, with his Mauser beside him, and his horse tethered to a thorn-tree.

Another story – subscribed to on doubtful authority by fellow members of the rebel commando that surrendered with Herklaas van Wyk in 1915, after General Kemp had failed to take Upington – seeks to account for that interval of a dozen years in a different fashion. In terms of this latter attempt at reconstructing the facts, all that happened to Herklaas van Wyk between 1902, the end of the Boer War, and 1914, the year of the outbreak of the rebellion, was that he lived on some farm in the Upington District as a *bywoner*. It is readily conceivable, protagonists of this standpoint declare, that he slept quite a lot during that period, especially on hot afternoons when his employer had sent him out to look for strayed cattle. Who has not heard – this school of doubters asks – of a *bywoner* lying asleep in his rondavel when he should be at the borehole pumping water?

I can only reply that this theory, which represents him as a decadent *bywoner*, does not fit in with my conception of Herklaas van Wyk as a person.

~

I still prefer Herklaas van Wyk's own story, which he told to anybody who would listen, after he had been captured by Botha's Government forces. For one thing, if we accept Herklaas van Wyk's account of his long sleep in the abandoned rondavel at the foot of a *koppie* in the Upington District, we have the material for a South African legend as stirring as the one that Washington Irving chronicled. This is surely no idle coincidence. Above all, there is a Gothic quality in Herklaas van Wyk's own story – a gloomy magnificence that is never absent from the interior of a rondavel at the foot of a *koppie*, if that *koppie* is composed of ironstone.

Herklaas van Wyk asleep in a dark corner, waiting, a

backveld Barbarossa, for his far-off awakening, in an hour filled with the thunder of horse-hooves and the noise of battle.

~

The old man with the white beard and the rusty Mauser and the walking skeleton of a horse had been with Kemp's rebel commando for the best part of a week of dispirited running away from the Government forces. It now began to dawn on the little band of 1914 rebels that Oom Herklaas van Wyk was – as they interpreted it – in his second childhood. It was clear that he thought the year was 1902. It was obvious that he did not know that he was a rebel who had taken the field against the Union troops. Instead, he spoke of himself as a Transvaal burgher, and he referred to Cronjé's surrender at Paardeberg scornfully, as though it had taken place yesterday.

He was very puzzled, also, when he learnt for the first time that the rebel commando was being pursued by a column of Botha-men.

'But if Botha is chasing us,' Herklaas van Wyk demanded, 'who is fighting Kitchener?'

Thus it came about, one evening when the rebels were encamped in a bluegum plantation on the road to Upington, that a lot of explanations were made.

'I remember the day you joined us, Oom Herklaas,' Jan Gouws, a young rebel, said after Herklaas van Wyk had told his story and they had persuaded him that the year was, indeed, 1915, and that he was not now fighting in the Boer War. 'Your white beard was blowing in the wind, Oom Herklaas, and several of us laughed at the awkward way your old horse cantered, throwing his legs all to one side. So you really say you slept for twelve years?'

'I believe now – now that you've told me,' Herklaas van

Wyk replied, 'that I must have lain asleep on the floor of that rondavel all those years. That must have been just at the end of the Boer War. And it's funny that I didn't wake up before my nation again needed me.'

The rebels received the old man's last remark in silence. They were beginning to doubt the wisdom of their armed uprising. They had been driven from pillar to post for many days. Incessant rain had damped their ardour.

'Did you remember to wind your watch before you went to sleep in that rondavel, Oom Herklaas?' Jan Gouws asked, trying to change the subject.

The others did not laugh at this sally. For one thing, the rain had started coming down again.

Some of the rebels seemed half-inclined to believe Herklaas van Wyk's story. And there seemed to be something inexplicably solemn in the thought of a burgher of the Transvaal Republic going to sleep in the corner of a deserted rondavel, with his Mauser at his side – and only waking up again a dozen years later, when men were once more riding with rifles slung across their shoulders.

'Did you dream at all during that time, Oom Herklaas?' another man asked, in a half-serious tone.

The old man thought for a little while.

'I remember dreaming about a *mossie* settling on a coral tree that was full of red flowers,' Herklaas van Wyk answered slowly, 'but I think I dreamt of it a long time back – after I had been asleep only four years or so.'

Jan Gouws shivered. The red flowers on that coral tree must be pretty well faded by now, he thought. And it gave him a queer feeling to think of that *mossie*, that an old man saw in a dream, flitting about in the sunshine of long ago. It made Jan Gouws feel uncomfortable, for a reason he could not explain.

'My Mauser is very rusty,' Herklaas van Wyk continued.

'I've tried oiling it, but that doesn't help. I'll have to hands-up or shoot one of the enemy, and take his Lee-Metford off him, like we used to do. How long will it take us to win this war, do you think?'

The rebels did not answer. They knew that their cause was already shot to pieces. In spite of the old man's senility, there seemed to emanate from his spirit a strange kind of assurance, a form of steadfastness in the face of adversity and defeat, that they themselves did not possess. It seemed that there was something inside the entrails of this burgher of the Transvaal Republic that they didn't have. Something firm and constant that they had lost. And they felt, sensing the difference between the previous generation and their own, without being able to express their feelings in words, that in that difference lay their defeat.

'What happened about your horse, Oom Herklaas?' a young rebel asked eventually.

Outwardly delapidated, Herklaas van Wyk still seemed to represent, somehow, the gloom and grandeur of a greater day.

'I tethered my horse to a thorn-tree,' Herklaas van Wyk said, 'and he, too, must have fallen asleep. I'm sure that the hoof-beats of a commando at full gallop must have awakened him, also. For when I got to the thorn tree – which hadn't grown much during that time: you know how slowly a thorn-tree grows – my old war horse was sniffing the wind and pawing the ground. And his neck was arched.'

31.

The Look in his Eyes

From 'Veld Maiden'

In *Mafeking Road*

I know what it is – Oom Schalk Lourens said – when you talk that way about the veld. I have known people who sit like you do and dream about the veld, and talk strange things, and start believing in what they call the soul of the veld, until in the end the veld means a different thing to them from what it does to me.

I only know that the veld can be used for growing mealies on, and it isn't very good for that, either. Also, it means very hard work for me, growing mealies. There is the ploughing, for instance. I used to get aches in my back and shoulders from sitting on a stone all day long on the edge of the lands, watching the labourers and the oxen and the plough going up and down, making furrows. Hans Coetzee, who was a Boer War prisoner on St Helena, told me how he got sick at sea from watching the ship going up and down, up and down, all the time.

And it's the same with ploughing. The only real cure for this ploughing sickness is to sit quietly on a *riempies* bench on the stoep, with one's legs raised slightly, drinking coffee until the ploughing season is over. Most of the farmers in the Marico Bushveld have adopted this remedy, as you have no doubt observed by this time.

But there the veld is. And it is not good to think too much about it. For then it can lead you in strange ways. And sometimes – sometimes when the veld has led you very far –

there comes into your eyes a look that God did not put there.

It was in the early summer, shortly after the rains, that I first came across John de Swardt. He was sitting next to a tent that he had pitched behind the maroelas at the far end of my farm, where it adjoins Frans Welman's lands. He had been there several days and I had not known about it, because I sat on my stoep then, on account of what I have already explained to you about the ploughing.

He was a young fellow with long black hair. When I got nearer I saw what he was doing. He had a piece of white bucksail on a stand in front of him and he was painting my farm. He seemed to have picked out all the useless bits for his picture – a *krantz* and a few stones and some clumps of khaki-*bos*.

~

Then John de Smidt showed me another picture he had painted; and when I saw that, I got a different opinion about this thing that he said was art. I looked from De Swardt to the picture, and then back again to De Swardt.

'I'd never have thought it of you,' I said, 'and you look such a quiet sort, too.'

'I call it the Veld Maiden,' John de Swardt said.

'If the *predikant* saw it, he'd call it by other names,' I replied. 'But I'm a broad-minded man. I've been once in the bar in Zeerust and twice in the bioscope when I should have been attending *Nagmaal*. So I don't hold it against a young man for having ideas like this. But you mustn't let anybody here see this Veld Maiden unless you paint a few more clothes on her.'

'I couldn't,' De Swardt answered, 'that's just how I see her. That's just how I dream about her. For many years now, she has come to me so in my dreams.'

'With her arms stretched out like that?' I asked.

'Yes.'

'And with …'.

'Yes, yes, just like that,' De Swardt said very quickly. Then he blushed and I could see how very young he was. It seemed a pity that a nice young fellow like that should be so mad.

'Anyway, if ever you want a painting job,' I said when I left, 'you can come and whitewash the back of my sheep-*kraal*.'

~

On several Sundays in succession, I took De Swardt over the *rant* to the house of Frans Welman. I didn't have a very high regard for Frans's judgment since the time he voted for the wrong man at the School Committee. But I had no other neighbour within walking distance, and I had to go somewhere on a Sunday.

We talked of all sorts of things. Frans's wife, Sannie, was young and pretty, but very shy. She wasn't naturally like that. It was only that she was afraid to talk in case she said something of which her husband might disapprove. So most of the time Sannie sat silent in the corner, getting up now and again to make more coffee for us.

Frans Welman was in some respects what people might call a hard man. For instance, it was something of a mild scandal the way he treated his wife and the labourers on his farm. But then, on the other hand, he looked after his cattle and his pigs very well. And I've always believed that this is more important in a farmer than that he should be kind to his wife and the labourers.

Well, we talked about the mealies and the drought of the year before last, and the subsidies, and I could see that in a short while the conversation would come round to the *Volksraad*. As I wasn't anxious to hear how Frans was going to vote at the General Election, believing that so irresponsible a person should not be allowed to vote at all, I quickly asked John de Swardt to tell us about his paintings.

He immediately started off about his Veld Maiden.

'Not that one,' I said, kicking his shin, 'I meant your other paintings. The kind that frighten the locusts.'

I felt that this Veld Maiden thing was not a fit subject to talk about, especially with a woman present. Moreover, it was Sunday.

Nevertheless, that kick came too late. De Swardt rubbed his shin a few times and started on his subject, and although Frans and I cleared our throats awkwardly at different parts, and Sannie looked on the floor with her pretty cheeks very red, the young painter explained everything about that picture and what it meant to him.

'It's a dream I've had for a long time, now,' he said at the end, 'and always she comes to me, and when I put out my arms to clasp her to me, she vanishes; and I'm left with only her memory in my heart. But when she comes, the whole world is clothed in a terrible beauty.'

'That's more than she is clothed in, anyway,' Frans said, 'judging from what you've told us about her.'

'She's a spirit. She's the spirit of the veld,' De Swardt murmured. 'She whispers strange and enchanting things. Her coming is like the whisper of the wind. She's not of the earth at all.'

'Oh, well,' Frans said shortly, 'you can keep these *Uitlander* ghost-women of yours. A Boer girl is good enough for ordinary fellows like me and Schalk Lourens.'

So the days passed.

John de Swardt finished a few more bits of rock and

drought-stricken khaki-*bos*, and I had got so far as to persuade him to label the worst-looking one 'Frans Welman's Farm'.

Then, one morning, he came to me in great excitement.

'I saw her again, Oom Schalk,' he said, 'I saw her last night. In a surpassing loveliness. Just at midnight. She came softly across the veld towards my tent. The night was warm and lovely, and the stars were mad and singing. And there was low music where her white feet touched the grass. And sometimes her mouth seemed to be laughing, and sometimes it was sad. And her lips were very red, Oom Schalk. And when I reached out with my arms, she went away. She disappeared in the maroelas, like the whispering of the wind. And there was a ringing in my ears. And in my heart there was a green fragrance, and I thought of the pale asphodel that grows in the fields of paradise.'

'I don't know about paradise,' I said, 'but if a thing like that grew in my mealie-lands, I would pull it up at once. I don't like this spook nonsense.'

I then gave him some good advice. I told him to beware of the moon, which was almost full at the time. Because the moon can do strange things to you in the Bushveld, especially if you live in a tent and the full moon is overhead, and there are weird shadows among the maroelas.

But I knew he wouldn't take any notice of what I told him. Several times after that, he came with the same story about the Veld Maiden. I started getting tired of it.

Then one morning, when he came again, I knew everything by the look he had in his eyes. I've already told you about that look.

'Oom Schalk,' he began.

'John de Swardt,' I said to him, 'don't tell me anything. All I ask of you is to pack up your things, and leave my farm at once.'

'I'll leave tonight,' he said, 'I promise you that by tomorrow morning, I'll be gone. Only let me stay here one more day and night.'

His voice trembled when he spoke, and his knees were very unsteady. But it was not for these reasons, or for his sake, that I relented. I spoke to him very civilly, for the sake of the look he had in his eyes.

'Very well, then,' I said, 'but you must go straight back to Johannesburg. If you walk down the road through the *poort* before sun-up, you'll be able to catch the Government lorry to Zeerust.'

He thanked me and left. I never saw him again.

Next day his tent was still there behind the maroelas, but John de Smidt was gone, and he had taken with him all his pictures. All, that is, except the Veld Maiden. I suppose he had no more need for it.

And, in any case, the white ants had already started on it. So that's why I can hang the remains of it openly on the wall in my *voorhuis*, and the *predikant* doesn't raise any objection to it. For the white ants have eaten away practically all of it except the face.

As for Frans Welman, it was quite a long time before he gave up searching the Marico for his young wife, Sannie.

32.

For the Transvaal

From 'The Traitor's Wife'

In *Unto Dust*

We did not like the sound of the wind that morning, as we cantered over a veld trail we had made much use of during the past year, when there were English forces in the neighbourhood.

The wind blew short wisps of yellow grass in quick flurries over the veld, and the smoke from a fire in front of a row of huts hung low in the air. From this we knew that the third winter of the Anglo-Boer War was approaching. We dismounted at the edge of a clump of camel-thorns, to rest our horses.

~

Our thoughts went immediately to Leendert Roux, who had been with us on commando for a long while, and who had been spoken of as a man likely to become a *veldkornet*. He had gone out scouting one night, and had never returned.

There were, of course, other Boers who had also joined the English, but none that we had respected as much as Leendert Roux.

Soon our small group of burghers was on the move again.

In the late afternoon, we emerged from the Crocodile Poort and came in sight of Leendert Roux's farmhouse. Next to the dam was a patch of mealies that Leendert Roux's wife had asked the labourers to cultivate.

'We'll camp on Leendert Roux's farm, and eat roast mealies tonight,' our *veldkornet*, Apie Theron, observed.

~

The road we were following led past Leendert Roux's homestead. The noise of our horses' hoofs brought Leendert Roux's wife, Serfina, to the door. She stood in the open doorway, watching us ride by. Serfina was pretty, taller than most women, and slender. There was no expression in her eyes that you could read, and her face was very white.

It was strange, I thought, as we rode past the homestead, that the sight of Serfina Roux did not fill us with bitterness.

Jurie Bekker said that something about Serfina Roux reminded him of the Transvaal. He said he didn't know what it was, but with the wind of early winter fluttering her dress about her ankles, that was how it seemed to him.

Kobus Ferreira then said that he had wanted to shout out something to her when we rode past the door, to let Serfina know how we, who were fighting in the last ditch, and in ragged clothing, felt about the wife of a traitor. 'But she stood there so still,' Kobus Ferreira said, 'I couldn't say anything.'

Then a remark by Jan Vermeulen reminded us that there was a war on. He had taken a mealie sack off his body and threaded a length of baling-wire above the places where the holes were. He was now restoring the grain bag to the use it had been intended for, and I suppose that, in consequence, his views also became more sensible.

'Just because Serfina Roux is pretty,' Jan Vermeulen said, flinging mealie heads into the sack, 'let us not forget who she is. Perhaps it is not safe for us to camp on this farm tonight. She is sure to be in touch with the English. She may tell them where we are, especially now that we've taken her mealies.'

But our *veldkornet* said that it wasn't important if the English knew where we were. Any person in the neighbourhood could go and report our position to them. What mattered was that we should know where the English were. And he reminded us that, in two years, he had never made a serious mistake in that regard.

'What about the affair at the *spruit*, though?' Jan Vermeulen asked him. 'My pipe and tinder-box were in the jacket I had to leave behind there, too.'

By sunset the wind had died down, but there was a chill in the air. We had pitched our camp in the tamboekie grass on the far side of Leendert Roux's farm. And I was glad, lying in my blankets, to think that it was the turn of the *veldkornet* and Jurie Bekker to stand guard.

Far away a jackal howled. Then there was silence. A little later, the stillness was disturbed by sterner sounds of the veld at night. They did not come from very far away, either. They were sounds made by Jurie Bekker, first when he fell over a beacon, and then when he gave his opinion of Leendert Roux for placing a beacon in the middle of a stretch of dubbeltjie thorns. The blankets felt very snug, pulled over my shoulders, when I reflected on those thorns.

And because I was young, there came into my thoughts, at Jurie Bekker's mention of Leendert Roux, the picture of Serfina as she had stood in front of her doorway.

The dream I had of Serfina Roux that night was that she came to me, tall and graceful, beside a white beacon on her husband's farm. It was that haunting kind of dream, in which you half-know all the time that you are dreaming. And she was very beautiful in my dream. And it was as though her hair was hanging half out of my dream and reaching down into the wind, when she came closer to me. And I knew what she wanted to tell me. But I did not wish to hear it. I knew that if Serfina spoke that thing, I would wake up from my dream. And in that moment, as always happens in a dream, Serfina spoke.

'*Opskud, kêrels!*' I heard.

But it was not Serfina who gave that command. It was Apie Theron, the *veldkornet*. He came running into the camp with his rifle at the trail. Serfina was gone, and in a few minutes we had saddled our horses and were ready to gallop away. Many times during the past couple of years, our scouts had roused us thus – when an English column was approaching.

We were already in the saddle when Apie Theron let us know what was afoot. He had received information, he said, that Leendert Roux had that very night ventured back to his homestead. If we hurried, we might trap him in his own house. The *veldkornet* warned us to take no chances, reminding us that when Leendert Roux had still stood on our side, he had been a fearless and resourceful fighter.

So we rode back during the night, along the same way we had come in the afternoon. We tethered our horses in a clump of trees near the mealie-lands, and started to surround the farmhouse. When we saw a figure running for the stable at the side of the house, we realised that Leendert Roux had been almost too quick for us.

In the cold, thin breeze that springs up just before dawn, we surprised Leendert Roux at the door of his stable. But when he made no resistance, it almost seemed as though Leendert Roux had taken us by surprise. Leendert Roux's calm acceptance of his fate made it seem, almost, as though he had never turned traitor, but that he was laying down his life for the Transvaal.

In answer to the *veldkornet*'s question, Leendert Roux said that he would be glad if we would read Psalm 110 over his grave. He also said that he did not want his eyes bandaged.

And he asked to be allowed to say goodbye to his wife.

Serfina was sent for. At the side of the stable, in the early morning breeze, Leendert and Serfina Roux, husband and wife, bade each other farewell.

Serfina looked even more shadowy than she had done in my dream when she set off back to the homestead, along the footpath through the thorns. The sun was just beginning to rise. And I understood how right Jurie Bekker had been when he had said that she was just like the Transvaal, with the dawn breeze fluttering her skirts about her ankles as it rippled the grass. And I remembered that it was the Boer women that had kept on when their menfolk recoiled before the steepness of the Drakensberg, and spoke of turning back.

I also thought of how strange it was that Serfina should have come walking over to our camp, in the middle of the night, just as she had done in my dream. But where my dream was different was that she had reported, not to me, but to our *veldkornet*, the whereabouts of Leendert Roux.

33.

The Voice of the Drum

From 'The Drum'

In *Unto Dust*

Old Mosigo was the last of the drum-men left at Gabarones – Oom Schalk Lourens said – when they brought the telegraph wires on long poles to this part of the country. But there was a time when the voice of the drum travelled right across Africa.

The peculiar thing about this was that, even when a message originated from a tribe with a completely alien language, the drum-man of the tribe receiving the message could still interpret it. In the old days there were two drum-men in each village. They were instructed in the code of the drum from boyhood, and then – in their turn – they taught the art of sending and receiving drum messages to those who came after them.

No white man has ever been able to learn the language of the drum. The only one who ever had any idea at all – and even his knowledge was of the slightest – was Gerhardus van Tonder, who regularly travelled deep into Africa with his brother, Rooi Willem.

Gerhardus van Tonder told me that he had asked the drum-men of several tribes to teach him the meaning of the sounds they beat out on their tom-toms. 'But I could never understand what the drum-men tried, over and over again, to explain to me,' Gerhardus van Tonder said to me. 'Even when a drum-man repeated the same thing up to ten times, I still couldn't grasp it. So thick-skulled are they.'

Nevertheless, Gerhardus said that, because he had heard the same message so often, he was able, later on, to understand whenever the drums broadcast the message that his brother, Rooi Willem, had shot an elephant dead. But one day an elephant trampled Rooi Willem to death. Gerhardus had listened to the message the drums had sent out after that. It was exactly the same as all the earlier messages, Gerhardus said, only it was the other way round.

Even in those days, the prestige of the drum-man had fallen considerably – because a mission station had been started at Gabarones, and the missionaries had brought with them their own message, which came into conflict with the more heathen news from Central Africa.

But when the telegraph wires were brought up from Cape Town, taken past the Groot Marico, and erected in the Protectorate, everyone knew that – so to speak – the days of the drum-man were numbered.

Yet on one occasion, when I spoke to Mosigo about the telegraph, what he had to say was this: 'The drum-man is better than the copper wire that you white men bring on poles across the world. I don't need copper wire for my drum's messages. Or long poles with rows of little white medicine bottles on them, either.'

But whatever Mosigo thought, the authorities had brought the copper wires as far as Nietverdiend. A little post office had then been built on Jurie Bekker's farm, and a young telegraph operator from Pretoria had been appointed to serve as postmaster. This young man had arranged for a colleague in Pretoria to telegraph to him, from time to time, items from the newspapers. By means of these telegrams, which were pinned up on a noticeboard in the post office, we who lived in this part of the Bushveld kept in touch with the outside world.

The telegrams were all very short. In one of them, we read

about President Kruger's visit to Johannesburg and what he said, at a public meeting, about the *Uitlanders*.

'If that's all that the President could say about the *Uitlanders*,' Hans Grobler said, 'namely, "that they are a pest stop and that they should be more heavily taxed stop and that a miner's procession threw bottles stop", then I think I'll vote for General Joubert at the next election. And why do these telegrams always repeat the word "stop" so monotonously?'

Those of us who were in the post office at the time agreed with Hans Grobler. We said, moreover, that not only did we need a better president, we also needed a better telegraph operator. And we agreed that extending the telegraph service to Nietverdiend had been a waste of hundreds of miles of copper wire, not to speak, even, of all those long poles.

When we mentioned this to the telegraph operator, he looked from one to the other of us, thoughtfully, for a few moments. Then he said: 'Yes. Yes, I think it has been a waste.'

~

'But look at this telegram,' Hans Grobler interjected. 'About "the fanatic who fired at the King of Spain stop and missed him by less than two feet stop". What use is a message like that to us Bushveld Boers? And what sort of a thing is a fanatic, anyway?'

As a result of these conversations at the post office, I decided to look up old Mosigo, the last of the drum-men at Gabarones.

I found him sitting in front of his hut. The wrinkles on his face were countless. They made me think of the footpaths that go twisting across the length and breadth of Africa, and that you can follow for mile after mile and day after day, and that never come to an end. And I thought of how the messages that Mosigo received through his drum came from somewhere along those farthest paths across Africa.

He was busy thumping his old drum. It sounded almost like a voice to me. Now and again it seemed as if there floated on the wind a sound from very far away, which was either an answer to Mosigo's message, or the echo of his drum. But it wasn't like in the old days, when you could clearly hear how the message of one drum was taken up and spread over *koppies* and *vlaktes* by other drums. Anyone could see that there were not so many drum-men left in the Bushveld. And the reduction in their numbers wasn't because the chiefs had thrown them to the vultures for bringing bad news.

More likely, it was due to competition from the white man's telegraph wires.

~

Looking at Mosigo's wrinkles, I thought that he must have more understanding of things than that young upstart of a telegraph operator, who had only been out of school for three or four years at the most, and who always put the word 'stop' in the middle of a message – a clear sign of his general uncertainty.

So I told Mosigo that the telegraph was still quite a new thing, and that it might improve with time. Perhaps it would improve considerably, I said, if – for a start – they sacked that young telegraph operator at Nietverdiend.

That young telegraph operator was too impertinent, I said.

Mosigo agreed that it would help. It was a very important thing, he said, that for such work you should have the right sort of person. It was no good, he explained, having news told to you by a man who was not suited to that kind of work.

'Another thing that is important is having the right person

to tell the news to,' Mosigo went on. 'And you must also consider well concerning whom the news is about. Take that King, now, of whom you have told me, that you heard of at Nietverdiend through the telegraph. He is a great chief, that King, is he not?'

I said to Mosigo that I should imagine that he must be a great chief, the King of Spain. I couldn't know for sure, of course; you never really can, with foreigners.

'Has he many herds of cattle and many wives hoeing in the bean-fields?' Mosigo asked. 'Do you know him well, this great chief?'

I told Mosigo that I did not know the King of Spain to speak to, since I had never met him. But if I did meet him – I was going to explain, when Mosigo said that that was exactly what he meant. 'What's the use of hearing about a man,' he asked, 'unless you know who that man is? When the telegraph operator told you about that big chief, he told it to the wrong man.'

And he fell to beating his drum again.

From then on I went regularly to visit Mosigo, in order to find out what was happening in the world. We still read what was on the noticeboard in the post office, for instance about what had happened in Russia – where a fanatic had opened fire on the Emperor 'and missed him by one foot stop'. We began to infer from the telegrams that a fanatic was someone who couldn't aim very well. But to get news that really meant something, I always had to go – afterwards – and visit Mosigo.

Thus it happened that one afternoon, when I visited old Mosigo on my way back from the post office, I again found him sitting in front of his hut, before his drum. He told me that there would be no more news coming over his drum, because of a message about the death of a drum-man that he had just received.

It was a message from a great distance, he said.

Still, the following week, I again rode over to Gaberones. It was after I had read a telegram on the noticeboard in the post office which said that a fanatic had missed the French President 'by more than twenty feet stop'.

And when I rode away from Gaberones – where, this time, I had not seen Mosigo, but had seen instead his drum, on which the skin stretched across the wooden frame had been cut, in accordance with the ritual carried out on the death of a drum-man – I wondered to myself, on my way home.

I wondered whether that last message received by old Mosigo had come from a really great distance – farther even than Spain or France or Russia.

Stop.

34.

A Time for Sowing

From 'Funeral Earth'

In *Unto Dust*

It was then – Oom Schalk Lourens said – that an unusual thing happened.

For we suddenly did see Mtosas. We saw them from a long way off. They came out of the bush and marched right out into the open. They made no attempt to hide. We saw in amazement that they were coming straight in our direction, advancing in single file. And we observed, even from a distance, that they were unarmed. Instead of assegais and shields, they carried burdens on their heads. And almost in that same moment, we realised – from the heavy look of those burdens – that the carriers must be women.

For that reason we took our guns in our hands and stood waiting. Since it was women, we were naturally prepared for the lowest form of treachery.

As the column drew nearer, we saw that at the head of it was Ndambe, an old tribesman whom we knew well. For years he had been Sijefu's chief counsellor. Ndambe held up his hand. The line of women halted. Ndambe spoke. He declared that we white men were kings among kings and elephants among elephants. He also said that we were ringhals snakes more poisonous and generally disgusting than any ringhals snake in the country.

We knew, of course, that Ndambe was only paying us compliments in the ignorant Mtosa fashion. And so we naturally felt highly gratified. I can still remember the way

Jurie Bekker nudged me in the ribs, and said: 'Did you hear that?'

When Ndambe went on, however, to say that we were filthier than the spittle of a green tree toad, several burghers grew restive. They felt that there was perhaps such a thing as carrying these tribal courtesies a bit too far.

It was then that *Veldkornet* Joubert, slipping his finger inside the trigger guard of his gun, requested Ndambe to come to the point. By the expression on our *veldkornet*'s face, you could see that he had had enough of compliments for one day.

They had come to offer peace, Ndambe told us then.

What the women carried on their heads were presents.

At a sign from Ndambe, the column knelt in the mud of the turf-land. They brought lion and zebra skins and elephant tusks, and beads and brass bangles and, on a long mat, the whole haunch of a red Afrikaner ox, hide and hoof and all. And several pigs cut in half. And clay pots filled to the brim with white beer. And also – and this we prized the most – witchdoctor medicines that protected you against *goël* spirits at night and the evil eye.

Ndambe gave another signal. A woman with a clay pot on her head rose up from the kneeling column and advanced towards us. We saw then that what she had in the pot was black earth. It was wet and almost like turf-soil. We couldn't understand what they wanted to bring us that for. As though we didn't have enough of it, right there where we were standing, sticking to our *veldskoens* and all. And yet Ndambe acted as though that was the most precious part of the peace offering that his chief, Sijefu, had sent us.

It was when Ndambe spoke again that we saw how ignorant he and his chief and the whole Mtosa tribe were, really.

He took a handful of soil out of the pot and pressed it

together between his fingers. Then he told us how honoured the Mtosa tribe was because we were waging war against them. In the past they had only had flat-faced Shangaans with spiked knobkerries to fight against, he said, but now it was different. Our *veldkornet* took half a step forward, then, in case Ndambe was going to start flattering us again. So Ndambe said, simply, that the Mtosas would be glad if we came and made war against them later on, when the harvest had been gathered in. But in the meantime, the tribe did not wish to continue fighting.

It was the time for sowing.

Ndambe let the soil run through his fingers, to show us how good it was. He also invited us to taste it. We declined.

We accepted his presents, and peace was made. And I can still remember how *Veldkornet* Joubert shook his head and said: 'Can you beat the Mtosas for ignorance?'

And I can still remember what Jurie Bekker said, also. That was when something made him examine the haunch of beef more closely, and he found his own brand mark on it.

~

It was not long afterwards that the war came against England.

By the end of the second year of the war, the Boer forces were in a very bad way. But we would not make peace. *Veldkornet* Joubert was now promoted to commandant. Jurie Bekker was still with us, and so was Fanie Louw. It was strange how attached we had grown to Fanie Louw during the years of hardship that we went through together in the field. But up to the end we had to admit that, while we had got used to his jokes, and we knew there was no harm in them, we would have preferred it that he should stop making them.

He did stop – and forever – in a skirmish near a blockhouse. We buried him in the shade of a thorn tree. We got ready to fill in his grave, after which the commandant would say a few words, and we would bare our heads and sing a psalm. And as you know, it was customary at a funeral for each mourner to take up a handful of earth, and fling it in the grave.

When Commandant Joubert stooped down and picked up his handful of earth, a strange thing happened. And I remembered the other war, against the Mtosas. And we knew – although we would not say it – what was now that longing in the heart of each of us. For Commandant Joubert did not straightaway drop the soil into Fanie Louw's grave. Instead, he kneaded the damp ground between his fingers. It was as though he had forgotten that it was funeral earth. He seemed to be thinking not of death then, but of life.

We patterned after him, picking up handfuls of soil and pressing it together. We felt the deep loam in it, and saw how springy it was, and we let it trickle through our fingers. And we could remember only that it was the time for sowing.

I understood then how, in an earlier war, the Mtosas had felt – they who were also farmers.

35.

Like an Orang-Outang, Even

From 'Reminiscences'

In *A Cask of Jerepigo*

I was engaged, for a couple of days last week, in going through old files of newspapers and magazines, making a collection of stories I had written over the past fifteen years.

In re-reading some of the Marico Bushveld stories I had written as long ago as the early years of the 1930s, I was surprised to find how intimate was my knowledge of life on the South African farm. I was also astonished at the extent of my familiarity with historical events – and the spirit of the times, and the personalities who had featured in them – that had taken place in the *ou* Transvaal.

~

Anyway, in again perusing those stories, written long ago, I realised where all that local colour came from. I had got it from listening to the talk of elderly farmers in the Marico district, who had a whole lot of information that they didn't require for themselves, any more, and that they were glad to bestow on a stranger. It was all information that was, from a scientific point of view, strictly useless.

That was how I learnt all about the First and Second Boer Wars. And about the tribal wars. And about the trouble, in the old days, between the Transvaal and the Orange Free State. And about the Ohrigstad Republic. And about the Stellaland Republic. If any contemporary South African historian would like some fallen-by-the-wayside information about any events in the early days of the South African Republics, I could supply him with all the facts he needs. And, what is more important, with a whole lot of surplus information, outside of just facts.

I regarded them as wonderful storytellers, the old Boers who lived in the Marico district twenty years ago. Most of them had moved into that part of the Transvaal, next to the Bechuanaland Protectorate, in 1917. It was a part of the Transvaal that had remained practically uninhabited since the Anglo-Boer War. I still have very vivid recollections of the Boers who lived in the Marico in those days. I was there as a schoolteacher for a little while. And I can only hope that the information I imparted to the children, in the way of reading, spelling and arithmetic, was – in a minute degree – as significant as the facts that were imparted to me by their parents, whom I went to visit at weekends.

I remember that there was old Oom Geel, who had been a Cape rebel, and who still used to display a fragment of red-striped jersey that he had worn as a prisoner-of-war in Bermuda.

Because he was a Cape rebel, Oom Geel said, he had been regarded by the English, not as a regular prisoner-of-war, but as a convict, and so he had been sent to Bermuda instead of to St Helena. And he said that, when he returned to South Africa after the Boer War, the former Free State and Transvaal burghers, who had been respectable POWs at St Helena, used to look on him with suspicion, as though he was going to pick their pockets, and so on, because he had worn a striped convict jersey in Bermuda. I can still remember the laughter that invariably greeted this straight-faced statement by Oom Geel.

Old Oom Geel had a very tall son, called At, and a shorter son, Jan, and a large number of grandchildren. And there was a family of Bekkers who lived on a farm, Drogedal. This farm seemed to be the size of a whole district.

I don't know how big the farm was, exactly, but in later years, when I was working for an educational establishment in London, and I had to interview the principals of schools in the southern English counties, I remember that we would approach Tunbridge Wells, or Sevenoaks, and the man who drove the car would ask me: 'Are we now in Sussex or in Surrey, do you think, or perhaps in Kent?' Then I would think to myself: 'Oh, well, all these counties together are less than the size of the Bekkers' farm in the Marico'.

There was an Afrikaner family named Flaherty, with whom I boarded; and old man Flaherty would regularly welcome me at breakfast with the greeting: *'Die beste van die môre'*, and it took me quite a while to realise that these words must have constituted a traditional family greeting, being a literal translation of what the family's original Irish forbear, the first South African Flaherty, must have said habitually at breakfast-time: 'Top of the morning to you'.

I must have known most of the families living in the Marico Bushveld at that particular time, and some of those farmers had most interesting stories to tell, relating, in a matter-of-fact way, all sorts of unusual circumstances. And my mind absorbed whatever they had to relate, provided that it was of a sufficiently unutilitarian order.

There was the legend of a spectre, in the form of a white donkey, that haunted the *poort* on the road to Ramoutsa. If you passed through that *poort* just around midnight, then, at the darkest part of the *poort*, near where the road skirts a clump of maroelas, you would be certain to encounter an apparition in the form of a white donkey, with his front legs planted firmly in the centre of the road. Nobody was quite certain where the hind legs of the donkey were planted because the lonely traveller would decide to turn back just about then.

(I visited that part of the Marico again about two years ago. The clump of maroelas by the side of the Government road has been cut down, since those days. But the donkey is still there.)

~

Amongst the hundreds of other stories I heard in the Marico, was a first-hand account by an elderly man – who had been a burgher in that particular commando – of the sartorial eccentricities of a certain Boer War commandant. This commandant was very fussy about his appearance, and always insisted on wearing white starched shirt-fronts and cuffs. No matter how adverse the conditions under which the commando was operating – in constant retreat from the enemy, fording swollen rivers under fire, or negotiating barbed-wire fences between blockhouses – every Monday morning was washing-day, with the burghers having to go into *laager*, beside some *spruit* or dam (or a jackal hole with muddy water at the bottom), while the commandant supervised the washing and starching and ironing of his linen by the *agterryers*. It wasn't that he was personally over-fastidious about such things, the commandant explained, but it was necessary, for the prestige of the Boer forces in the field, that a commandant should not go about looking like a Bapedi.

My informant – as mentioned, a burgher in this commando – said that he could never feel that the commandant's arguments carried any weight. Himself, he didn't care if he looked like a Bapedi, or a Shangaan, or an orang-outang even, he said, as long as he didn't get shot. But the commandant was a capable officer, he said, and the burghers trusted him and admired him, although, in their ragged clothes, they would be aware of a certain sense of inferiority beside the commandant's starched magnificence. It was observed that, when the commandant addressed a *veldkornet* directly, giving him instructions, the *veldkornet* would say: '*Ja, Kommandant,*' but at the same time he would be standing, shuffling somewhat awkwardly.

There was something fine, I thought, about the way the commandant led his force into a Northern Cape village that the English had just evacuated. He did it all in great style. He wore his best white shirt-front for the occasion. And he sat up very straight on his horse, riding at the head of his commando, with an occasional stray bullet still whistling down the street.

It was only when they got to the church square, in the centre of the village, that the burghers realised, from the circumstance of his shirt-front having gone limp, and not being white any longer, that their commandant would ride at their head no more.

36.

Hiding their Weaknesses

From 'Bushveld Romance'

In *The South African Opinion*

It's a queer thing – Oom Schalk Lourens observed – how much trouble people will take to hide their weaknesses from the world. Often, of course, they aren't weaknesses at all, only the people who have these peculiarities don't know that. Another thing they don't know is that the world is aware all the time of these things they imagine they're concealing.

I remember a story my grandfather used to tell – of something that happened when he was a boy. Of course, that was a long time ago. It was before the Great Trek. But it seems that, even in those days, there was a lot of trouble between the Boers and the English. It had much to do with slaves. The English Government wanted to free the slaves, my grandfather said, and one man who was very prominent at the meetings that were held to protest against this was Gert van Tonder.

Now Gert van Tonder was a very able man, and a good speaker. He was at his best, too, when dealing with a subject about which he knew nothing at all. He always spoke very loudly then. As you can see, he was a fine leader.

So, when the slaves were freed, and a manifesto was drawn up to be sent to the King of England, the farmers of Graaff-Reinet took it first to Gert van Tonder for his signature.

You can imagine how surprised everyone was when he refused to sign. He sat with the manifesto in front of him, and the pen in his hand, and said that he had changed his mind.

He said that perhaps they were a bit hasty in writing to the King of England about so trivial a matter.

'Even though the slaves are free now,' he said, 'it doesn't make any difference. Just let one of my slaves try to act as though he's free. I'll show him. That's all. Just let him try.'

The farmers told Gert van Tonder he was quite right. It didn't really make any difference whether the slaves were free or not. They said they knew that already. But there were a lot of other grievances in the manifesto, they explained, and they were sending it to let the King of England know that, unless the Boers got their wrongs redressed, they would trek out of the Cape Colony.

My grandfather used to say that everybody was still more surprised when Gert van Tonder put down the pen, very firmly, and told the farmers that they could trek right to the other end of Africa, for all he cared. He was quite satisfied with the way the King of England had done things, Gert said, and there was a lot about English rule for which they should all be thankful.

The upshot of all this was that, when the farmers of the Cape Colony trekked away, into the north, with their heavily laden wagons, and ther long spans of oxen, and their guns, Gert van Tonder did not go with them.

My grandfather often spoke about how small a thing it was that kept Gert van Tonder from being remembered in history as one of the leaders of the nation. It was all on account of that one weakness of his – not wanting people to know that he couldn't read or write.

~

When I speak of people and their peculiarities, it always makes me think of Stoffel Lemmer. He had a weakness of an altogether different sort. What was peculiar about Stoffel Lemmer was that if a girl, or a woman, so much as looked at him, he was quite certain that she was in love with him. And what made it worse was that he never had the courage to go up and talk to the girl he thought was making eyes at him.

Another queer thing about Stoffel Lemmer was that he was just as much in love with the girl as he imagined she was with him.

~

'I could see by the look in Minnie Bonthuys's eyes that she loved me, Oom Schalk,' Stoffel Lemmer went on, once, 'and by the firm way that her mouth shut when she caught sight of me. In fact, I can hardly even say that she looked at me. It all happened so quickly. She just gave one glance in my direction, and slammed the window shut. All girls who are in love with me do that.'

This was just one example of the sort of thing that Stoffel Lemmer would relate to me, sitting on my stoep. Mostly it was in the evening. And he would look out into the dusk, and say that the shadows that lay on the thorn-trees were in his heart also. As I have told you, I had frequently heard him say exactly the same thing. About other girls.

And always it would end up the same way – with him saying what a sorrowful thing it was that he would never be able to tell her how much he loved her. He would also say how grateful he was to have someone like me who would listen to his sad story, with understanding. That, too, I had heard before. Often.

What's that? Did he ever tell her? Well, I don't know.

The last time I saw Stoffel Lemmer was in Zeerust. It was in front of the church, just after the ceremony. And by the determined expression that Minnie still had on her face when the wedding guests threw rice and confetti over Stoffel and herself – no, I don't think he ever got up the courage to tell her.

37.

Opposite Sides of the Law

From 'Man to Man'

In *A Bekkersdal Marathon*

Because young Bothma was, after all, a mounted policeman in a khaki uniform, with brass letters on his shoulders, we did feel a measure of constraint in his company. The circumstance of our not feeling quite at ease manifested itself in the way most of us sat on our *riempie* chairs – a little more stiffly than usual, with our shoulders not quite touching the backs of the chairs. It also manifested itself in the unconventional way in which Gysbert van Tonder saw fit to sprawl in his seat, an affectation of mental contentment that would have awakened mistrust in any policeman with some experience.

It was then that Chris Welman made a remark that went a good way towards relieving the tension. Afterwards, in talking it over, we had to say that we could not but admire the manner in which Chris Welman had worked out the right words to use. Not that there was anything clever in the way that Chris Welman had spoken, of course.

No, we all felt that the statement Chris Welman had made, then, was something that was easily within the capacity of any of us, if we had just sat back a little and thought, and then made use of the common sense that comes naturally to anybody who has lived long enough on a farm.

'The man you should really ask questions of,' Chris Welman said to Constable Bothma, 'is Gysbert van Tonder. That's him there. Sitting with his legs taking up half the floor, his hands behind his head, and his elbows all stretched out. Just from the way he's sitting, you can see he's the biggest cattle-smuggler in the district.'

Well, that gave us all a good laugh. For everyone knew that Gysbert van Tonder had smuggled more cattle across the border than any other man in the Marico. What was more, we knew that Gysbert van Tonder's father had regularly brought in cattle, over the line from Ramoutsa, before there had even been a proper barbed-wire fence there. And we also knew that, in the long years of the future, when we were all dead and gone, Gysbert van Tonder's sons would still be doing the same thing.

What was more, nothing would ever stop them, either. Not even if every policeman from Cape Town to the Limpopo knew about it.

For the Bechuanas from whom he traded cattle felt friendly towards Gysbert van Tonder, and that was a sentiment they did not have for a border policeman – unreasonable though such an attitude might seem to be. This was an outlook on life that, to a considerable degree, Gysbert van Tonder shared with the Bechuanas.

Consequently, in speaking the way he did, Chris Welman had cleared the air for us all – Gysbert van Tonder included. As a result, Gysbert van Tonder could, for one thing, sit more comfortably in his chair, relaxing as he sat. There was no longer any need for him to adopt a carefree pose, which must have put quite a lot of strain on his neck and leg muscles, not to mention how hard it must have been for his spine to maintain the posture that was intended to suggest indifference.

Anyway, Gysbert van Tonder joined in the laughter that greeted Chris Welman's words.

And Constable Bothma laughed, too. It was clear from his

laughter that the sergeant at Bekkersdal had told him to keep an eye on Gysbert van Tonder.

~

After that it was Oupa Bekker who spoke. And although his story related to the distant past, when the functions of a police constable were exercised (apparently not unsuccessfully) by the local *veldkornet*, it seemed that the difficulties Constable Bothma was experiencing were not dissimilar from the vicissitudes of the young *veldkornet* in Oupa Bekker's story.

'Many a man would have been satisfied with the position of *veldkornet*,' Oupa Bekker said, 'because of the honour that went with it in those days. For one thing, even if you didn't have a uniform, or an office with a telephone, or a mounted-police horse with a white star on his forehead – that could keep time to the music at the Johannesburg Show – and even if you had to ride one of your own horses on a patched saddle, with a patch on the seat of your trousers too, you still had a printed certificate, signed by the President, to say that you were the *veldkornet*. And you could hang that certificate in a gold frame on the wall of your *voorkamer*.'

But the glitter of rank and the burden of office were as nothing to that young *veldkornet*, Oupa Bekker said. What worried him far more was that, because it was his job to maintain law and order, he had to act as an informer on his neighbours, however delicately. And the thought that, because of his job, he was cut off from intimate contact with them, saddened him. He liked having friends, but found that he couldn't have friends – well, not real friends – any more, now that he was the *veldkornet*.

'In the end ...' Oupa Bekker said.

We would have preferred Oupa Bekker not to continue to

the end, for the only true friend the young *veldkornet* had, in the end, was Sass Koggel – a scoundrel, the likes of which the Groot Marico had had but few in its history.

Only with Sass Koggel could the *veldkornet* be himself. They each took the other for what he was; and neither, in his relations with the other, had to maintain any sort of pretence. They were on opposite sides of the law.

Vocationally speaking, the *veldkornet* was devoted to apprehending Sass Koggel; and Sass Koggel was determined that the *veldkornet* would never come across anything against him. Outside of that technicality, however, it would have been hard to find two firmer friends in the whole of the Marico.

It was a long story that Oupa Bekker told, and we listened to it with fluctuating levels of attention. But Constable Bothma and Gysbert van Tonder did not listen to Oupa Bekker at all. They were too engrossed in what each had to say to the other. And while talking to Gysbert van Tonder, the cattle-smuggler, it was necessary for young Bothma, the policeman, to open his policeman's notebook only once.

Constable Bothma opened his notebook in order to extract a photograph, which he handed to Gysbert van Tonder. Gysbert studied the likeness for some moments, and then he asked: 'Takes after you, does he?'

And in his voice, there was only sincerity.

38.

Nobody Even Interested

From 'Home Town'

In *Selected Stories*

Oupa Bekker told us about how he had once gone back – very many years later – to revisit a village where he had lived as a child. Jurie Steyn asked him how many years, but he did not answer. He pretended to be too deaf to hear Jurie Steyn's question.

That was a peculiarity of Oupa Bekker. He not infrequently, by implication, made claims to great age. But he never allowed himself to be pinned down into stating how old he actually was, in terms of years. It seemed that he wanted to give himself a certain measure of room for manoeuvering in, on that score.

Nor did Oupa Bekker acquaint us with the name of the little place that he went back to, to have a look at, after an interval of many years. But that did not matter. Since, for each of us, they were the remembered scenes of our own childhood that Oupa Bekker spoke about.

'Of course, there was a railway station now, which, of course, there hadn't been before,' Oupa Bekker said.

'Yes, and tarred streets, and a filling station with petrol pumps,' Chris Welman said.

'And a fish and chip shop, and a milk bar with high stools,' Gysbert van Tonder said.

'And where there had been an old garden wall of red bricks with honeysuckle growing over it ... ' Jurie Steyn began.

'No, not honeysuckle,' Chris Welman interrupted him,

'but a creeper with those broad leaves and blue flowers. I forget what it's called now.'

'And the wall isn't red brick,' Gysbert van Toner said, 'but a whitewashed earth wall.'

~

They were in general agreement, however, that whatever building had been erected on the site of that old garden wall must be something pretty awful, anyway.

Oupa Bekker took our remarks in bad part.

'Who's telling this story – me or the lot of you?' he asked.

Then he went on to say that from the station there was a bit of a rise before you got to the village itself.

'And so you decided to walk,' Jurie Steyn said, 'so you could enjoy each moment of it, recalling how you had run over the veld there as a carefree boy.'

'Yes,' Oupa Bekker snapped. 'That's what I did do. I did walk. But the way you're carrying on, I'm sorry now that I didn't take a taxi instead.'

That shut Jurie Steyn up for a while. And so Oupa Bekker told us how, having deposited his suitcase in the railway cloakroom, he set off along that road, which was tarred now (as Chris Welman had said it would be), and there was a soft wind blowing, that was always there, on the rise, when in the village, in the hollow, the air was very still.

And Oupa Bekker said that he thought what a strange thing it was that, after all those years, the same wind should still be there. You think of wind as something that blows and is gone, Oupa Bekker said. And yet, after so many long years, there, on the rise, there that wind still was, and not changed in any way.

So Chris Welman said that was how it always was. When

you revisited a place after a long interval, the first impression you always got was that it hadn't changed. The first building you would see, as likely as not, would be the church. And the church steeple would look just like it did when you were a child, except not so tall any more. Only afterwards did you find out how much the place had really altered.

'And when you were a child the steeple, even then, needed paint on it,' Gysbert van Tonder observed.

~

'What I had noticed,' Oupa Bekker proceeded, getting bitter at all the interruptions, 'what I noticed, as I walked up the rise, was that the rise was not as high as it had seemed when I was a boy. Only, when I was a boy I could get up over it easier. Maybe that was the fault of the tarred road. But when Chris Welman says that the church steeple did not look so tall any more, he's quite wrong. Because the church steeple looked taller, when I got there. And the church looked three times bigger than it used to be. And it seemed to be standing right at the other end of the *kerkplein* from where it had stood in the old days. And why it all looked like that to me was because the church had been rebuilt on the other end of the *plein*. And it was three times bigger.

~

That should have put Chris Welman in his place. But it didn't. Instead, a twinkle came into his eye.

'Where was the bar, Oupa Bekker?' he asked. 'I hope you found that all right. I mean, they didn't go and shift the saloon bar too, did they, where you couldn't find it?'

Oupa Bekker said he was coming to that.

First he had walked about the *kerkplein* a good while, searching for the site of the old church.

Then he came across a row of stones that were half-buried in the long grass, and that he knew were the foundations of the old church. He went and sat on a stone, Oupa Bekker said, and a ...

'And a host of childhood memories came back to you,' Jurie Steyn said.

Then Oupa Bekker got really huffy.

'Look here,' Oupa Bekker said, 'I only hope the same thing happens to you, all of you, as happened to me. I only hope that one day, when you take it into your heads to go and visit your childhood homes again, you'll also find everything as changed as I found it, that's all. Then you won't see anything to laugh at, in it.

'And I only hope you also feel as lonely as I felt when I turned away from the *kerkplein*, and walked down the main street of the village, and everywhere I saw only strange faces, and strange buildings, and there was nobody to whom I could say – and there was nobody who was even interested – that this was my home town.

But, of course, it wasn't the place, any more, that I had spent my childhood in. Not the way they had changed it, it wasn't.'

39.

Unchanged

From 'Home Town'

In *Selected Stories*

Chris Welman started feeling sorry for Oupa Bekker then. 'Was it really as altered as all that, Oupa?' he asked.

'Altered?' Oupa Bekker repeated. 'Take the hotel, now. It used to be a wood and iron building with a long verandah. Now it was a double-storey brick building. And where there had been a hitching-post in front of that, that we children used to swing on, there was now one of those upright iron box things that have to do with electricity. Electricity – why, in the old days, we hardly even had paraffin-lamps.'

It all sounded quite sad. But then, as Gysbert van Tonder remarked, there had to be such a thing as progress. We couldn't expect the world to just stand still, for Oupa Bekker's sake, or for any of our sakes, for that matter, either.

'I went to look for the place that we children used to call the river,' Oupa Bekker went on, 'and that we used to fish in, and that people used to lead water into their gardens from, and that had a bridge over it.'

Well, we knew what was coming, of course. And we almost wished that Oupa Bekker wouldn't go to the length of telling us about it. Because they would have put pipes there, of course. And the stream would have been covered up. And where the bridge had been, there would now be a new power station. Or a glue factory.

We would rather not think what there was on the site of the garden wall that Jurie Steyn and Chris Welman and

Gysbert van Tonder had spoken about earlier. The piece of garden wall that every person who spent his childhood in a village remembers. A red-brick and honeysuckle wall, or a white-washed wall wildly rich with convolvulus.

'After I had had dinner in the hotel,' Oupa Bekker proceeded – and without his having to say so, we gathered that he did not eat much: his voice told us all that – 'I went to the bioscope. I had been there earlier in the day, and it had said that there would be an afternoon show.

'It was a picture about cowboys and Indians, or about cowboys and something. Or it might not even have been cowboys. I'm not sure. Seeing that the talking was all in English, I couldn't understand very much of it.

'But there was a coach in the picture, like the Zeederberg coaches they used to have here in the old days, before they had trains. And there was a fat man in the picture with a black *manel* who had other fat men under him. And he looked important, like a *raadslid* that they had had in that village when I was a boy. And that fat-man-with-the-*manel*'s job seemed to be to work out for the other fat men what was the best way to rob that Zeederberg coach, every time.

'And after a while, sitting in that bioscope, I began to get quite happy again, and I didn't mind so much that my home town had changed. Because the places they had there, on the picture, where all those things were going on, were just like my village had been when I was a boy. And there was the same sort of riding on horses, that I remembered well. And the hotel in the picture had the same kind of verandah. And although I didn't actually see any children swinging on the hitching-post, they might have been, but the picture just didn't show it. Anyway, I knew it was the same hitching-post. I mean, I would know it anywhere.

'And I was pleased to see the bridge, too. It was exactly

the same bridge that we had had over our stream, in the old days. And there was a young fellow who wasn't as fat as the fat-man-in-the-*manel*'s men, and who seemed to be on the opposite side from what they were on, and got in their way, every time. And the young fellow stood on that very bridge that I remembered from my childhood. He stood on the bridge with a lovely girl in his arms. And if you had looked under the bridge, I'm sure there would have been the same pieces of tree-trunk washed up under the side of it.

'And afterwards, when there was shooting in the hotel, it was exactly the same paraffin lamps and candles that they had there that used to be in the village hotel in the old days, before they made it into two storeys.'

~

Afterwards, Oupa Bekker said, when it came to the end of the picture, and that lovely girl got married to the young fellow who wasn't as fat as the man-in-the *manel*'s men were fat, he felt happier than he had done for a considerable while – happier than he had felt at any time since he had got off the train that morning, and seen that the road over the rise was tarred.

'Because the church they got married in was the old church just as I had known it,' Oupa Bekker said. 'It was like the church used to be, before they made it three times bigger and moved it to the other end of the *plein*.'

~

And when he went back to the station in the evening, Oupa Bekker said, descending the rise with the light wind that he knew so well blowing about him, it was with much satisfaction that he realised how, through all those years, his home town had not changed.

'But that bioscope itself,' Jurie Steyn said. 'That must be quite a new thing, I should imagine. They certainly couldn't have had a bioscope in that village when you were a boy.'

'No,' Oupa Bekker said. 'Where they built that bioscope there was, before that, when I was a boy, a stretch of garden wall with a creeper over it.'

40.

Psycho-Analysis I

From 'Psycho-Analysis'

In *Selected Stories*

'Koos Nienaber got a letter from his daughter, Minnie, last week,' Jurie Steyn announced to several of us sitting in his *voorkamer*, that served as the Drogevlei post office. 'It's two years now that she's been working in an office in Johannesburg. You wouldn't think it. Two years …'

'What was in the letter?' At Naudé asked, coming to the point.

'Well,' Jurie Steyn began, 'Minnie says that …'

Jurie Steyn was quick to sense our amusement.

'If that's how you carry on,' he announced, 'I won't tell you anything. I know what you're all thinking, laughing in that silly way. Well, just let one of you try and be postmaster, like me, in between milking and ploughing and getting the wrong statements from the creamery and the pigs rooting up the sweet potatoes – not to talk about the calving season, even – and then see how much time you'll have left over for steaming open and reading other people's letters.'

Johnny Coen, who was young and more than a little interested in Minnie Nienaber, hastened to set Jurie Steyn's mind at rest.

'You know, we make the same sort of joke about every postmaster in the Bushveld,' Johnny Coen said. 'We don't mean anything by it. It's a very old joke.'

~

'It must be that Koos Nienaber told you what was in his daughter's letter,' Johnny Coen said. 'Koos Nienaber must have come round here and told you. Otherwise you would never have known, I mean. You couldn't possibly have known.'

That was what had happened, Jurie Steyn acknowledged.

Thereupon Jurie Steyn acquainted us in detail with the contents of Minnie Nienaber's letter, as retailed to him by her father, Koos Nienaber.

~

'Koos says that Minnie has been,' Jurie Steyn said, 'has been – well, just a minute – oh yes, here it is – I got old Koos Nienaber to write it down for me – she's been psycho … psycho-analysed. Here it is, written down and all – *sielsontleding*.'

I won't deny that we were all much impressed. It was something we had never heard of before. Jurie Steyn saw the effect his statement had had on us.

'Yes,' he repeated, sure of himself – and more sure of the word, too, now – 'Yes, in the gold-mining city of Johannesburg, Minnie Nienaber got psycho-analysed.'

After a few moments of silence, Gysbert van Tonder made himself heard. Gysbert often spoke out of turn, that way.

'Well, it's not the first time a thing like that has happened to a girl living in Johannesburg on her own,' Gysbert said. 'One thing, the door of her parents' home will always remain open for her. But I'm surprised at old Koos Nienaber mentioning it to you. He's usually so proud.'

I noticed that Johnny Coen looked crestfallen for a moment, until Jurie Steyn made haste to explain that it didn't mean that at all.

According to what Koos Nienaber told him – Jurie Steyn said – it had become fashionable in Johannesburg for people to go and be attended to by a new sort of doctor, who didn't worry about how sick your body was, but saw to it that he got your mind right. This kind of doctor could straighten out anything that was wrong with your mind, Jurie Steyn explained. And you didn't have to be sick, even, to go along and get yourself treated by a doctor like that. It was a very fashionable thing to do, Jurie Steyn added.

Johnny Coen looked relieved.

'According to what Koos Nienaber told me,' Jurie Steyn said, 'this new kind of doctor doesn't test your heart any more, by listening through that rubber tube thing. Instead, he just asks you what you dreamt last night. And then he works it all out with a dream book. But it's not just an ordinary dream book that says if you dreamt last night of a herd of cattle, it means that there is grave peril ahead for some person that you haven't met yet …'

'Well, I dreamt a couple of nights ago that I was driving a lot of Afrikaner cattle across the Bechuanaland Protectorate border,' Fritz Pretorius said. 'Just like I have often done, on a night when there isn't much of a moon. Only, what was funny about my dream was that I dreamt I was smuggling the cattle into the Protectorate, instead of out of it. Can you imagine a Marico farmer doing a foolish thing like that? I suppose this dream means that I'm going mad or something.'

~

After At Naudé had said how surprised he was that Fritz Pretorius should have to be told in a dream what everybody knew about him in any case, and after Fritz Pretorius's invitation to At Naudé to come and repeat that remark outside the post office had come to nothing, Jurie Steyn went on to explain further about what the new kind of treatment was that

Minnie Nienaber was receiving from a new kind of doctor in Johannesburg, and that she had no need for.

'It's not the ordinary kind of dream book, like that *Napoleon Dream Book* on which my wife set so much store before we got married,' Jurie Steyn continued. 'It's a dream book written by professors. Minnie has been getting all sorts of fears, lately. Just silly sorts of fears, her father says. Nothing to worry about. I suppose anybody from the Groot Marico who has stayed in Johannesburg as long as Minnie Nienaber has, would get frightened in the same way.

'What puzzles me is only that it took her so long to start getting frightened.'

41.

Psycho-Analysis II

From 'Psycho-Analysis'

In *Selected Stories*

'It's very funny,' Jurie Steyn said, 'but all this talk of yours fits in with what Minnie Nienaber said in her letter. That's the reason why, in the end, she decided to go and get herself psycho-analysed. I mean, there was nothing wrong with her, of course. They say you've got to have nothing wrong with you, before you can get psycho-analysed. This new kind of doctor can't do anything for you if there's something the matter with you …'

'I don't know of any doctor that can do anything for you when there's something the matter with you,' Oupa Bekker interrupted. 'The last time I went to see a doctor was during the rinderpest. The doctor said I must wear a piece of leopard skin behind my left ear. That would keep the rinderpest away from my oxen, he said, and it would at the same time cure me of my rheumatism. The doctor only said that after he had thrown the bones for the second time. After the first time he threw the bones, the doctor said …'

By that time we were all laughing very loudly. We didn't mean that kind of doctor, we said to Oupa Bekker. We didn't mean a Shangaan witchdoctor. We meant a doctor who had been to university, and all that.

Oupa Bekker was silent for a few moments.

'Perhaps you're right,' he said at last. 'Because all my cattle died of the rinderpest. Mind you, I've never had rheumatism since that time. Perhaps all the witchdoctor could cure was rheumatism. From what Jurie Steyn tells us, I can see that the witchdoctor was just old-fashioned. It seems that a doctor is of no use today, unless he can cure nothing at all.

'But I still say, I don't think much of that doctor who threw the bones upward of fifty years ago. I was more concerned about my cattle's rinderpest than I was about my own ailments. All the same, if you want a cure for rheumatism – there it is. A piece of leopard skin tied behind your left ear. The skin from any ordinary old leopard will do.'

With all this talk, it was quite a while before Jurie Steyn could get a word in. But what he had to say, then, was quite interesting.

'You don't seem to realise it,' Jurie Steyn said, 'but you've been talking all this while about Minnie Nienaber's symptoms. The reason why she went to get herself psycho-analysed, I mean. It was about the awful dreams she's been having of late.

'Chris Welman has mentioned his prize cow, that got chased out of the Rand Show, and At Naudé has told us about his silver-medal bull, and Oupa Bekker has reminded us of the old days, when this part of the Marico was all leopard country. Well, that was Minnie Nienaber's trouble. That's why she went to that new kind of doctor. She'd had the most awful dreams – Koos Nienaber told me.

'She dreamt of being ordered to leave places – night clubs, and so on, Koos Nienaber said. Also, she dreamt regularly of being chased by wild bulls. And of being chased by Natal Indians with long sugar-cane knives. And lately she's been having nightmares almost every night, dreaming she's being chased by a leopard. That's why, in the end, she went to have herself psycho-analysed.'

~

We discussed Minnie Nienaber's troubles at some length. And we ended up saying that we'd like to know where the Afrikaner people would be today if our women could run to a new sort of doctor every time they dreamt of being chased by a wild animal. If Louis Trichardt's wife had dreamt she was being chased by a rhinoceros, we said, she'd jolly well have had to escape from that rhinoceros in her dream. She wouldn't have been able to come to her husband with her dream troubles the next day, seeing that he already had so many Voortrekker problems on his mind.

42.

When You're a Member of the Family

From 'Secret Agent'

In *Voorkamer Stories*

Well, anyway, here was this stranger, Losper, a middle-aged man with a suitcase, sitting in the post office and asking Jurie Steyn if he could put him up in a spare room for a few days, while he had a look around.

'I'll pay the same rates as I paid at the boarding-house in Zeerust,' *Meneer* Losper said. 'Not that I think you'd overcharge me, of course, but I'm only allowed a fixed sum by the Department for accommodation and travel expenses.'

'Look here, *Neef* Losper,' Jurie Steyn said, 'you didn't tell me your first name, so I can only call you *Neef* Losper.'

'My first name is Org,' the stranger said.

Well then, *Neef* Org,' Jurie Steyn went on. 'From the way you talk I can see that you're unacquainted with the customs of the Groot Marico. In the first place, I'm a postmaster and a farmer. And I don't know which is the worst job, what with money orders and the blue-tongue. I've got to put axle-grease on my mule cart and sealing wax on the mailbag. And sometimes I get mixed up. Any man in my position would. One day I'll paste a revenue stamp on my off-mule and brand a half-moon and bar on the Bekkersdal mailbag. Then there'll be trouble. Trouble with my off-mule, I mean. The post office won't notice any difference. But my off-mule is funny, that way. He'll pull the mule-cart, all right. But then everything's got to be the way he wants it. He won't have people laughing at him because he's got a revenue stamp stuck on his behind.

I sometimes think my off-mule knows that a shilling revenue stamp is what you put on a piece of paper after you've told a justice of the peace a lot of lies ...'

'Not lies,' Gysbert van Tonder interjected.

'A lot of lies,' Jurie Steyn went on, 'about another man's cattle straying into a person's lucern lands while that person was taking his sick child to Zeerust ...'

Gysbert van Tonder, who was Jurie Steyn's neighbour, half rose out of his *riempie* chair, then, and made some sneering remarks about Jurie Steyn and his off-mule. He said he'd never had much time for either of them. And he said he'd prefer not to describe the way his lucern lands looked after Jurie Steyn's cattle had finished straying over them. He said he would not like to use that expression, because there was a stranger present.

Meneer Losper seemed interested, then, and he sat forward to listen. It looked as though Gysbert van Tonder would have said the words, too, only At Naudé, who had a wireless to which he listened in regularly, put a stop to the argument. He said that this was a respectable *voorkamer*, with family portraits on the wall.

'And there's Jurie Steyn's wife in the kitchen, too,' At Naudé said. 'You can't use the same sort of language here as in the *Volksraad*, where there are only men.'

Actually, Jurie Steyn's wife had left the kitchen, about then. Ever since that young schoolmaster with the black hair parted in the middle had come to Bekkersdal, Jurie Steyn's wife had taken a good deal of interest in matters educational. Consequently, when the stranger, Org Losper, had said that he was from the Department, Jurie Steyn's wife thought right away – judging from his shifty appearance – that he must be a school inspector. And so she sent a message to the young schoolmaster to warn him in time, so that he could put away the saws and hammers that he used for the private fretwork he did in front of the class while the children were writing compositions.

In the meantime, Jurie Steyn was getting to the point.

'So you can't expect me to be running a boarding-house as well as everything else, *Neef* Org,' he was saying. 'But all the same, you're welcome to stay. And you can stay as long as you like. Only, you mustn't offer to pay again. If you'd known more about these parts, you'd also have known that the Groot Marico has got a very fine reputation for hospitality. When you come and stay with a man, he gets insulted if you offer him money. But I'll be glad to invite you into my home as a member of my own family.'

Org Losper then said that that was exactly what he didn't want, anymore. And he was firm about it, too.

'When you're a member of the family, you can't say no to anything,' he explained. 'In the Pilansberg I tore my best trousers on the wire. I was helping, as a member of the family, to round up the donkeys for the water-cart. At Nietverdiend a Large White bit a piece out of my second-best trousers and my leg. That was when I was a member of the family and was helping carry buckets of swill to the pig troughs. The farmer said that the Large White was just being playful that day. Well, maybe the Large White thought I was also a member of the family – his family, I mean. At Abjaterskop I nearly fell into a disused mine-shaft on a farm there. Then I was a member of the family, assisting to throw a dead bull down the shaft. The bull had died of anthrax and I was helping to pull him by one haunch, and I was walking backwards, and when I jumped away from the opening of the mineshaft, it was almost too late.

'I can also tell you what happened to me in the Dwarsberge when I was also a member of the family. And also about what happened when I was a member of the family at Derdepoort. I didn't know that that family was having a misunderstanding with the family next door about water rights. And it was when I was opening a water furrow with a shovel that a load of buckshot went through my hat. As a member of the family, I was standing ankle-deep in the mud at the time, so I couldn't run very fast.

'And so you see, when I say I would rather pay, it's not that I'm ignorant of the very fine tradition that the Marico has for the friendly and bountiful entertainment it accords the stranger. But I don't wish to presume further on your kindness. If I have much more Bushveld hospitality, I might never see my wife and children again. It's all very well being a member of somebody else's family, but I have a duty to my own family. I want to get back to them alive.'

Johnny Coen remarked that the next time Gysbert van Tonder had an American tourist on his hands, he need not take him to the Limpopo, but could just show him around the Marico farms.

It was then that Gysbert van Tonder asked Org Losper straight out what his business was. And, to our surprise, the stranger was very frank about it.

'It's a new job that's been made for me by the Department of Defence,' Org Losper said. 'There wasn't that post before. You see, I worked very hard at the last elections, getting people's names taken off the electoral roll. You've no idea how many names I got taken off. I even got some of our candidate's supporters' names crossed off. But you know how it is, we all make mistakes. It's a very secret post. It's a top Defence secret. I'm under oath not to disclose anything about it. But I am free to tell you that I'm making certain investigations on behalf of the Department of Defence. I'm trying to find out whether something has been seen here. But, of course, the post has been made for me, if you understand what I mean.'

We said we understood, all right. And we also knew that, since he was under oath about it, the nature of Org Losper's investigations in the Groot Marico would leak out sooner or later.

As it happened, we found out within the next couple of days. A Mahalapi, who worked for Adriaan Geel, told us. And then we realised how difficult Org Losper's work was. And we no longer envied him his Government job – even though it had been specially created for him.

If you know the Mtosas, you'll understand why Org Losper's job was so hard. For instance, there was only one member of the whole Mtosa tribe who had ever had any close contact with white people. And he had unfortunately grown up among the Trekboers, whose last piece of crockery, that they had brought with them from the Cape, had got broken almost a generation earlier.

We felt that the Department of Defence could have made an easier job for Org Losper than to send him around asking those questions of the Mtosas – they who did not even know what an ordinary kitchen saucer was, let alone a flying one.

43.

Real Money

From 'Five-Pound Notes'

In *Voorkamer Stories*

'It explains in the newspaper,' At Naudé said, 'how you can tell the difference between a good five-pound note and those forged ones. There are a lot of forged notes in circulation, the paper says, and the police are on the point of making an arrest.'

'Bad as all that, is it?' Gysbert van Tonder asked. 'I've noticed that when the papers say that about the police, it means that unless somebody walks into the charge office to confess that he did it, the police are writing that case off as yet another unsolved African mystery. There's only one thing worse, and that's when they write in the papers about a dragnet, and that the police are poised and ready to swoop. That means the guilty person left the country a good while before with a lot of luggage that he didn't have when he came into the country, and with his passport in order.'

Gysbert van Tonder's lip curled as he spoke. It was sad to think that an occasional misunderstanding with a mounted man on border patrol should have led to his acquiring so jaundiced a view of the activities of the forces charged with the state's internal government.

'How you can tell,' At Naudé continued patiently, 'that it's a counterfeit five-pound note is that it's actually a very good imitation note. The only way you can tell it's a forgery is that it's better printed than the genuine note, and it's got the word "*geoutoriseerde*" spelled right.'

The schoolmaster looked interested.

'Well, they keep on changing Afrikaans spelling so much,' he said, 'that I don't know where I am, half the time, teaching it. Anyway, I'd be glad to know what the right way is to spell that word. But, unfortunately, I haven't got a five-pound note on me at the moment – I don't suppose anyone here would care to lend me one?'

His tone was pensive, wistful. But he was quite right. Nobody took the hint.

'Just until the end of the month?' young Vermaak asked again, but not very hopefully.

After an interval of silence, At Naudé said that even if somebody were to lend the schoolmaster a fiver – which, in his own opinion, did not seem very likely – it would still not help him with the spelling of that word. Because it was the genuine banknote that had the spelling wrong – spelling it the old way. Only the counterfeit note had the correct, new spelling.

Jurie Steyn said that that was something that had him beat, now: calling it a counterfeit note just because it had better printing and spelling than the genuine note. It was one of those things that made his head reel, Jurie Steyn added. No wonder a person sometimes felt that he didn't know where he was in the world.

'Saying that just because it's better than the real note,' Jurie Steyn continued, 'then, for that reason, it's no good – that's got me floored all right.'

A situation like that opened up possibilities on which he, personally, would rather not dwell, Jurie Steyn went on.

'By and by,' Jurie Steyn said, 'it will mean that if a respectably dressed stranger comes here to my post office, driving an expensive motor car, and he hands me a banknote that I can see nothing wrong with, except that it looks properly printed, then it means I'll have to notify the police at Nietverdiend. But if a Shangaan in a blanket comes round here and he doesn't buy stamps, even, but he just wants change for a five-pound note, then I'll know it's all right, because the banknote has got bad spelling and the lion on the back is rubbed out in places, through the pipe in his mouth having been drawn wrong the first time.'

Oupa Bekker nodded his head, thoughtfully.

'Yes, there were certain matters relative to currency, as passed from person to person, that did not always admit of facile comprehension,' he declared, somewhat pompously.

'Take the time the Stellaland Republic issued its own banknotes, now,' Oupa Bekker said. 'Well, of course, the Stellaland Republic didn't last very long. And it might have been different if it had gone on for a while. But I'm just talking about how it was when we first got our own Stellaland Republic banknotes, and about how pleased we all were about it.

'The trouble in that part of the country was that there were never enough gold coins to go around, properly. Even before the Stellaland Republic was set up, there was that trouble. You could notice it easily, too, by the patches a lot of the men had on the back parts of their trousers.

'And so, when the Stellaland Republic starting printing its own banknotes, it looked as though everything would come right. But the affairs of the nation did not altogether follow the course that we had expected. I remember the boarding-houses landladies. What they wanted at the end of the month, they said, was – I remember very clearly – money. I don't think I've ever, in my life, either before or since, heard quite that same kind of sniff. I mean, the kind of sniff a Stellaland Republic landlady would give at the end of a month when she saw you feeling in an envelope for banknotes.

'Then there was the Indian storekeeper.

'I was once with my friend, Giel Haasbroek, in the Indian store, and I'll never forget the look that came over the Indian's face when Giel Haasbroek produced a handful of Stellaland Republic banknotes to pay him. Among other things, what the Indian said was that he had a living to make, just like all of us.

'"But these banknotes are perfectly good," Giel Haasbroek said to the Indian. "Look, there's a picture of the Stellaland Republic eagle across the top, here. And here, underneath, you can read for yourself the printed signatures of the President and the Minister of Finance – signed with their own names too."

'I'll never forget how the Indian shopkeeper winced then, either. The Indian said that he had nothing against the eagle. He was willing to admit that it was the best kind of eagle that there was. He wouldn't argue about that. Where he came from, they didn't have eagles. And if you were to show him a whole lot of eagles in a row, he didn't think he'd be able to tell the one from the other, hardly, the Indian said. We must not misunderstand him on that point, the Indian took pains to make clear to us. He had no intention of hurting our feelings in any way. He would not take exception to the eagle in any shape or form.

'But when it came to the signatures of the President and the Minister of Finance, it was quite a different matter, the Indian said. For he had both of their signatures in black and white – for old debts that he knew he'd never be able to collect, the Indian said. And of the two, the President was worse than the Minister of Finance, even. The President had got so, the Indian said, that for months now, on his way to work in the morning, he would walk three blocks out of his way, round the other side of the *plein*, just so that he didn't have to pass the Indian's store.'

Oupa Bekker interrupted his story to get a match from the schoolmaster. That gave us a chance to ponder over what he had said. For they had fallen strangely on our ears, some of his words. There appeared to have been a certain starkness about the texture of life, in the old days, that our present-day imaginings could not too readily embrace.

'But they never caught on, really, those Stellaland Republic banknotes,' Oupa Bekker continued. 'Afterwards the Government withdrew the old banknotes, and brought out a new issue. But even that didn't help very much, I don't think. Although, I must say, the new series of banknotes looked much nicer. The new banknotes were bigger, for one thing. And they were printed in more colours than the old ones. And they had a new kind of eagle on top. The eagle seemed more imposing, somehow. And he also had a threatening kind of look, that you couldn't miss. It was like the Stellaland Republic threatening you, if you got tendered one of those notes for board and lodging, and you were hesitating about taking it.

'But, all the same, those banknotes never really seemed to circulate very much. Maybe the Indian storekeeper was right in what he said. Perhaps, after all, it wasn't the eagle, so much, that they should have changed, as those two signatures on the lower portion of the banknote. Perhaps they should have been signed so that you couldn't read them.

'And, as I have said, the queer thing is that there was nothing wrong with those Stellaland Republic banknotes. They weren't counterfeit notes in any way, I mean. They were absolutely legal. The eagle and the printing were both all right – they were the smartest-looking eagle and the smartest printing you could get in those days. And yet ... there you are.'

We agreed with Oupa Bekker that the problem of money

was pretty mixed up, and always had been. Shortly afterwards, the Government lorry arrived from Bekkersdal, and the lorry driver's assistant went up to the counter.

'Change this fiver for me please, Jurie,' he said.

Now it was Jurie Steyn's turn to be funny. He took full advantage of it. He turned the note over several times.

'The printing looks all right,' Jurie Steyn said. 'And for all I know, the spelling's also all right. And the lion hasn't got a pipe in his mouth.

'What kind of fool do you think I am, handing me a note like this? About the only thing it hasn't got on it is an eagle.'

The lorry driver's assistant looked at Jurie Steyn, mystified.

44.

Cattle Thieves and Herdboys

From 'Idle Talk'

In *Voorkamer Stories*

'What about the time our *Volksraad* member's brother-in-law himself went down to the station and spoke to the stationmaster very firmly?' Gysbert van Tonder went on. 'And he asked the stationmaster if he thought that every farmer in the Groot Marico was a cattle thief. He asked him that straight out, because he had brought witnesses with him. And the stationmaster said no, but he knew that every Marico farmer was a cattle farmer, and he knew that any cattle farmer could make a mistake.'

We all said, then, that that was quite a different thing. And we said that if you weren't there to see to it yourself, and you left it to a Bechuana herdboy to go and have a lot of cattle railed to Johannesburg, why, mistakes were almost sure to happen, we said. Thereupon At Naudé started telling us about a mistake that one of his Bechuana herdboys had made on a certain occasion, as a result of which six of Koos Nienaber's best trek-oxen had got railed to Johannesburg along with some scrub animals that At Naudé was sending to the market.

'That was the time Koos Nienaber went to Johannesburg to have his old Mauser mended,' At Naudé explained. 'And it just so happened that because he didn't know where to get off, Koos Nienaber was shunted onto a siding, somewhere past Johannesburg station. And what should take place, but that Koos Nienaber alighted from his second-class compartment at just the same time that his six trek-oxen were walking out of a truck on the other side of the line. That caused quite a lot of trouble, of course. And before he got his six trek-oxen back, Koos Nienaber had had to explain to a magistrate what he meant by loading all five chambers of his Mauser on a railway platform, even though the bolt action and foresight of the Mauser were in need of repair. I believe the magistrate said that there were quite enough brawls and ugly scenes that had to do with gun-play taking place in Johannesburg every day, without a farmer having to come all the way from the Marico with a rusty Mauser to add to all that unpleasantness. Naturally, I gave my Bechuana herdboy a good straight talking-to about it afterwards, for being so ignorant.'

At Naudé paused, as though inviting one of us to say something. But we had, none of us, any comment to make. For we had, long ago, heard Koos Nienaber's side of the story. And from what he had told us, it would appear that all the fault did not lie with At Naudé's herdboy. At Naudé seemed to fit a little into the story, himself.

'Anyway,' At Naudé added – smiling in a twisted sort of way – 'what Koos Nienaber was most sore about, in court, was that that Johannesburg magistrate spoke of his Mauser as a rusty old fowling-piece.'

Koos Nienaber didn't object to the fowling-piece part of it, so much, At Naudé said, because he wasn't quite sure what a fowling-piece was. But it took him a long time to get over the idea of the magistrate saying that his Mauser was rusty.

There was an uncomfortable silence, once again. It was broken by young Johnny Coen. Often, in the past, when there had been some misunderstanding in Jurie Steyn's post office, Johnny Coen had said something to smooth matters over.

'Maybe it's like what it says in the Good Book,' Johnny Coen remarked. 'Perhaps it's to do with Mammon. Perhaps if we sought the Kingdom of Heaven more, then we wouldn't have such thoughtless things happening. Like a farmer sending some of his own neighbour's cattle to the market, by mistake. It's a mistake that happens with every truck-load, almost. I worked at Ottoshoop siding, and I know. It used to give the stationmaster there grey hairs. Loading a lot of cattle into a truck and then not knowing how many would have to be unloaded again before the engine came to fetch that truck. And all the time it was through some mistake, of course. A mistake on the part of an ignorant Bechuana herdboy.'

It was then that some of us remembered the mistakes that the herdboy of Deacon Kirstein had made, long ago, along those same lines. We felt not a little pained at having to mention those mistakes, considering the high regard in which we held Deacon Kirstein, who was Jurie Steyn's wife's cousin. We only made mention of it because of the circumstance that that mistake on the part of the deacon's herdboy had gone on over a period of years, before it was detected. And maybe the mistake would never have been found out, either, if it wasn't that, along with a truck full of Deacon Kirstein's Large White pigs, there was also loaded a span of mules belonging to a near neighbour of Deacon Kirstein.

And because he was already a deacon, we all felt very sorry for Deacon Kirstein, to think that his herdboy should be so ignorant. And we winked at each other a good deal, too, in those days, one Marico farmer winking at another. And we said that it was just too bad that Deacon Kirstein should have so uneducated a herdboy, who couldn't tell the difference between a Large White and a mule. And we would wink a lot more.

That was the line that the conversation suddenly took, in Jurie Steyn's *voorkamer*. We were just recalling the old days, we said to each other.

And we were enjoying this talk about the past. And we could see that Jurie Steyn was enjoying it also. And then Johnny Coen tried to spoil everything. Johnny Coen, without anybody asking him, began to talk about the Sermon on the Mount. And let any of us that was without sin, Johnny Coen added, cast the first stone.

Jurie Steyn summed it all up.

'Maybe a lot of sense gets talked here in my post office,' Jurie Steyn said, 'but a lot of crap also.'

Jurie Steyn said that word softly, because he didn't want his wife to hear.

45.

A Pale Wind in a Tall Tree

From 'The Wind in the Tree'

In *Unto Dust*

It was a simple story that Gerrit van Biljon told me, and he took a long time over it, and when he had finished with the telling, it was like no story at all. And that was one of the reasons why I liked his story.

'I am planting bluegum trees,' Gerrit van Biljon said, 'in those holes that I am digging. For shade.'

I was speechless.

'But trees, *Neef* Gerrit,' I said, 'trees! Surely the whole Marico is full of trees. I mean, there's nothing here but trees. We can't even grow mealies. Why, you had to chop down hundreds of trees to clear a space for your homestead and the cattle-*kraal*. And they're all shady trees, too.'

Gerrit van Biljon shook his head. And he told me the story of how he met his wife, Sarie, on her father's farm in Schweizer-Reneke, in front of the farmhouse, under a tall bluegum. It was a simple story of a boy and a girl who fell in love. Of initials carved on a white tree-trunk. Of a smile in the dusk. And hands touching, and a quick kiss. And tears. Oh, it was a very simple story that Gerrit van Biljon told me. And as he spoke, I could see that it was a story that would go on for ever. Two lovers in the evening, and a pale wind in a tall tree. And Sarie's red lips. And two hearts haunted for ever by the fragrance of the bluegum trees. No, there was nothing at all in that story. It was the sort of thing that happens every day. It was just something foolish about the human heart.

'And if it had been any tree other than a bluegum,' Gerrit van Biljon said, 'it wouldn't have been the same thing.'

I knew better, of course, but I did not tell him so.

Then Gerrit explained that he was going to plant a row of bluegums in front of his house.

'I've ordered the plants from the Government Test Station in Potchefstroom,' he went on. 'I'm getting only the best plants. It takes a bluegum only twelve years to grow to its full height. For the first couple of years the trees will hardly grow at all, because of the stones. But after a few years, when the roots have found their way into the deeper parts of the soil, the trunks will shoot up very quickly. And in the late afternoons I shall sit under the tallest bluegum, with my wife beside me, and our children playing about. The wind stirring through a bluegum makes a different sound from when it blows through any other tree. And a bluegum's shadow on the ground has a feeling altogether different from any other kind of shadow. At least, that's how it is for me.'

Gerrit van Biljon said that he didn't even care if a pig occasionally wandered away from the trough at the back of the house, at feeding time, and scratched himself on the trunk of one of the trees. That was how tolerant the thought of the bluegums made him feel.

'Only,' he added, rather quickly, 'I only hope the pig doesn't overdo it. I don't want him to make a habit of it, of course.'

'Perhaps I will even read a book under one of the trees, some day,' Gerrit said, finally. 'You see, outside of the Bible, I have never read a book. Just bits of newspaper and things. Yes, perhaps I will even read a book. But mostly – well, mostly I will just rest.'

So that was Gerrit van Biljon's story.

~

As he had prophesied, the bluegums, after not seeming to want to grow at all, at first, suddenly started to shoot up, and they grew almost to their full height in something over eight years.

And I often saw Sarie sitting under the tallest tree, with her youngest child playing on the grass beside her, and I was sure that Gerrit van Biljon rested as peacefully under the withaak by the foot of the *koppie* at the far end of the farm as he would have done in the bluegum's shade.

46.

A Sigh from very Far Away

From 'Potchefstroom Willow'

In *A Bekkersdal Marathon*

'The trouble,' At Naudé said, 'about getting the latest war news over the wireless, is that Klaas Smit and his *boeremusiek* orchestra start up right away after it, playing *Die nooi van Potchefstroom*. Now, it isn't that I don't like that song.'

So we all said that it wasn't as though we didn't like it, either. Gysbert van Tonder began to hum the tune. Johnny Coen joined in, singing the words softly – '*Vertel my neef, vertel my oom, is dit die pad na Potchefstroom?*' In a little while, we were all singing. Not very loudly, of course. For Jurie Steyn was conscious of the fact that his post office was a public place, and he frowned on any sort of out-of-the-way behaviour in it. We still remembered the manner in which Jurie Steyn had spoken to Chris Welman the time Chris was mending a pair of his wife's *veldskoens* in the post office, using the corner of the counter as a last.

For that reason we did not raise our voices very much when we sang *Die nooi van Potchefstroom*. But it was a catchy song, and Jurie Steyn joined in a little, too, afterwards.

Not that he let himself go in any way, of course. He sang in a reserved and dignified fashion, that made you feel he would yet go far. You felt that even the Postmaster-General in Pretoria, on the occasion of a member of the public coming to him to complain about a registered letter that had got lost – well, even the Postmaster-General would not have been able to sit back in his chair and sing *Die nooi van Potchefstroom* in as elevated a manner as Jurie Steyn was doing at that very moment.

Before the singing had quite died down, Oupa Bekker was saying that he knew Potchefstroom when he was still a child. It was in the very old days, Oupa Bekker said, and the far-side foundations of the church on *Kerkplein* had not sunk nearly as deep as they have done today. He said he remembered the first time that there was a split in the Church. It was between the *Doppers* and the *Hervormdes*, he said. And it was quite a serious split. And because he was young, then, he thought it had to do with the way the brickwork on the wall nearest the street had to be constantly plastered up, from top to bottom, the more the foundations sank.

'I remember showing my father that piece of church wall,' Oupa Bekker continued. 'And I asked my father if the *Doppers* had done it. And my father said, well, he had never thought about it like that, until then. But all the same, he wouldn't be surprised if they had. Not that anybody would ever see the *Doppers* kneeling down there on the sidewalk, loosening the bricks with a crowbar, my father added. Whatever they did was under the cover of darkness.'

At Naudé started talking again about the news of the war in Korea, that he had heard over the wireless. But because so much had been spoken in between, he had to explain right from the beginning again.

'It's the way the war news gets crowded by Klaas Smit and his orchestra,' At Naudé said. 'You're listening to what the announcer is making clear about what part of the country General MacArthur is fighting in now – and it's hard to follow all that, because it seems to me that sometimes General MacArthur himself is not too clear as to what part of the country he is in – and then, suddenly, while you're still listening, up strikes Klaas Smit's orchestra with *Die nooi van*

Potchefstroom. It makes it all very difficult, you know. They don't give that General MacArthur a chance at all. *Die nooi van Potchefstroom* seems to be crowding him even worse than the Communists are doing – and that seems to be bad enough, the Lord knows.'

This time we did not start singing again. We had, after all, taken the song to the end, and even if it wasn't for Jurie Steyn's feelings, we ourselves knew enough about the right way of conducting ourselves in a post office. You can't go and sing the same song in a post office twice, just as though it's the quarterly meeting of the Mealie Control Board. We were glad, therefore, when Oupa Bekker started talking once more.

'This song, now,' Oupa Bekker was saying. 'Well, as you know, I remember the early days of Potchefstroom. The very early days, that is. But I would never have imagined that someday a poet would come along and make up a song about the place. Potchefstroom was the first capital of the Transvaal, of course. Long before Pretoria was thought of, even. And there's an old willow tree in Potchefstroom that must have measured I don't know how many feet around the trunk where it goes into the ground. It measured that much only a little while ago, I mean. I am talking about the last time I was in Potchefstroom. But I never imagined that anybody would ever write a poem about the town. It seemed such a hard name to make verses about. But I suppose it's a lot different today. People are so much more clever, I expect.'

Oupa Bekker would have gone on a good deal longer, maybe, if it wasn't that Jurie Steyn's wife came in just about then with the coffee. Consequently, Oupa Bekker had to sit up properly and stir the sugar round in his cup.

'I heard that song you were singing, just now,' Jurie Steyn's wife remarked to all of us. 'I thought it was – well, I liked it. I didn't catch the words, quite.'

Nobody answered. We knew that it was school holidays, of course. And we knew that young Vermaak, the schoolmaster, had gone to his parents in Potchefstroom for the holidays. Because we knew that Potchefstroom was young Vermaak's home town, we kept silent. There was no telling what Jurie Steyn's reaction might be.

Oupa Bekker went on talking, however.

'All the same, I would like to know how many feet around the trunk that willow tree is today,' Oupa Bekker said. 'And they won't chop it down either. That willow tree is right on the edge of the graveyard. You can almost say it's inside the graveyard. And so they won't chop it down. But what beats me is to think that somebody could actually write a song about Potchefstroom. I would never have thought it possible.'

Oupa Bekker's sigh seemed to come from very far away. From somewhere a good deal further away than the *rusbank* he was sitting on. We understood, then, why that Potchefstroom willow tree meant so much to him.

And the result was that when Gysbert van Tonder started up the chorus of the song again, we all found ourselves joining in – no matter what Jurie Steyn might say about it. '*En in my droom,*' we sang, '*is die vaalhaarnooi by die wilgerboom.*'

47.

A Kind of Sweetness in the Air

From 'Young Man In Love'

In *Jurie Steyn's Post Office*

'You won't listen to me,' Oupa Bekker said. 'You never let me finish what I'm trying to say. Always, you just let me get so far. Then somebody says something foolish, and so I can't get to the important thing.

'Now, what I wanted to say is that At Naudé is quite right. And Johnny Coen will come here. He'll come this afternoon because he wants to know what we think. A young man in love is like that. He wants to know what we've got to say. But all the time he'll be laughing to himself, secretly, about the things we're saying. A young man in love is like that. And his titivating himself – with the short blade of a pocket knife and a handful of dry grass – well, you've no idea how vain a young man in love can be.

'And he's not making himself all stylish for the girl's sake, but for his own sake. It's himself that he thinks is so wonderful. He knows less than anybody what she's like – the girl he's in love with. And it's only the best kind of pig's fat he'll mix with soot to shine his bought shoes with. Because he's in love with the girl, he thinks he's something. Oh yes, Johnny Coen will come here this afternoon all right. And what I want to say ...'.

At this point, Oupa Bekker was interrupted once more. But because it was Jurie Steyn who broke in on his dissertation, Oupa Bekker yielded with good grace. The post office we were sitting in was, after all, Jurie Steyn's own *voorkamer*.

There was something of the spirit of old-world courtesy in the manner of Oupa Bekker's surrender.

'... you, Jurie Steyn,' Oupa Bekker said. 'You talk.'

Several of us looked in the direction of the kitchen. We were relieved to see that the door was closed. This meant that Jurie Steyn's wife had not heard the low expression Oupa Bekker had just used.

'What I'd like to say,' Jurie Steyn said, 'is that I had the honour to drive *Juffrou* Pauline Gerber to her home in my mule-cart, that day she arrived here at my post office, getting off from the Government lorry and all ...'.

'What do you mean by "and all"?' Gysbert van Tonder demanded.

Jurie Steyn looked around him with an air of surprise.

'But you were all here,' Jurie Steyn declared. 'All of you were here. Maybe that's what I mean by "and all". I'm sure I don't know. But you did see Pauline Gerber. You, each one of you, saw her. When she alighted here that day from the Zeerust lorry, on her return from the Cape finishing school. You saw the way she walked around here in my *voorkamer*, picking her heels up high – and I don't blame her. And her chin up in the air. And as pretty as you like. You all saw how pretty she was, now, didn't you? And the way she smelled. Did you smell her? You must have. It was too lovely. It just shows you the kind of perfume you can get in the Cape.

'And I'm sure that if a church elder smelled her – even if he was an *Enkel Gereformeerde* Church elder from the furthest part of the Waterberge, I'm sure that the Waterberg elder would have known that Pauline Gerber had class – just from smelling her, I mean. I'm sure that the scent that Pauline bought at the Cape must have cost at least seven shillings and sixpence a bottle.

'Take my wife, now. I once bought her a bottle of perfume at the Indian store at Ramoutsa. And I can assure you – you can smell the difference between my wife and Pauline Gerber.'

Chris Welman, who had not spoken much so far, hastened to remark that there were other ways, too, in which you could tell the difference.

It was an innuendo that, fortunately, escaped general attention.

For it was at that moment that Johnny Coen came in at the front door of the post office. In one way it was the Johnny Coen we'd always known; and yet it also wasn't him. Somehow, in some subtle fashion, Johnny Coen had changed.

After greeting us, he went and sat on a *riempie* chair, and he sat very upright.

From his manner he seemed almost unaware of our presence as he whittled a matchstick to a fine point, and commenced scraping out the grime from under one of his fingernails.

Gysbert van Tonder, who always liked getting straight to the point, was the first to speak.

'Nice bit of rain you've been having out your way, Johnny,' Gysbert remarked. 'Your dams must be pretty full.'

'Yes, indeed,' Johnny Coen answered.

'Plenty of water in the *spruit*, too, I'd imagine,' Gysbert continued.

'Yes, that's very true,' Johnny Coen replied.

'New grass must be coming along nicely in the *vlakte* where you burnt,' Gysbert van Tonder went on.

'Yes, very nicely,' Johnny agreed.

'What's the matter with you, man – can't you talk?' Gysbert demanded. 'You know very well what I'm trying to say. Have you seen her at all since she's been back?'

'I saw her yesterday,' Johnny Coen said, 'on the road near their house. I had to go quite a long distance out of my way to be passing by there, at the time.'

Gysbert van Tonder made a swift calculation: 'About eleven miles out of your way, counting in the short cuts through the withaaks,' he announced. 'Did she have much to say?"

Johnny Coen shook his head. 'Please don't ask me,' he almost implored Gysbert, 'because I really can't remember. We did speak, I know. But after she'd gone, there was nothing we said that I could recall. It was all so different after she had gone. I wish I could remember what we said. What I said must all have sounded so foolish to her.'

Gysbert van Tonder was not going to allow Johnny Coen to get off that easily.

'Well, how did she look?' Gysbert asked.

'I also tried to remember that, afterwards,' Johnny Coen declared. 'How she looked. What she did. All that. But I just couldn't remember. After she'd gone, it was as if it had all been a dream, and there was nothing that I could remember. She was picking yellow flowers, there by the side of the road, to stick in her hair. Or she was carrying a sack of firewood over her back for the kitchen fire. It would have been all the same to me, the way I felt. But I don't know. Afterwards, all I was able ...'.

'That's what I was trying to explain to them, Johnny,' Oupa Bekker interjected, 'but they never let me finish anything I start to say. They always ...'.

'Afterwards,' Johnny Coen repeated, 'after she'd gone, that is, there was a kind of sweetness in the air. It was almost hanging in the air, sort of. At one stage I even thought it might be a kind of scent, like what some women put on their clothes when they go to *Nagmaal*. But, of course, it couldn't have been that. Pauline wouldn't wear scent ... I mean, she's just not that kind.'

'What I wanted to say earlier on, when you all interrupted me,' Oupa Bekker declared, then – with an air of triumph – 'is that a young man in love is like that.'

48.

Gutters

From 'Rebuilding Europe's Cities'

In *A Cask of Jerepigo*

Now that peace has come to Europe – or has it? – it is not uninteresting to speculate on the faces that the cities of Europe will now be wearing. There will be changes in some of them, of course; and of a quite startling nature, obviously enough.

For one thing, there will be rebuilding to be done and on a scale for which we can find, off-hand, only the word 'unprecedented'. This applies to a by no means insignificant area of Europe. Cities that have been laid in ruin and for whose reconstruction totally new plans have to be drawn up.

It is to be trusted that the commissionaires of public works in the various countries will apply a measure of imagination to the exercise of their official functions – a difficult task for works commissionaires, whose imaginative powers appear to have declined considerably since the Egyptian dynasty that saw the building of Thebes. At all events, we hope that the works commissionaires, in resurrecting ruins, will distinguish between ancient and modern. We hope that they don't go erecting pillar-boxes where a Gothic castle used to stand, or replacing the fallen pillars of the Parthenon with steel and concrete structures, or macadamising the Appian Way.

Anyway, it must be a tough job, after a city has been destroyed, to have to build it up all over again – from scratch, as it were. And I bet the new lot of architects and town planners and building contractors will make just about the same mistakes as the old ones did. They will create the same ugliness and the same chaos. It may be difficult to achieve all that – but they will. That much is comforting.

Civic authorities will once more have to wrack their brains in planning the thoroughfares, so as to ensure the creation of bottle-necks and the maximum amount of congestion. They will have to put railway stations in all the wrong places. Law courts will once more have to be constructed to look like museums, town halls to look like town halls, and art galleries to look like gas-works. As a result, the cities of bombed Europe will again become impossible bedlams – and therefore places you can live in.

In a city centrally planned in terms of Utopian conceptions, the soul of man perishes.

~

The cities of Europe will rise again out of their rubble. Their streets will wind along the banks of the rivers on which they are situated. They will conform with sea-fronts and hills and valleys, and the demands of propertied and privileged interests. And from a peaceful movement, one will again become confronted with a spectacle as violently *outre* as the Arches of Adelphi. In spite of the planners, life will creep back into the cities. And into the buildings, drama of a kind the architects did not intend.

I believe that the war will have made no difference to the cities of Europe. A city gets its individuality from the people who live there. The streets are torn up, the buildings are destroyed, but the soul of the place remains.

The city in which a genius has lived becomes recreated into something that is more than the inanimate background to his source. The streets he has walked; the scenes amid which the incomprehensible pattern of his life has unfolded; above all, the places where sublime inspiration came to him. It doesn't matter what happens to such a place, afterwards. That spot on the earth's surface remains impregnated with a spirit of beauty that is, forever, rich and rare. Take a stroll through the streets of Brussels, and you will see what I mean.

The artistic soul of a city is the contribution that genius makes to it. Its incongruities are the things that life brings along: the architects and the city planners and the landowners and human nature. And you can't do without either influence.

When a city has enough incongruities, I feel that you can live in it.

Above all, a city must have strong and bizarre contrasts. Ermines and rags. Beauty and filth. The sublime and the diabolical. A well-conducted night club next door to a, perhaps, not-so-well conducted morgue.

~

I have thought of a story that I would like to write someday, when I get the time.

It is about people who live in Johannesburg and people who live, say, in the Marico Bushveld. These two sets of people, those who live in city flats and those who live on the farm, don't know each other. They never meet. But life does exactly the same things to each of them. Life is like that. And the story ends with the heroine of this little group of people in the city, smashed into pieces by the things life has done to her, declaring that she can't stand it any longer: she's got to get away, somewhere. And the girl on the farm, to whom exactly the same things have happened, says that this has been too terrible. She is going to Johannesburg. What she means is … life.

Life ...
The difference between the city and the farm is, alas, age-old: the city has gutters.

49.

Why Durban is so Uncivilised

From 'Student of Divinity'

In *Jurie Steyn's Post Office*

At Naudé acted in what we could not help feeling was a quite singular fashion. First he half rose to his feet, emitting a long moan. Then he suddenly slumped back again into his *riempie* chair, at the same time smacking the open palm of his right hand in a despairing manner against his forehead. His visage was noticeably contorted.

'All this same old childishness,' At Naudé exclaimed, 'that's supposed to be clever, or that's supposed to be funny. I can't stand it anymore, this heavy what's assumed to be Marico fun. If it's not Jurie Steyn doing it, it's Chris Welman. Or it's Gysbert van Tonder. And if it's not Jurie Steyn's wife, it's Oupa Bekker, or it's me. And if it's not me, it's ... oh, I tell you, it's driving me mad. And when I switch on the wireless, it's the same thing.'

~

So Oupa Bekker said that if it was civilisation that At Naudé wanted to get away from, well, there was always Durban. He had been to Durban only once, Oupa Bekker said, but that was enough. It was quite a story, too, how he got to Durban, in the first place, Oupa Bekker added. But Durban was quite a good place to go, if you were sick and tired of civilisation.

'The same old thing,' At Naudé remarked to Oupa Bekker. 'And I know exactly what you're going to say, too. It was in the old days. And you went there by mule-cart. Or you were a transport-driver, and you went there by ox-wagon. And on the way back you gave a young student of divinity a lift as far as Kimberley.'

~

'Every time Oupa Bekker speaks it sounds to me as though he's being introduced by a wireless announcer, and as though there's somebody playing the piano, for background effect. I mean, Oupa Bekker isn't real to me anymore.

'Even the way he spits behind his chair – well, it looks to me like a put-on kind of spit, if you know what I mean. I don't feel that Oupa Bekker is spitting just because he has to.'

We looked at At Naudé in amazement. It was clear that he was in a pretty bad way, through too much civilisation – that he was getting over the wireless and from reading newspapers. There was no telling how far this sort of thing could go. We felt that we wanted to help him, if we could.

~

It came as a relief to us – for At Naudé's sake – to hear Oupa Bekker's voice once more.

'The last time I went to Durban wasn't in the old days, but two years ago,' Oupa Bekker said. 'And why I said that it was like a story was because I went there by train. I had never before in my life travelled so far by train. And that was a wonderful thing for me. Because I would never have believed, otherwise, that you could journey so far by train. We didn't once have to get out and walk. Or change to a post-cart. Or mount a horse ready-saddled that would take us along a bridle-path over the worst part of the *rante* …'

'Then it couldn't have been in the Union,' Chris Welman

shouted out, trying to be really funny. 'You couldn't have been travelling on the S.A.R.'

We were pleased that Oupa Bekker ignored Chris Welman.

'No trouble over the whole journey,' Oupa Bekker continued. 'It was only when I got off at the station and a Zulu came and pulled my portmanteau out of my hands. I had never in my life seen a Zulu like that. He had bull's horns on his head, and sea-shells on his feet. That was just how my grandfather had told me the Zulus were dressed at Vechtkop.'

We laughed at that, of course. After all, those of us who had been to Durban knew that about the rickshaw-pullers – the way they dressed up to look ferocious. But all they did was to transport you and your luggage to a hotel.

'That sort of talk,' At Naudé began, his lip curling, 'and I suppose when you got to the hotel …'

'That's why I say that Durban is so uncivilised,' Oupa Bekker explained. 'Because it was only when we got to the hotel that the rickshaw-puller started apologising for all the boot-polish brown that was coming off his chin. He was working his way through college, he told me. He said it was steadier work than looking after babies or mowing lawns, and the sea-shells on him rattled as he spoke.

'He was a divinity student, the rickshaw-puller said.'

50.

Good Stuff

From 'Street Processions'

In *A Cask of Jerepigo*

For almost as long as I can remember, street processions have been in my blood. When I see a long line of people marching through the streets – the longer the line, the better I like it – something primordial gets stirred inside me and I am overtaken by the urge to fall in also, and take my place somewhere near the end of the procession. And it's been like that with me all my life. There is something about the sight and the thought of a long line of people marching through the streets of a city that fills me with an awe I can't easily define. It has got to be through a city – a procession through a village or over the veld wouldn't be the same thing.

The ideal conditions for a procession are grey skies and wet streets. And there should be a drizzle. My tastes don't run to the extremes of a blizzard or a tropical downpour. Thunder and lightening effects are out of place. All you want is a steady drip-drip of fine rain that makes everything look bleak and dismal, without the comfortable abandonment of utter desolation. Then through these drab streets there must come trailing a long line of humanity, walking three or four abreast, their boots muddy and their clothes (by preference) shabby and shapeless in the rain, and their faces a grey pallor. They can sing a little, too, if they like, to try and cheer themselves up – without ever succeeding, of course. And in this sombre trudging of thousands of booted feet on cobbles or tarred road, there goes my heart, also. I get gripped with an intense feeling of being one with stupid, struggling, rotten, heroic humanity, and in this grey march there is a heavy symbolism whose elements I don't try to interpret for fear that the parts should together be less than the whole; and I find myself, contrary to all the promptings of good sense and reason, yielding to the urge to try and find a place for myself somewhere near the tail-end of the procession.

Oh, and of course, there is another thing, something I had almost forgotten, and that is the cause operating as the dynamism for getting a procession of this description organised and under way. Frankly, I don't think the cause matters very much. I have a natural predilection for an unpopular cause and, above all, for a forlorn cause – a lost hope, and whether this peculiar idiosyncrasy of mine springs from ordinary perversity, or from a nobility of soul, is something I have not been able to ascertain. And so, while I always feel that it is very nice, and all that, if the march is undertaken by the participants in a spirit of lofty idealism, because a very important principle is at stake, I am equally satisfied – provided that the muddy boots and the grey skies are present – if the spiritual factors behind the demonstration are not so very high or altruistic.

The last time I marched in a procession was as recently as last Saturday afternoon. I was on my way home when, from the top of the Malvern tram, I spotted in front of Jeppe Station a street procession in the course of formation. I could see straight away that the conditions were just right. It was drizzling. The streets were wet and grey and muddy. The sky was bleak and cheerless. I prepared to alight. Unfortunately, however, the tram was very crowded, with the result that I wasn't able to get off before the Berg Street stop. From there I took another tram back to Jeppe Station, arriving there just as the procession was moving off. I took my place somewhere near the rear. We marched in a northerly direction and swung into Commissioner Street. Trudge. Trudge. Drizzle. Mud. Wet boots and shapeless clothes. I didn't ask what the procession was about. I didn't want to reveal my ignorance and chance getting sneered at. I'd been sneered at by a procession before, and I don't like it.

~

This weakness of mine – in the way of desiring to make one with street processions, identifying myself with and merging my personality in a mass of humanity, moving to no clearly defined goal – has in the past resulted in my becoming, on more than one occasion, involved in a considerable measure of embarrassment. In my youth, for instance, when the Salvation Army had moved up from the town hall steps at the termination of a Sunday evening open-air meeting, and I found myself marching at the back, in a sort of trance, it happened, at least twice, that I followed the procession right into the Hope Hall in Commissioner Street, with the result that, each time, I wasn't able to get out again until I had been converted.

And then, only a couple of years ago, with the annual Corpus Christi procession to the End Street Convent, when I had again, from force of habit, taken my place near the end of the line and was proceeding down Bree Street, feeling very solemn as I always do on such occasions, I realised, suddenly, the incongruity of my presence in the company of priests in black vestments and stoles, and choirboys in white surplices, all carrying missals, while I was dressed in civvies with half a loaf of bread under my arm, which I was taking home for supper – as I explained to an abbot-looking gentleman in a mitre, who hadn't said anything about my being in that procession, but who seemed unhappy, nevertheless, in a peculiar sort of way.

Similarly I have, at different times, marched through the streets of London with Communists, Mosleyites, Scotchmen on their way to the Cup-Tie, unemployed Welsh miners, and the Peace Pledge Union.

~

'It's that (so-and-so) Steyn,' the man on the left of me remarked, by way of conversation.

'You're telling me,' I answered.

He was telling me, of course. Otherwise I wouldn't know what it was all about.

'If it wasn't for him,' the man on my left continued, 'us miners wouldn't be on strike.'

'Us miners wouldn't be,' I agreed, relieved to have discovered, so soon, what the procession was all about.

A middle-aged man in front of me, in a khaki overcoat, was singing rather a lot. A young fellow, with a free-and-easy sort of look, marched next to him. On my right was a stocky man with a grey moustache and a red rosette.

'You know,' this stocky, grey-moustached man remarked to me after a while, 'in 1922 I was shooting yous. In 1922 I was in the police. Now I'm one of yous.'

The imp of perversity inside me egged me on to pick a quarrel with Grey-Moustache.

'How do I know that you aren't still one of thems?' I enquired.

Grey-Moustache's neck went all red.

'I'm a rock-buster on the Crown Mines,' he retorted. 'There's half-a-dozen men in this procession as knows I'm a rock-buster on the Crown Mines.'

In this way, what had at first promised to be an unpleasant

incident was settled peaceably. Only, I couldn't help feeling that, in the depth of his most secret sincerities, Grey-Moustache was still one of thems. As the old saying goes, if you're once one of thems, you're always one of thems.

So the march continued in the grey drizzle. Wet clothes and boots and mud-splashed trouser-tops. A number of low songs were sung. Various obscene remarks were made. Everything was in order.

A big fat man in a black overcoat was acting as a sort of linesman for our part of the procession. They called him Oom Tobie. He was a kind of cheerleader. He would hurry on until he got about fifty yards ahead of our rank, and then he would stand on the pavement and shout out the slogans. These were in the form of questions, to which the procession would roar out the answers. As far as I could make out, it all had a lot to do with the miners' democratic rights.

'Do we want Steyn?' Oom Tobie would ask.

'No!' the procession would roar. That seemed to be the right answer.

'Do we want the capitalists?' Oom Tobie would ask again.

'No!' would come the thunderous reply.

Then Oom Tobie would look sort of arch, like a schoolteacher trying to tip his class off as to the right answer, when the school inspector is present, and he would shout out: 'But – do we want democracy?'

I make the acknowledgement – gladly – that a considerable proportion of the miners shouted: 'Yes!' But it was also a fact that an equal number answered, with the same degree of determination: 'No!'

It seemed to me that Oom Tobie had not properly rehearsed them in their responses. He didn't seem to have given them the proper instructions on this point. I came to the conclusion that Oom Tobie, himself, wasn't too sure as to what the right answer was, either.

~

It was after we had passed the *Rand Daily Mail* offices that I realised why the man in the khaki overcoat and the free-and-easy youth were singing more loudly than anybody else. By that time they were not only singing, but also staggering. They had a bottle of Jereipgo which they were passing backwards and forwards, and from which they were taking surreptitious swigs. Grey-Moustache reported the matter to Oom Tobie. (As I have remarked, once one of thems, always one of thems.) Nevertheless, I have rarely seen a man as indignant as Oom Tobie was at that moment. And I am sure that not even an underground foreman had ever dressed down Khaki Overcoat and the free-and-easy youth in terms of vituperation such as Oom Tobie then employed.

'You're giving us all a bad name,' he shouted, finally. 'Drinking wine like that, out of the bottle, and in the street. And in front of the *Rand Daily Mail*, too. What if they'd taken your photograph, drinking wine, when all the boys was booing? What if they got your photo like that in the *Rand Daily Mail* on Monday morning?'

'But we did boo, too,' the free-and-easy youth explained. 'In between.'

'Won't you have a pull at the bottle, too, Oom Tobie?' the man in the khaki overcoat asked. 'Just a small one, Oom Tobie?'

'Well, seeing it's you,' Oom Tobie replied, 'and because it's raining today – but not for any other reason, mind you – I don't mind if I have just a small mouthful. But don't let anybody see. Don't pass me the bottle until that tram has gone round the corner.'

A few minutes later the procession reached the town hall steps, and I made a dash for home. But as there wasn't a Malvern tram in sight, I sauntered into a pub. I asked for a Jerepigo. And I found that it was good stuff.

51.

The Awakening of Gigantic Laughter

From 'Humour and Wit'

In *A Cask of Jerepigo*

How shall we define the wayward and mysterious and outcast thing that we term humour – that is forever a pillar-to-post fugitive from the stern laws of reality, and yet forms so intimate a part of – and even embodies – all truth about which there is an eternal ring?

There isn't so much humour in the world today as there was of yore, I think; and through the realms of culture, there do not sweep those gusts of great laughter that blew the lamp smoke away from thought, and left behind an intoxication. The material for splendid mirth is still here, of course – right in our midst. Turn but a stone and the diamonds coruscate. Yet the man who could make out of this material a supremely godlike brand of jesting, we seem not to have with us any more.

~

Lots of people have tried to analyse humour: writers, comedians, clergymen, psychologists, undertakers, political cartoonists, crooks, prison superintendants – in fact, all sorts of men in whose private or professional lives humour plays an important role. But I have never come across any attempt, trying to explain what it is that makes us laugh, that has impressed me very much. You can work out what are the important ingredients that go towards the compounding of that rare and subtle thing that stirs the risible faculties. But that doesn't get you anywhere. You can analyse the elements that embrace laughter, but you can't make anybody laugh with your analysis.

It's the same thing with those distinctions that people draw between humour and wit. Is there any difference? I don't know. If that rather generally accepted, rough-and-ready attempt at classificiation holds water – namely, that humour is born out of the emotions and wit springs from the intellect – then I would naturally be prone to look upon wit as being, to some extent, an intruder. I am by nature suspicious of the intellect, fancying that in its dark recesses there lurks a specious cunning, whose purpose is to gloss over – with trickery – the soul's deficiencies.

With this deep-seated distrust of the intellect, therefore, I would be inclined to move warily within the domain of wit, if the abovementioned definition were correct. But, funnily enough, I don't think there is much truth in it. When something makes me laugh, I would have to think twice about whether I'm laughing intellectually or whether it is just low, moron joy. And if I had to pause, in order to reflect on this problem, I wouldn't want to go on laughing any more.

Humour we find all over the place. But with writers of humour (at least with the kind of humour that appeals to me), it seems to be different. You seem to find them at particular times and in particular places. The Elizabethans had a sense of humour that I can respond to, as readily as to a backveld joke about rinderpest and drought. I regard Shakespeare as the greatest humourist I have ever come across. And the singular thing about it is that he seems to me to have been a humourist, primarily, in the literary sense – as the Americans of the nineteenth century were humourists, primarily, in the literary sense – for his jests seem to have a spontaneous magic in the form of the written word that they lack spoken, or dramatised. I have always derived much more pleasure from reading Shakespeare's humour than from seeing it on the stage, but perhaps I have never yet seen Shakespeare – when he is being funny – properly acted.

But with the exception of the Elizabethans, there have been no English writers who have risen to such dazzling heights of fantasy, or have reached to genius through such an utter abandonment of the spirit, that I would be willing to make for them the claim that they should be admitted – without reservation – to the wearing of the true humorist's garland. There are a large number that I would be willing to accept, making allowances for this and for that. But when it comes to my response to humour, I prefer to be with those for whom I have to make no concessions.

And here I feel I am in godly company: the American humorists of the nineteenth century. Mark Twain and those who preceded him, and those who came after, too, some of them. I feel that there has never, in the whole history of the world, been anything so shocking, so sublime, and truthful and starlike and inspired, as what those men wrote, who contributed to that immortal beauty of literature that comprises American humour. It began shortly after the American War of Independence, this particular expression of a literary spirit whose goal was the awakening of gigantic laughter.

~

By the time of the American Civil War, this new kind of humour (new, not in its essence, but in its strength and stark objectivity) had blossomed into quite unimaginable beauty; and it lasted in the hands of one or two men of genius, right into the early years of the twentieth century. But for as long as a generation before that, it had already begun to manifest, deep within its structure, the elements of a dark decay. The writers stopped creating humour for its own sake. They began to apply this powerful weapon to the serving of causes that a creative artist can't believe in. In this respect O. Henry, coming in right at the other end of the epoch, kept his art untainted in a way that Mark Twain, ultimately, did not.

~

All the ordinary attempts at evaluating the significance of humour in terms of its social use and its psycho-physiological functioning seem, of necessity, to end in sterility.

Humour is something that stands apart from these things. I feel that, to get at the true essence of humour, it must be approached from the side of the eternities, where it stands as some sort of battered symbol of man's more direct relationship with God.

Humour is one of mankind's most treasured possessions, one of the world's richest cultural jewels.

But it came among us when the flowers were already fading, and it came too late.

52.

With Studied Nonchalance

From 'Paysage De La Highveld'

In *A Cask of Jerepigo*

During the past weeks I have been living on a farm on the Muldersdrift Road, thirteen miles out of town. A private bus passes the farm at about six o'clock in the morning, on the way to the city. At that hour it is still dark, and it is not always easy to distinguish, from the glare of their headlights, between the bus and the farm trucks carrying agricultural produce to market. Consequently, since there are no regular bus stops on the route, I have to describe the accepted hitchhiker's arc with my thumb each time I see headlights. Sometimes, when I have signalled a lorry, and the vehicle happens to draw up, I get a lift as far as Newtown.

The fascination of driving along the country roads on the outskirts of Johannesburg in the early dawn has not yet begun to pall on me. And I have several times wondered why our South African artists don't paint the early morning landscape more often. When the *koppies* and the valleys are swimming in mists. And plantations are dark masses with soft grey light behind them. And the blurred horisons are wrapped in theology. Instead of which, our painters almost invariably limit themselves to canvases of landscapes in the full glare of day or with flamboyant sunrise or sunset effects. Perhaps they leave that part of the day alone – that part of the day before the sky is red – because it is so much more difficult to catch those griseous tones, leaden and ashen-silver tints and neutral greens, and patches that are the colour of doves' wings; it is not just anybody that can cover a canvas with different kinds of slatey greys and still not make the thing look like a night scene. It takes a real artist to paint a landscape in dun shades – and yet to reveal it as a world filled with morning's clean light.

It is also difficult to get that particular part of the morning onto canvas because it is an effect that doesn't stay very long. In about ten minutes' time the sky is streaked with crimson and the magic of the grey light is gone, and you are left with the orthodox 'Sunrise on the Veld'. Another reason why paintings of the misty pre-sunrise morning are rare in South African art is because it is hard for the South African artist to get up that early.

When I was at the Cape recently I was often made acutely unhappy, in the course of a ramble along, say, Camps Bay beach – or, for that matter, the Muizenberg or the Somerset Strand – through the circumstance that every hundred yards or so I would be confronted with a typical South African artist's painting of a seascape. Azure skies and ultramarine ocean and brown rocks in the left foreground. It was all such obvious beauty – colour, composition, everything – just the sort of painting that the general public thrills to. Every other hundred yards I was confronted by yet another picture painted by a second-rate artist.

I saw thousands of these second-rate paintings along the Cape beaches, and they were an interminable source of distress to me. All they needed were frames. After a while it seemed to me that a lot of those paintings actually were framed, and that some of the frames even had little red tabs on them. One day, after I had passed a large number of daubs like that, all in a row, I found myself absent-mindedly putting my hand in my pocket for the catalogue. I knew then that I must never again take a stroll along any part of the Cape Peninsula seafront.

But it's different speeding along Transvaal highveld roads,

a few miles outside Johannesburg, by bus or farm-lorry, in the dew-drenched light of a new day, before the sun is up. This is a different class of work altogether. For one thing, a lot of it is in watercolours: swift strokes with a full brush – as often as not flung down, apparently just anyhow, on soaking wet paper, with breathtaking mastery, and with the superb carelessness of certainty. And it is all early impressionism, before the impressionists became mathematicians. And just outside the Johannesburg municipal area there is a magnificent example of near-fauvism, an extraordinary piece of work, a thrilling smudge of dark trees with silver light breaking through them, against a background of blurred hills and earthy sky.

There is also an interesting painting, higher up along the Muldersdrift Road, with rows of trees and a couple of farmhouses carefully laid out in accordance with a complicated system of receding planes. But while I can admire the cleverness of this canvas very much, it doesn't make a strong and direct emotional appeal to me. I can sense in it the beginning of the *trompe l'oeil* decadence of the last years of the nineteenth century.

The last piece of early impressionism on the road comes into view at the very moment of sunrise. I can't, just at the moment, recall the name of this picture. And I can't make out the artist's signature, which looks like a scrawled 'G' with some wrigglings after it (which makes me think that it might be Gauguin before he went to the South Seas). On the other hand, it might equally be an 'S' with some scribbling after that. Seurat, perhaps? I have often wondered.

I have asked the bus-driver, but he says he doesn't know.

Postscript
It is springtime on the farm. The almond trees and the apple trees, the peach and apricot and cherry trees, are covered in

pink and white blossom. And I, neurotic city-dweller, whom the springtimes of the last four or five years have passed by with studied nonchalance – bringing me neither enchantment nor rapture nor heartache – gaze upon the annual miracle of bursting blooms without the awakening of memories and without wonderment.

53.

A Quality of Granite

From 'The Disappearance of Latin'

In *A Cask of Jerepigo*

A few days ago, in the course of a conversation with a couple of people connected with education, I learnt, with sincere feelings of regret, that Latin is gradually disappearing from the curriculum of our South African schools. Latin is being replaced by other languages or by commercial subjects. And the scholars who take Latin for matriculation are declining in number every year.

This is all wrong, somehow. Apart from its cultural value, the study of Latin is essential to the moulding of character.

Of course, a great deal of rubbish has been talked and written through the centuries about the value of various subjects in the school syllabus in the direction of developing moral virtues. When cardboard modelling was introduced in the primary school, for instance, it was claimed by its protagonists that cardboard modelling exercised an elevating influence on the young mind, and that pupils who studied this subject for two hours a week would grow up into good and upright citizens.

The moral virtues you acquired through doing cardboard modelling included, I believe, those of honesty, tenacity of purpose, spiritual concentration, a high idealism, determination and chastity. You also learnt physical courage, that way.

Woodwork was even better for building character, for developing the nobler qualities of mind and soul, the loftier attributes of the spirit.

The point is that cardboard modelling was tried out. And the children who studied cardboard modelling in the lower standards grew up into men and women who were not in any way noticeably better human beings than the previous generation of pupils who had not been privileged to practise the art of making things out of cardboard and gummed paper.

In spite of cardboard modelling, a whole generation of scholars went into the world and didn't cut life's cardboard straight. The real trouble with cardboard modelling is that it makes for cynicism at too tender an age: it teaches the child that life is all just lath and plaster – sawdust and cardboard.

But it's different with Latin.

If the present tendency in our system of education continues, Latin will, in the course of the next few years, have become a dead language. And this isn't right. For one thing, the interests of good fellowship demand that we keep the ancients with us: as foreigners, maybe, but as foreigners with whose tongue we are tolerably familiar and whose accents do not fall jarringly on the modern ear. Unfamiliarity with the stranger's home language is one of the most potent causes of xenophobia. And we don't want the people who wrote the western – if less enchanting – half of classic literature to be excluded from our society merely because their language sounds uncouth and falls harshly on the polite ear.

I don't mean that we have to accept the whole literature. I can understand anybody drawing the line at Virgil: '*Aut redit a nobis aurora diemque reducit*', or '*… tremens procumbit humi bos*'.

No, I feel that Virgil is a foreigner who will never really become assimilated. Not even: '*Quidquid id est, timeo Danaos et dona ferentes*' – colloquially, 'beware of Greeks bearing gifts' – no matter how often it is quoted by high school headmasters, is quite free from that inelegance, that infelicity bordering on vulgarity, which we so mistakenly associate with the foreigner.

But there is Cicero. There is also Horace. Above all, there is Ovid. No matter what Ovid is like on the outside, he has an inner refinement that we cannot do without. He is quite unmistakably one of the boys of the game. We have just got to invite him to the party.

~

But part from purely cultural considerations, there is another reason why our educational authorities must insist on Latin being retained in the curriculum. The study of Latin builds character. If you have Latin throughout your school years, and you have enough of it, you will never, in later life, become decadent – no matter how weak-willed you are naturally, or to what extent your bloodstream is tainted with the various forms of congenital depravity. And no matter how checkered your life may be, a thorough grounding in Latin during the formative years will pull you through every subsequent vicissitude.

The mental effort you have to put into acquiring a mastery of the rules of Latin grammar – prose, syntax, conjugations, declensions, 'ut' with the subjunctive, the ablative absolute, indirect statement – all that can only make your mind foursquare and imbue your nature with a purposeful earnestness and impart to your character a quality of granite that will remain inside of you, irrespective of what surface qualities of gaiety and apparent irresponsibility you acquire later on, for purely decorative purposes.

The iron introduced into your soul through the weary hours of slogging away at Latin will remain.

That is where, when it comes to character building, Latin is so superior to mathematics. Mathematics teaches you to be slick, the use of ingenuity, to look for quick ways – saying a dozen times so many pennies is the same number of shillings, and using logarithm tables, instead of multiplying out. But there is no nonsense like that about Latin. There is only hard, honest toil. The result when you have studied Latin is that in later life you approach an issue in an honest, stupid, straightforward fashion, which is the right way, in the long run, for approaching any issue. You don't look for loopholes. Evasions are all right for securing short-range results. Honest stupidity is the only thing that brings you lasting satisfaction – even if it is only for the reason that you are too stupid to know any better.

Penology and education being, for obvious reasons, closely interrelated sciences, it is as well to consider, for a moment, the advisability of introducing the study of Latin as a prison task for our convicts along with the more orthodox activities of packing oakum, sewing mail-bags and breaking stones. The compulsory study of Latin in prisons could go a long way towards reforming our criminal classes. How the convicts would hate those dreary hours of drudgery. Hours spent in the hall with grammars and textbooks, under the supervision of broken-down and retired Latin teachers.

The compulsory study of Latin as a routine part of the hard labour course would lead to the reform of many otherwise incorrigible criminals. 'The stone-pile was nothing,' I can imagine a reformed recidivist saying, 'and I could always do solitary. But that fourth-year Latin class left me a broken man. I am only fifty-two – and look at me. *O tempora, o mores.*'

No, Latin is not a dead language. There is a great future for it.

54.

The Poet's Embroidered Lie

From 'Johannesburg'

In *A Cask of Jerepigo*

Fiction is different from history. At least, I suppose, that is what an historian would maintain, ignoring for the moment the immortality that characterises good fiction. Because when all is said and done, it is not dull fact – recorded in terms of historical truth – that survives. If you wait long enough, you'll see that in the end historical fact, carefully checked and audited by the historian, cedes pride of place to the poet's embroidered lie.

~

Frankly, I believe that as a source of new cultural inspiration to the world, Europe is finished.

Europe has a background of unrivalled magnificence. Almost every town and city of Western Europe is impregnated with ancient splendour, but as far as the spirit of the peoples of Western Europe is concerned, these glories have run to seed.

For this reason it is most depressing to find painters in this country – some of them not without a good measure of creative talent – slavishly following the tricks of technique that contemporary European artists are employing with ever-increasing complication of subjective subtleties, as a substitute for individuality. Nothing can take the place of the raw inspiration of life itself, expressed with all the strength of a creative personality. And nobody knows this better than the European artists themselves. They're not glad that their inner force has decayed; it's just that they can't help themselves.

It is therefore all the more regrettable that our South African artists, as a whole, should have no clear sense of values in this matter. You can learn all the technique you like from Europe – that's what Europe is there for – but if you don't put your own spirit into what you paint, either because you have no spirit of your own or because you don't know how to express it, then what you produce cannot be anything more than synthetic rubbish.

I believe, however, that this is only a passing phase. South African artists are not trying to meet Europe on her own ground, which in itself would be an impossible enough task, they're actually trying to copy Europe on her own ground. This is pure clownishness.

But this stage will pass. After that, I believe, South Africa – with Johannesburg as its cultural centre – will find itself in an era of inspired creation, sprung forth from the passion of love for this country. Then we'll produce art that reaches real heights of grandeur because the note it strikes is authentic, and this beauty will endure because it is our own.

We have everything for it here. What has already been achieved in Afrikaans literature augurs well for the future. America has produced Edgar Allan Poe and Mark Twain, two sublime literary figures whose true influence is being felt only today.

But Africa has not yet spoken.

~

I believe it is possible to see Johannesburg as it really is only when we view it as a place of mystery and romance – as a city wrapped in mist. Is there any other city that is less than sixty years old, and the origin of its name is already lost in the shadows of time?

People who were present at the christening of Johannesburg say the town was named after the second baptismal name of President Kruger. Others with equal authority say it was called Johannesburg after Johan Rissik. Other candidates – and in each case their names are put forward on the most excellent authority – include Christiaan Johannes Joubert, *Veldkornet* Johannes Meyer, Johannes Lindeque, and Willem Gerhardus Christoffel Pelser (the latter, possibly, because his seemed to be the only set of names that didn't have Johannes in it).

There are at least another dozen claimants. And you need have no hesitation in supporting any one of them. The evidence in each case is indisputable.

With its skyscrapers, Johannesburg is today no mean city. These tall edifices of concrete and steel would look highly imposing anywhere, let alone just being dumped down in the middle of the veld. But we still bear one or two traces of our mining-camp origin.

Take, for instance, the Public Library.

55.

A Place for the Soul's Abiding

From 'Universities'

In *A Cask of Jerepigo*

You can only know a university if you have attended classes in it as a student. Otherwise you can only prowl around it as a visitor, and that, of course, doesn't count.

I have frequently prowled around Oxford as a visitor, but I was not able to gather much about the place except that it was conveniently situated in fairly close proximity to Morris-Cowley's motorworks. I thought that this was rather useful, because if an apprentice to the motor industry found that the task of turning out brass screws of various intricate dimensions on a lathe was beyond the range of his intelligence, he could switch over, instead, to the University, and learn something easy, like Latin and Greek.

Every time I returned from a visit to Oxford I felt glad that I had not gone there as a student. Because I was satisfied that I would never have been able to learn anything there. I would have been too much impressed with the buildings, which were not in any way what I had expected them to be, but were all low unto the earth, with rough-looking walls – real mediaeval bricks covered over with a yellowed mediaeval plaster.

~

I have seen many a stately pile, heavily encrusted with history, thick with dust and tradition, sanctified through the intimacy of its association with a nation's fortunes, through the centuries a silent witness of dooms and splendours – I have seen such a building, cathedral, abbey, palace, mausoleum, and I have not been impressed.

But because the walls of Oxford did not tower, but seemed sunk into the earth, almost, and because with what was venerable about the masonry that had lasted from the Middle Ages there went also a warmth and richness of life that time could not chill, I realised that if I had gone there as a student, I would never have been able to do any work in the place. I would have gone to Oxford and spent too many years in the more idle kind of dreaming.

~

Then there is Wits. I was a student at the University of the Witwatersrand in the early days, when there was still the smell of wet paint and drying concrete about the buildings at Milner Park. There was something in my eighteen-year-old soul that revolted at all this newness. When I went there recently, to attend a play in the Great Hall, I was still appalled at the feeling that Wits had not acquired any of the external characteristics of poise and suavity. The girl who sold me the programme was gauche.

When I was a student at Wits I had a contempt, both for the buildings and for the professors. I could not reconcile myself to the idea that any really first-class man from Europe would bring himself to apply for so obscure and – as I then thought – Philistine an appointment as a professorship in a South African mining-town university where the reinforced concrete slabs were still wet inside.

Needless to say, my views in this regard have since that time undergone a very profound change. I have seen some of the things that first-class men get reduced to doing in this life.

Myself included. And I feel only a sense of humble gratitude towards those men from overseas who came to the University of the Witwatersrand when it was first started, bringing with them that vital breath of culture that includes the Near East and Alexandria and the Renaissance, that rich Old World of thought in whose inspiration alone the soul of man can find a place for its abiding.

~

It is strange how the past all looks like the other day. Before they erected the main gate you could wander all over without knowing when you were inside the University grounds. I remember once when I went to look for a department that was housed away from the main building. I must have got to the wrong place. Because I asked a man in charge there: 'Is this the Wits Philosophy Department?' And he said: 'No, this is the filling-up section of the Lion Brewery.'

It was only then that I noticed all those bottles stacked around, and I realised that not even a philosophy class could get through that quantity.

~

It all depends, of course, on what your view is as to what a university should be. If you believe that a university is an institution where you go to acquire technical knowledge, then it does not particularly matter what the buildings and their surroundings are like. On the other hand, if you believe that you go to a university in order to have things done to you that will make you useless for the requirements of practical life, deepening and enriching your spirit in the process – and either view of the functions of a university is legitimate –

then the atmosphere of the place in which you are to spend a number of years is highly important.

There must be tall, old trees through whose branches the sunshine falls dappled on the walks. There must be winding lanes and unexpected vistas and sequestered nooks. There must be mildew and ruin and dilapidated façades. There must be aged and crooked corridors, and aged and crooked professors. All these advantages – or disadvantages – will no doubt accrue to the University of the Witwatersrand in time. For while there are two schools of thought on the question as to whether or not a university that is a non-technical seat of learning should be lousy – and I can quote highly venerable authority in this connection – it is unanimously conceded that it should be mouldy.

The University of the Witwatersrand will grow mellowed with the centuries, with the generations of men and women passing through the doors, and I wish that its future may be fortunate, that the enduring things of the mind may remain, that the imperishable nobilities of the spirit will live on, when the gold mines of the Rand have been worked out and forgotten, when the mills that crushed the ore have fallen into a long stillness.

And those solecisms about the University of the Witwatersrand that distressed me as a student will belong with the unremembered past, also.

56.

A Great Tragedy

From 'Writing'

In *A Cask of Jerepigo*

The older I grow, the more puzzled I get as to what life is for, and how to live it.

Since my early adolescence, I have had one fervent longing: to have twelve months of leisure in which I should be able to devote myself, in exclusiveness and abandonment, to the task of writing the things that have surged blindly inside me for expression. Just a quiet room somewhere, and a piece of floor-space to lie down on, and pen and ink, and a ream of 34 lb. cream-laid paper, cut into quarto size. That is the one thing I have wanted all my life, and always it has evaded me. There have been times when I have seemed on the verge of achieving this ambition, and then, on each occasion, what has seemed to be the beginning of this period of leisure has in actual fact been but the prelude to fresh turmoil – the calm before the storm.

I can always get the ream of cream-laid easily enough, and my connections with the printing industry make it a simple matter for me to get a quad-cap ream cut up into the right size sheets, and ink is cheap. A piece of quiet floor-space and a strip of hessian to lie on, though more difficult to procure, are not completely beyond the range of my organisational capacity. But it is then, when I have got all these things together, and I am well set on Act 1, Scene 1 of a sublime, high tragedy, and I have got to 'Enter Bernadus van Aswegen' – it is then that the outside world enters, with shouting and banners, and I proceed to roll up my strip of hessian, and I sighfully set a light to the 34 lb. cream-laid, and I take the nib out of the pen-holder, and break off the point, and fasten a strip of folded paper to the back of it, and shoot it into the ceiling.

I don't remember, just off-hand, how many times in my life I have got as far as 'Enter Bernadus van Aswegen' – and at that point the world has entered, swearing and flat-footedly trampling. Sometimes it has been creditors. On one occasion, it was the bailiffs. Once, it was a demolition gang, come to tear down the building. Once, also, it was the police. And always, I have had to get up from the floor, with Bernadus's momentous opening speech unwritten.

I have got so, now, that I accept it as inevitable that there is a curse on Bernadus van Aswegen. He is bad luck. He will never be allowed to walk onto the centre of the stage, his brow furrowed in thought, his right arm raised dramatically to say: '...'. But it is O.K. I won't write down the opening words of his speech, which I know off by heart, just as well as he does. I don't want this article to be interrupted, also. I have learnt cunning with the years.

~

And with the years I have begun, in some strange fashion, to identify myself with Bernadus van Aswegen. I feel that the world won't allow him to have his say, any more than it will allow me to have my say. This gives me a queer sense of intimacy with Bernadus. What he feels, I feel. His hopes are my hopes. And we have both learnt this same truth from life, Bernadus and I – and it is knowledge as ineluctable as death – and that is that we are both doomed to eternal frustration every time we really want to open our mouths.

And I regret to say that, with the years, Bernadus van

Aswegen has begun to grow embittered. There is today a cynical twist to the left part of his upper lip that I don't like. It doesn't help him to win and keep friends. And it's no use my trying to reason with him, either.

'Aren't I as good as Lear?' he asks of me. 'What does Othello have that I haven't got? And you know I can run rings around Hamlet, can't I?'

'Well, Bernadus,' I reply, 'I wouldn't say rings. But as good, yes. And there's that soliloquy I've got for you, on the death of your little daughter. But I started it all so long ago, and we have both grown so old in the meantime, that I'm afraid it will now have to be your little granddaughter. And there's that opening speech, right in the beginning, in the first scene, when you say …'.

'Oh, cut it out,' Bernadus replies petulantly. 'I never get that far. If it isn't creditors, it's men with picks and shovels. Or it's a couple of "johns" from Marshall Square.'

'Don't use such dreadful solecisms, Bernadus,' I answer soothingly. 'Remember you're a character in a great tragedy. Don't say "johns".'

And so it goes on.

~

But I am trying to write of life and its meaning, if any, and I have reluctantly come to accept a conclusion that has been persistently forced on me by external circumstances. I cannot evade this conclusion. Within my own experience, the same situation has repeated itself over and over again. I believe that, speaking strictly for myself, personally, the practice of the creative art of letters is contrary to the laws and the demands of life. It is always when I have turned out my best work, and I have received the right sort of recognition for it, too – in terms of people dubiously enquiring as to whether I think I should go on writing at all – it is at these times, when my creative powers, such as they are, have been at their peak, that the worst kinds of disaster have invariably overtaken me.

And this is something I cannot understand. I have become afraid to pick up my pen. Or when I do, to dip it too deep into the ink.

And this is something that, I have noticed, applies to other writers as well. Recently I read another biography of Edgar Allan Poe, in which the story of his life is related with strict regard to chronology. I got to 1845. This year, states the biographer, was a year of great literary creativeness for Edgar Allan Poe. 'Next year, 1846,' I thought, 'Edgar Allan Poe will have dropped in the …'. I read on, and found that, by 1846, he had.

Taking it by and large, it is far better not to write.

But I think I have solved the problem of Bernadus van Aswegen. I shall keep him out of the play until right at the end. He will enter only in the last scene of Act V. He will come on at the opposite-prompt side. He knows his lines. He walks onto the centre of the stage. He raises his right hand. And just as he opens his mouth, the curtain falls.

Title: *Bernadus van Aswegan, a Tragedy in Five Acts*.

57.

Too Much like the Real Thing

From 'Toys in the Shop Window'

In *Selected Stories*

'You ought to see David Policansky's store,' the lorry driver's assistant said. 'My, but it does look lovely. All done up for Christmas. It's worth going all the way to Bekkersdal, just to see it. And the toys in the window – you've no idea.'

Thereupon, speaking earnestly to him because this was no time for foolishness, Gysbert van Tonder said to the lorry driver's assistant that he hoped he hadn't been talking about the toys at every Bushveld farmhouse and post office that the lorry had stopped at on the way north from Bekkersdal. Because if he had, why, the children would make their parents' lives impossible between now and Christmas. He himself had several children of school-going age, Gysbert van Tonder said. So he knew.

The lorry driver's assistant looked embarrassed.

'Well, I did talk a little,' he admitted. 'But I didn't say too much, I don't think. Except maybe at Post-bag Laatgevonden. Yes, now I come to think of it, I did, perhaps, say one or two things I shouldn't have said, at Post-bag Laatgevonden. You see, the driver had trouble with a sparking plug there, and so, in between handing the driver a spanner or a file, I might have said a few things more than I should have done.'

~

The lorry driver's assistant was in the middle of telling us about something else that Policansky was arranging to have in the toy department of his store for Christmas, when the lorry driver called through the door, asking whether the assistant thought they could waste all day at a third-rate Dwarsberge post office, where the coffee they got was nearly all roasted kremetart root?

By the time Jurie Steyn had walked around, from behind his counter, to the front door, the lorry was already driving off, so that most of the long and suitable reply that Jurie Steyn gave was lost on the driver.

Before that, with his foot on the clutch, the lorry driver had been able to explain that his main grievance was not the coffee, which he was not by law compelled to drink. But he did have to handle Jurie Steyn's mailbag, the lorry driver said. And although he was pressing down the accelerator at the time, we could still hear what it was that the lorry driver took exception to about Jurie Steyn's mailbag.

~

By the time Jurie Steyn had finished talking to the driver, the lorry was already halfway through the *poort*.

'What do you think of that for cheek?' Jurie Steyn asked of us, on his way back to the counter. 'He's just a paid servant of the Government, and he talks to me like I'm a Mtosa. I mean, he's no different from me, that lorry driver isn't. I mean, I am, after all, the postmaster for this part of the Dwarsberge. I also get paid to serve the public. And that lorry driver talks to me just like I talk to any Mtosa that comes in here to buy stamps.'

We felt that it was a pity that this unhappy note should have crept into what had, until then, been quite a pleasant summer afternoon's talk. What made it all the more regrettable, we felt, was that it was only another few weeks to Christmas. The way Jurie Steyn and the lorry driver had spoken to each other did not fit in with the friendly spirit of Christmas, we felt. Nor did it fit in, either, with the even more friendly spirit that there should be at New Year.

'And did you hear what he said about my mailbag?' Jurie Steyn demanded, indignantly. We confessed that we had. Indeed, we would have had to have been more deaf than Oupa Bekker to miss any of the lorry driver's remarks about the mailbag. Even though the engine of his lorry was running at the time, the driver had spoken so clearly that we could hear every word he said. And what had made what he said even more distinct was that kind of hurt tone in his voice. When a lorry driver talks like he's injured, you can hear him a long way off.

'But what about my fowls?' Jurie Steyn burst out. 'That's what I can't get over. When he spoke about the mailbag that my fowls had ... had been on.'

Jurie Steyn was expressing it, well, more politely that the lorry driver had done, we thought.

'And he said that he had to handle that mailbag,' Jurie Steyn continued.

Several of us spluttered, then, remembering the way in which the lorry driver had said that.

'And he declared that my fowls were a lot of speckled, mongrel, dispirited Hottentot *hoenders*,' Jurie Steyn finished up, 'with sickly hanging-down combs. Well, that got me all right. There isn't a hen or a rooster on my farm that isn't a pure-bred Buff Orpington. Look at that hen pecking there, next to At Naudé's foot, now. Would you call it a speckled ...'

Words failed Jurie Steyn, and he stopped talking.

~

It was then that Chris Welman remembered what the lorry driver's assistant had been saying, just before the lorry driver shouted at him to get a move on. And it was as though the cloud, that had come over us, suddenly lifted.

For David Policansky had said that he was going to get a Father Christmas at his store again, that year. He said he had to have a Father Christmas. The toy trade was no good without a Father Christmas with a red cap and overcoat and white whiskers, shaking hands with the children in the toy department, Policansky said. We laughed, and said we would have thought that the toy trade was no good with a Father Christmas. We also said we hoped, for his own sake, that Policansky wouldn't get old Doors Perske to be Father Christmas again, as he had done the previous year.

We went on discussing the previous year's Father Christmas at Policansky's store for quite a long time.

As far as looks went, Doors Perske should have made a very good Santa Claus. He was fat, and he had a red face. The circumstance of his face being, on some occasions, more red than on others would, as likely as not, escape the innocent observation of childhood.

But where Doors Perske went wrong was in his being, essentially, an odd-job man. For years he had contrived to exist in the small town of Bekkersdal by getting a contract to erect a sty, or to chop wood, or to dig a well. And that was how he had learnt to sub.

So, when he was Santa Claus in Policansky's store, Doors Perske would, every so often, go and get a small advance against his pay from the bookkeeper. After a bit, the sight of Santa Claus entering the local public bar, for a quick one, no longer excited comment. The bartender no longer thought it funny to ask if he had come down the chimney. And no scoffing customer asked, any more, whether he could go and hold Doors Perske's reindeer.

In Policansky's store, too, everything was, at first, all right. If, in shaking hands with Doors Perske, a small child detected his beery breath, the small child would not think much of it. Since he had a father – or, maybe, a stepfather – of his own, the small child would not see anything incongruous in Father Christmas having had a few.

One day Doors Perske's wife had come charging into the toy department, swearing at Father Christmas and loudly accusing him of subbing on his wages, on the sly. And Doors Perske had called his wife an old ... and had ungraciously clouted her one on the ear before bundling her out of the store. But even that incident had not had a disillusioning effect on the minds of David Policansky's juvenile clientele.

For the altercation had taken place at a counter where there were prams and dolls' houses and little crockery sets, and the children thronging that part of the shop were familiar with domestic scenes of the sort they had just witnessed. All they thought was that Father Christmas had just had a fight with Mother Christmas.

~

It was the day before Christmas Eve that Doors Perske got the sack. He had just come back from the bar, again. And the first thing he did was to stumble over the shilling dips. Then, to save himself, he grabbed at an assortment of glassware stacked halfway up to the ceiling. This was foolish – as he realised the next moment. The glassware offered him no sort of purchase at all. All that happened was that the whole shop shook when it fell. The next thing that went was the counter with the toy soldiers. And there wasn't anything martial in the way the little leaden soldiers – no longer in their neat toy rows

– were scattered about, lying in heaps, with pieces broken off them. It looked too much like the real thing. Grim, it looked.

When Policansky came rushing in, it was to find Doors Perske sitting in the wash-tub, with a teddy bear in his arms. His red cap had come off, and his Father Christmas beard was halfway round his neck. And from the position of his beard, the children in the shop knew that he wasn't Father Christmas, but just a dressed-up drunk.

'I couldn't get a proper grip on those glasses,' Doors Perske explained. 'That's how I fell.'

Policansky got a proper grip on Santa Claus, all right. And he ran him out of his shop, and when he got to the pavement, he kicked Father Christmas, and told him not to come back again.

'Go on, there isn't any Father Christmas,' Doors Perske jeered, suddenly recovering himself, when he got to the corner. 'It's just a lie that you make up for the kids.'

David Policansky's face twisted into a half-smile.

'I wish I could believe you,' he said, surveying the wreckage of his shop through the door. 'I wish I could believe that there wasn't a Father Christmas.'

58.

The Dappled Pattern of Shadow and Light

From 'The Cape Revisited'

In *A Cask of Jerepigo*

The circumstances surrounding the historical trouble between Governor Willem Adriaan van der Stel and Adam Tas seemed so intricately threaded through the early days of the Dutch and Huguenot settlement at the Cape. So many legends were still current about it. So many relics of it remained, scattered over the Western Province, as though flung there by the violence of the administrative explosion that resulted in a governor being sacked, and a large number of colonists going to prison. There were so many remembrances of the affair extant – in the form of documents, and pieces of furniture, and the outside walls of houses, and in the shape of oaks and pines and camphorwood trees – that I felt the need to consult a school history book about it.

I can still remember as a child – in standard two, I think it was – at about the fifth lesson in South African history, when the teacher got to Willem Adriaan van der Stel.

No doubt the story made an equally painful impression on the minds of other scholars, because everything at the Cape had been going so smoothly until then – the landing of Jan van Riebeeck and the founding of the Colony for the purpose of provisioning ships sailing between Europe and the East. Everything was so respectable. Idealistic, even. Jan van Riebeeck was a good man. And then Simon van der Stel, who founded Stellenbosch. A good man, too. He planted oak trees and completed the Castle started by Jan van Riebeeck to keep out the Hottentots. A good man and a fine governor. And then it was announced that the next governor was Willem Adriaan van der Stel. The child's mind, eager to learn even nobler things about him than his predecessors, suffered the disillusionment that the next governor at the Cape was a crook.

~

It was on a pleasant morning in the late summer that we set off on a four-mile stroll through leafy avenues in quest of the farm Vergelegen, where Willem Adriaan van der Stel had built his mansion, and had set a thousand slaves to till the soil two and a half centuries before.

Ambling through the lanes of this valley in the Hottentot's Holland, cool with the shade of old pines and oaks, we had no difficulty finding our way to Vergelegen. Where we were in doubt, we addressed ourselves to passers-by. Our questions were always the same.

'Is this the road to the place where that scoundrel Willem Adriaan van der Stel stayed?' we would enquire.

And we would be assured that we were going the right way. The form that our questions took occasioned no surprise. Sometimes, for the word 'scoundrel' we would substitute 'embezzler' or 'thief' or, more simply, 'cad'. And the response, made with hardly so much as the raising of an eyebrow, would always be the same. Yes, we were on the right road.

In so natural a manner did they answer our two-hundred-and-fifty-year-old questions about Vergelegen that it was almost as though Willem Adriaan van der Stel was still dishing out placards from there.

About four miles from the village of Somerset West, on

a tree by the side of the road, was a board bearing the name Vergelegen. We passed through a gate, and within a few minutes found ourselves on a path thickly shaded by oaks of immense girth: old trunks, gnarled and twisted and hollowed, and contemporaneous in appearance, almost, with the oaks that had grown, until a few years before, in the Cape Town Gardens, whose planting was ascribed to the time of Simon van der Stel. I could readily believe that the oaks forming the avenue to the Vergelegen homestead had been planted by Simon van der Stel's son, Willem Adriaan.

Some distance down the avenue, where the foliage seemed especially dense, we sat down by the roadside and lunched off sandwiches and beer. I cast about and discovered, without much difficulty, a hollow oak to sit down in. The day was silent; the thick leafage sheltered us from the heat of high noon; no wind stirred the dappled pattern of shadow and light spread at our feet; our minds were at peace; in our thinking was the calmness of the moss on the oak tree's hollow bole.

For a while we rested there, watching the smoke from our cigarettes rising in slow spirals through the placid air, interested only in the smoke-wreaths that were like frail ghosts haunting and getting lost in the green ceiling that the oaks had erected above us. And such was the feeling of time long passed that was borne in upon us in the avenue laid out by Willem Adriaan van der Stel, that it seemed to me that the three of us, seated at the foot of that ancient oak, were phantoms also, 'palely loitering' by the side of the seventeenth and the eighteenth centuries.

Vergelegen was the first of the old Cape houses that we were to visit. And as we sojourned by the roadside, it was almost as though we sensed that it was meet that we should tarry there awhile, waiting without the portals, because when we crossed the threshold, it would not be that of Vergelegen only – our feet would carry us over a wider doorstep. We would be entering a region that was separated from Johannesburg not merely by a thousand miles, but by a quarter of a millennium. We would be passing through a lintel in which, like in the dust of the road beside which we were seated, there was imprisoned the sunshine and the shadow and the fragrance of two and a half centuries.

~

I should like to say, right at the start, that as regards the main feature of the place, the house itself, I was fated to be disappointed in Vergelegen. I was expecting to find the house that had been built on that farm, at the close of the seventeenth century, by Willem Adriaan van der Stel. (I hadn't read Theal then, and so I was ignorant of the Dutch East India Company's instructions for the demolition of Willem Adriaan van der Stel's home. The instructions were very detailed, too, even going to the extent of specifying what had to be done with the timber salvaged from the ruins.)

The homestead at Vergelegen is surrounded by an old wall that I liked. In front of the house are a number of magnificent camphorwood trees. I believe implicitly that they were planted in 1666. They are grand, stately things. If somebody were to tell me that Vasco da Gama, through some whim, went and planted those camphorwood trees in the Hottentot's Holland valley two hundred years before Willem Adriaan van der Stel got there, I would believe that, also. It is difficult, without going into unseemly raptures, to convey something of the impression that those trees make on the visitor's mind. Perhaps the Dutch East India Company didn't notice those camphorwood trees growing on the other side of the wall. Obviously, they neglected to give instructions for the trees to be chopped down.

~

If the house that is now standing on Vergelegen had been inspected by the Dutch East India Company, they would not have bothered to tear it down.

But there is an old wine cellar immediately behind the main building. That long wine cellar, with its low, whitewashed walls and its enormous black door, is unforgettable. I would not mind going many miles out of my way to revisit it.

I was told that in the early years of the twentieth century, when a number of alterations were being made to the place, the workmen at Vergelegen unearthed a lot of foundations. I should imagine that those foundations date back to the original building erected by Willem Adriaan van der Stel. There is also a very old, decaying wall some little distance removed from the site of the present farmhouse. It is a thick wall constructed of very small bricks that you can't prise out of the mortar, even today. I know, because I tried.

I stood before that battered relic, that venerable and discoloured ruin, and I felt that the shapeless pile of masonry, about twelve feet high and perhaps twenty yards long and over three feet in thickness, was all that remained of the palatial mansion that Willem Adriaan van der Stel had built in the palmy days of the Dutch East India Company. That weather-beaten structure, green with age, a piece of wall that, standing alone, seemed a formless decapitation, had nevertheless survived the hands of the Dutch East India Company's demolition gang, and the wind and rain of two and a half centuries. So my feelings, when I stood by that wall, were feelings of awe.

That weed-garmented reminder of the past evoked in me a reverence which I feel I would not have known in the roomy halls of the old Vergelegen long ago, when Willem Adriaan van der Stel's star was still in the ascendant, and before Adam Tas got to work on him.

59.

No Crime to be Poor

From 'Easy Circumstances'

In *A Bekkersdal Marathon*

'Poverty is no crime,' Chris Welman declared. He declared it loudly, a shade aggressively, at the same time pushing the toe of his broken *veldskoen* under his chair. 'Nor is it a matter for shame, either,' he added, 'to be poor.'

'No, I don't care who knows that I'm not particularly rich, myself,' At Naudé remarked, withdrawing from general view a trouser turn-up that had been mended with string. 'Of course, it's not like I've been brought up poor. When my father trekked into these parts, coming up from the Cape, he was well-to-do. I won't say diamonds, and a sitting-up chair with blue curtains that you got carried around in, and such like, as they used to have in the old days in the Cape. No doubt my grandfather, in his time, would have been carried around in a sitting-up chair.

'But my father, when he came up from the Cape – why, we were just people in quite easy circumstances, that's all. Perhaps in the Transvaal – with the class of farmer living in the Transvaal then, I mean – we would have been thought to be rich, even.'

So Chris Welman said, yes, in the same way when his grandfather came up from the Cape, his grandfather was reckoned to be a man of no little affluence – especially so, perhaps, in comparison with what was the financial standing of the general run of Transvaler then resident in the Transvaal. In fact, he wouldn't have been surprised if his grandfather had actually been carried up from the Cape into the Transvaal Bushveld, sitting in one of those sitting-up chairs with blue curtains.

'Yes, I can quite believe it,' Gysbert van Tonder interjected in a sarcastic voice. 'And it's easy to see that that's what your *Nagmaal* suit is patched with, too – a piece of that same blue curtain. Well, I'm not exactly penniless today, and I don't care who knows it. Also, I was brought up poor, and I'm not ashamed of that either.'

So Jurie Steyn said, well, there were different ways of making money. And he wasn't sure that it would meet with everybody's approval, the way some people made their money. At the same time, he couldn't but think that it was a strange thing how some people would talk about how well-to-do their forebears were, compared with the Transvalers there that lived in reed-and-mud-daubed houses.

After all, where did the Transvalers that lived in reed-and-mud-daubed houses come from, if they didn't come from the Cape? He was sure he didn't know, Jurie Steyn said.

But what he would not seek to deny about his own family, when they came up from the Cape, Jurie Steyn said, was that they enjoyed a greater than ordinary measure of prosperity. Compared with most of the Transvalers, that was.

'Not that I won't admit that I, myself, am a bit on the poor side, today,' Jurie Steyn added, before Gysbert van Tonder could make another interjection. 'And it's not that I'm ashamed of being poor, either. There's nothing about it that I've got to try and hide.'

That was true enough. Shielded as his apparel was by the post office counter, there were no flaws in his garments that Jurie Steyn needed to retire from the gaze of vulgar curiosity.

~

Before the discussion grew really acrimonious, however, Oupa Bekker began to relate an old Transvaal story that introduced a good many of the features we had already touched on. It was a story of a poor girl, Miemie de Jager, who lived with her parents, in the Groot Marico, in the kind of hartbees house we had already been talking about.

'It was the kind of dwelling ...' Oupa Bekker started.

'You don't need to say that part of it again. We already know all that,' Jurie Steyn interjected. For Jurie Steyn had noticed that At Naudé was again surveying his *voorkamer*, in a thoughtful manner.

'Very well, in that case, I'll say only that Miemie de Jager's parents did not exactly live in a palace ...' Oupa Bekker proceeded.

'Yes,' At Naudé nodded. 'I can imagine just the kind of hovel she stayed in. I must say, I think I've got a pretty good idea, now. And I think the less said about it, the better.'

Thereupon Jurie Steyn burst out that At Naudé should be the last person to talk. If Miemie de Jager had ever seen At Naudé's kitchen, and the kind of plates he ate out of, Jurie Steyn said, then Miemie de Jager would feel, next to it, that her parents were rich people from the Cape who had just arrived in sitting-up chairs.

Jurie Steyn talked as though he already knew what Miemie de Jager was like.

Only after Gysbert van Tonder had spoken at some length, and in a sneering way – saying that for people who weren't ashamed of being poor, it was surprising how fussy some of us were – was Oupa Bekker able to get on with his story.

'Miemie de Jager,' Oupa Bekker said, 'lived with her parents in a ... in a plain house that was near the first sawmill they had in this part of the Transvaal. And one morning, when she was on her way home from the sawmill ...'

'Good Lord!' Chris Welman ejaculated suddenly. 'You don't mean to say they were that poor. You don't mean she worked in the sawmill – those heavy thirty-foot logs – that's no work for a young girl with fair hair and dimples – sawing …'

It was apparent that Chris Welman had already formed a picture in his own mind of how Miemie de Jager looked.

But Oupa Bekker said no, it was Miemie de Jager's father who worked in the sawmill. Miemie went there every morning to fetch firewood in a sack.

'And then, one morning, on her way home through the bluegums,' Oupa Bekker continued, 'she saw a young man approaching along the path – a young man she did not know. She guessed right away that he must be a son of the new people who had bought up the sawmill and the whole property. Rich people from the Cape, they were.

'So she let the sack of firewood fall from her shoulders, quickly, and she hid the sack behind a bluegum. She did not mind the young man seeing her walking barefoot, but she did not want him to see her carrying that sack of wood. It went against her womanly pride. Not that she was ashamed of her parents being poor …'.

No, no, we said. Poverty wasn't a crime, we said. But we had noticed Chris Welman hiding his broken *veldskoen*. And we had seen what At Naudé had done, furtively almost, with his trouser turn-up, a little earlier on. So we knew just how Miemie de Jager felt about that sack, a symbol of the fact that her parents were none too well off.

'She decided to walk straight on, and pass that young man; and then, after he was out of sight, she woud go back and fetch the sack,' Oupa Bekker said. 'But after she had passed the young man – keeping her eyes down on the ground as she passed him – and she turned round to see if he was out of sight yet, she saw that he had turned round, to look back at her. And when he saw her turning round, he thought – oh well, they were both young. And so they walked slowly towards each other, Miemie de Jager walking much more slowly than the young man, and blushing a good deal.

'And the young man said that he was going to look at the sawmill his father had just bought. And Miemie said that she had come out for a walk through the bluegums and to pick yellow veld flowers. And they stood talking a long while in the pathway. And afterwards, the girl said she had to go home. And then the young man said, oh, but what about her firewood. And he asked whether he could carry it home for her. And she said, yes. And when she saw him lift the sack of firewood onto his broad, young shoulders, she knew she would never need to carry a sack of firewood home again.'

Jurie Steyn wanted to know how Oupa Bekker knew all that. About what went on in Miemie de Jager's thoughts, Jurie Steyn said.

'She told me after we were married,' Oupa Bekker answered. 'You see, I was that young man. It was my father who had just bought the sawmill. You must understand that, when we came up from the Cape, my parents were in easy circumstances.'

60.

Mountain Retreat of the Smugglers

From 'Rolled Gold'

In *Jurie Steyn's Post Office*

It was the first time young Vermaak had come to visit us, in Jurie Steyn's post office, since his marriage to Pauline Gerber. We could see, in several ways, the difference it had already made to the schoolmaster, to be married to the daughter of a wealthy Bushveld farmer like old Gerber.

For one thing, young Vermaak was now smoking expensive cigarettes out of a cigarette case, made of a yellowish metal, that he passed round to us, so that we could help ourselves to a cigarette and, at the same time, see the big curved lines of his initials engraved on the lid.

We knew that the schoolmaster's initials had certainly not been, by any means, so important before he had married Pauline Gerber.

'If I had a cigarette case like that,' Gysbert van Tonder said to young Vermaak, in handing it back to him, 'I wouldn't have had the letters of my Christian name and my surname cut into it so big and so fat. And so deep. I mean, think how much gold gets scooped off, that way. It's a wonder that the Zeerust watchmaker who did the job didn't write his own name on it as well, and his address, so that he could prune off a whole lot more gold for himself.'

Young Vermaak gazed at Gysbert van Tonder with a thin smile.

If the jeweller's engraver had been set that shallow, there would have been no mark at all made on the cigarette case lid.

'It wasn't a Zeerust watchmaker,' young Vermaak announced. 'My monogram was engraved by a Johannesburg firm.'

'I don't know whether I shouldn't give up teaching for a while,' he said. 'I would like to improve my mind, so that I can fit in better – in the world of intellect and culture. I want to have breadth to my mind, and outlook. I've been reading a book that describes the cramping influences that fetter the spirit, like a *vinculum*. A *vinculum* is the Latin word for a chain.'

Gysbert van Tonder said that if that was all that was worrying the schoolmaster, then he was certainly in the right place, now, at Welgevonden, for being able to enlarge his knowledge of the world. Oom Koos Gerber, young Vermaak's father-in-law, Gysbert van Tonder said, was easily the most broadminded man in this part of the Marico.

'I mean, just take the way Oom Koos Gerber made all his money,' Gysbert van Tonder proceeded. 'Well, if that's not broadminded, then I don't know what is. I mean, the Bechuanas – as far as Malopolole – know how broadminded Oom Koos Gerber is – to this day – about what brand-marks there are on the cattle he brings back to the Transvaal. That's why the Bechuanas have given him the name of *RaSakèng*. It means "He-Who-Walks-Too-Near-The-Cattle-*Kraal*". And if Oom Koos can teach you a few things in that line, then maybe you'll get just as broadminded. Only, I think your father-in-law will tell you that the police pay more attention today, than they did in the old days, to a Bechuana's complaint about missing cattle.

'So you should perhaps not start getting too broadminded, straight away. Otherwise you'll find your wrists fastened together with a … what was that foreign word you used?'

'*Vinculum*,' interjected At Naudé, who was quick at picking up languages.

After an interval of silence, the schoolmaster, having first self consciously cleared his throat, proceeded to deal with the matters on which we could sense he had really come to enlighten us.

'I've booked for a number of the Grand Operas in Johannesburg,' he said. 'I feel that that will open up a new world of culture to me. Vision is what I'll get, I think.'

We could see, from the way he opened his mouth, that Gysbert van Tonder was going to ask if that was a new word for time.

'It's some of the true glory of European culture coming here to South Africa,' young Vermaak went on quickly, before Gysbert van Tonder could make any more disguised references to the penalties for cattle-theft.

'And I think I'll be a better schoolteacher, and more of a credit to the Education Department, for having gone. You've got to wear an evening dress-suit, with tails.'

That was how you had to go to the Grand Opera in Johannesburg today, the schoolmaster added. And that was what gave Chris Welman, who had once worked on the mines, his chance to be sarcastic.

'I suppose you've also got to carry the right sort of dinner-pail,' Chris Welman said, thinking of the times when he had been wont to present himself for the night-shift at number three shaft (and of how his colleagues would laugh at an underground man who wasn't *de règle*, but had his sandwiches wrapped in an odd piece of newspaper). 'And at the Opera, I suppose, you've also got to wear the right kind of bicycle-clips with your evening dress-suit pants.'

Nevertheless, no matter what we might have pretended to the contrary, the fact was that we stood in a good deal of awe of what young Vermaak had said about the culture of Europe.

It was in recognition of this that Jurie Steyn, as though doffing his hat to the traditions of the old cities, enquired of the schoolmaster, reluctantly, as to what an Opera was, exactly.

So young Vermaak got his chance to spread himself, after all.

'An Opera,' he said, 'is a play, just like *Vertrapte harte* or *Die dominee se verlossing* or *Liefde op die ashoop*. It's like any play they have in the hall next to the flour-mill at Bekkersdal, except that it's all songs and music.

'When the warder tells the condemned man that the noise of falling bricks is the hangman's footsteps on the stairs, the warder sings it. And when the condemned man gets a sack pulled over his head before being hanged – like in the play *Frikkie se laaste ongeluk* – then the condemned man comes to the front of the stage and sings his last words.

'But what it sounds like, coming through a black sack and all, I wouldn't know. I've just learned about Opera from reading books about it. That's why I'd like to see how it's actually done on the stage.'

Gysbert van Tonder looked pleased with himself, suddenly. It seemed as though he had not been too far wrong, in having warned the schoolmaster of the dangers that lay in being too broadminded.

'You don't only get those *vinculum* things on your feet, from having your ideas go too wide,' Gysbert van Tonder assured young Vermaak, solemnly. 'There's that sack over your head, also. It's how one thing just sort of leads to another.'

The schoolmaster flared up, then. He said he hadn't come to Jurie Steyn's post office to be insulted. And here was Gysbert van Tonder talking about him as though he were already a cattle-smuggler and a cattle-thief – and worse. A lot worse, the schoolmaster added – thinking, no doubt, of that sack.

Thereupon At Naudé advised young Vermaak to ignore Gysbert van Tonder. He needn't talk, was the way At Naudé phrased it. In any case, At Naudé said, we were all eager to learn more about Opera, and if people in the Operas got *vinculums* put on them, also, well, he was sure it was for more high-minded things than just cattle-smuggling and stock-theft.

But the schoolmaster said that, strangely enough, from what he had read in his book, there was one Opera that was just like that, more or less.

The cattle part, he said, came in the scene that was called 'Exterior of the Bull-Fighting Arena'. And he said that when that Opera was first produced in Paris or Munich or Rome or Sweden, or somewhere – he forgot where, exactly, now, but it was some foreign place … Moscow likely – then, when the curtain went up on the 'Exterior of the Bull-Fighting Arena' scene, the audience all applauded when they heard a bellowing, because they expected a real live bull to come prancing onto the stage, right up to the footlights.

But the audience was very disappointed when they found that it was just the *Basso-Profundo* at the back of the stage, practising some notes – *arpeggios*, the schoolmaster called them.

'And it's queer,' young Vermaak went on, 'that there actually is a scene in the Opera, too, that is called "Mountain Retreat of the Smugglers". Only, there is a beautiful girl in that Mountain Retreat, and she is concerned only with the pleasure and the passion of the passing moment.'

'Well, that was something like …' Chris Welman began to say. Several of us sat up very straight on our *riempie* chairs, then, to hear more. This was something quite new to us. It looked as though those Europeans had something, after all.

'She makes them aware of her charms,' young Vermaak

went on.

Yes, quite, we thought.

It was certainly something that had never come the way of a Bushveld farmer on a cloudy night when he had cut some strand of barbed-wire, to let a herd of cattle into the Transvaal.

We doubted whether anything like that had ever happened, even to Oom Koos Gerber himself, although everybody knew how lucky he was in such matters. In matters relating to cattle-smuggling, that was.

'This Opera is full of colour and movement,' the schoolmaster went on.

And we thought, yes, we could believe that. We could also understand young Vermaak having booked seats, then, even though it was all just music and singing.

'Then a gentle peasant girl arrives with a message for the officer, who is now a smuggler,' the schoolmaster proceeded.

Well, we didn't really care what he was – whether he was an officer or anything else – before he became a smuggler. Nor were we much interested to hear about that peasant girl, either. It was the other one that the schoolmaster couldn't tell us enough about.

'It's a very moving song that the smuggler, who was once an officer, sings,' young Vermaak continued. 'I'm looking forward to hearing it. He sings it by a hole in the wall. It's through reading the message that the simple-minded girl brings him.'

The schoolmaster spoke a good deal more about Opera, after that. But somehow, it never sounded quite the same again as when he had first started.

Even what he said about the lovely Rhine-maiden with the lily in her hair didn't come up to the level of that other one.

All the same, as the schoolmaster went on speaking, our attitude towards him began to change, in a singular way, with the result that we started feeling more human about him, and it seemed that there was something in what he called European culture, after all.

The result was that, afterwards, he set our feelings at rest with some quite simple words.

'I'm going to the Opera in Johannesburg with my own money,' the schoolmaster said, 'that I have saved up. I know I sort of tried to lie to you at the start.

'But I don't want you to think I've changed just because I've now got a rich father-in-law. I wouldn't take his money, even if …'

'Even if he offered you some,' Gysbert van Tonder said, trying to sound sardonic.

Young Vermaak smiled.

'Yes,' he said, 'even if he offered me some – which he hasn't. And this cigarette case of mine is only rolled gold. What's more, it *was* engraved by a Zeerust watchmaker. What Jo'burg engraver can make scrolls and flourishes like that today, I mean? Here … take a look.'

Glossary

agterryer	-	after-rider
baas	-	master, boss
beskuit	-	rusk
bessie	-	berry
bitter-bessie	-	bitter-berry
blouklip	-	bluestone
blou oge	-	blue eyes
boeremusiek	-	Boer music
boom	-	tree
boomslang	-	tree-snake
bos	-	bush
brak	-	mongrel
bult	-	ridge, rise
bywoner	-	share-cropper
dagbreek toe	-	until daybreak
dagga	-	marijuana
debatsvereniging	-	debating union
dominee	-	minister of religion
Dopper	-	member of the Reformed Church
droom	-	dream
enkel	-	single
geoutoriseerde	-	authorised
Gereformeerde	-	Reformed
goël	-	white magic
harde	-	hard
Hef, Burghers, Hef	-	reference to the Orange Free State National Anthem
hensopper	-	handsupper

Hervormdes	-	Reformed
hoenders	-	chickens
hoogte	-	height
hoor hoor	-	hear, hear
huisbesoek	-	house call
jong	-	young man
juffrou	-	miss
kappie	-	sun bonnet
kêrel	-	fellow, chap
Kerkbode	-	church magazine
kerkplein	-	church square
kleinbaas	-	little master
kloof	-	ravine, gorge
kommandant	-	commandant
konsistorie	-	consistory, vestry
koppie	-	hillock, small hill
kraal	-	pen, fold
krantz	-	cliff, precipice
laager	-	Boer military camp
lacuna	-	gap
landdrost	-	magistrate
manel	-	frock-coat
mealie	-	maize, corn
mealie-meal	-	maize porridge
mealie-pap	-	maize porridge
meneer	-	mister
mevrou	-	Mrs
middag	-	afternoon
miltsiekte	-	anthrax
mossie	-	sparrow
nagmaal	-	Holy Communion
nee	-	no
neef	-	nephew, cousin,

Glossary

nooi	-	young lady, sweetheart
o tempora, o mores	-	oh the times, oh the customs
oom	-	uncle
opskud	-	get moving
ou	-	old
ouderling	-	elder
ouma	-	grandmother
oupa	-	grandfather
outre	-	eccentric
pad	-	road
platteland	-	countryside
plein	-	square
polgras	-	tuft-grass
poort	-	gateway, entrance
pouse	-	pause, break
predikant	-	minister of religion
raadslid	-	council member
rant	-	ridge, range
riempie	-	leather thong
riempiesbank	-	leather-thong couch
riempiesstoel	-	leather-thong chair
rooinek	-	redneck, slang for Englishman
rusbank	-	couch
seksie	-	section
sielsontleding	-	soul-searching
span	-	team
spoor	-	track
spruit	-	small stream
uitlander	-	foreigner
vaalhaarnooi	-	fair-haired young woman
vaal hare	-	fair hair

vas staan	–	stand firm
vastrap	–	hop-dance
veldkornet	–	field-cornet
veldskoen	–	veld-shoe
vlakte	–	plain
volksraad	–	parliament
voorhuis	–	living-room
voorkamer	–	sitting-room
voorloper	–	leader (of a team of oxen)
voorwaarts	–	forwards
wilgerboom	–	willow tree